BLOOD LOSS

A VAMPIRE STORY

ANDY MASLEN

TYTON PRESS

For the family.

Die facht fich an gar ein grauffen
liche erfchröckenliche Hyftorien. von dem wilden wü-
trich Dracole weyde Wie er die leüt gefpift hot vnd
gepraten vñ mit den haüptern yn einë keffel gefotten

Translation of the image text (from Old German). Here begins a very cruel frightening story about a wild bloodthirsty man Prince Dracula. How he impaled people and roasted them and boiled their heads in a kettle.

"There was a deliberate voluptuousness that was both thrilling and repulsive. Lower and lower went her head. I closed my eyes in a languorous ecstasy and waited."
Bram Stoker, Dracula

"I felt a stinging pain as if two large needles darted, an inch or two apart, deep into my breast. I waked with a scream."
J. Sheridan Le Fanu, Carmilla

HUNT BOOK OF LILY BAX, 24TH AUGUST 2010

I followed the female along Shaftesbury Avenue and then into the warren of narrow streets that makes Soho such a good hunting ground for the O-One, as they call themselves. She was wearing a soft red biker jacket over black clothes and left a scent-trail in her wake – the usual musky stink, though overlaid this time with expensive perfume. Her heels clicked on the pavement; she had a long, easy stride. I lost her in a knot of tourists then saw her turn down a dingy side street – little more than an alley, really – where she found her victim, a boy, maybe 14 or 15. She leant down to him and I could see a bank note in between her fingers. Her nails were long, and red, of course. I crept closer, keeping downwind, even though her stench was rank, and slipped into a doorway, dark except for a dull blue lamp above the porch.

The lamia leaned in closer to the boy, until her lips brushed the edge of his ear.

"You don't have to sleep outside tonight," she said. "Come home with me. I'll feed you. You'll have a bed of your own."

The scrawny mutt lying next to the boy on the layered sheets of cardboard scrambled to its feet as she approached. It stood now, stiff-legged, hackles bristling, ears flat against its skull, growling way back in its throat.

The boy tried to quieten it.

"Hush, Coco. The lady means no harm. I'm sorry, I don't know what's got into him. I think he's trying to protect me," he said.

"That's perfectly all right," the lamia said. She leaned towards the dog and hissed a command. "Lie down."

The dog complied, whimpering, its bony tail tucked so far between its legs it protruded forward from under its thigh.

"You can leave him with a friend just for one night, can't you?" she asked him.

"I don't have any friends. Not round here. I only got here a couple of days ago."

She smiled, her lips stretching wide. "He'll be fine," she said. "Leave him here. Now, up you get."

She held out a hand, the banknote no longer gripped between her fingers. He reached out and she pulled him easily to his feet.

"You're tall," he said. He was average height, but the lamia towered above him.

"Just my heels," she said. But that wasn't it. Even without the shoes, she would have been three or four inches taller than him.

I stepped out from the doorway and pulled my knife from its sheath. It is an old, old weapon; the curving patterns in the blade remind me of oil swirling on water. The blade, honed to a razor-edge, was coated in *salcie usturoi* – the old remedy we cutters have always used against the lamia: a concentrated distillation of salicylic acid from the willow tree and wild garlic oil. The whisper of steel against leather was quiet but the lamia heard it and whirled around, letting the boy's hand drop. He stumbled back against the wall and sat down, thin pale arms wrapped around the dog's ribs.

Seeing me, she opened her mouth wide and exposed her fangs: long, needle-like teeth dripping with that disgusting liquid they secrete before feeding. She hissed and sprang, claws reaching for my neck. But she was new to the ways of the cutters – a recent convert, I guessed. I moved quickly, lunging inside her grasping arms, surprising her; their victims are usually either paralysed with fear or running for their lives. A fast upwards stab with my knife under the ribs and into her heart. Then I stepped back out of reach and watched. I like to see the realisation in their faces before they go.

The lamia clutched at her bleeding chest, hand snaking inside the bloody rent in the jacket. Her eyes were blood-filled and her mouth was stretched so wide I could see the puffy red throat tissue. Then the *salcie usturoi* worked its way fully into the creature's circulation. She emitted a thin scream as every blood cell, vessel and chamber of her black heart exploded. The boy gasped and flinched as the tide of blood soaked him and his dog. I cleansed the blade carefully on the cloth I keep for the purpose and resheathed it. I walked quickly to him and told him to find somewhere to clean himself up. Then I left. It does not do to remain at the killing ground for too long. This was one of the daughters of Peta Velds, and I knew she would sense the destruction.

2

CAROLINE MURRAY'S JOURNAL, 25TH AUGUST 2010

I'd been in about 30 minutes, hadn't changed – there didn't seem much point – when the knocker clacked loudly against the front door. Which is odd, because nobody ever uses it. Our friends call from the doorstep and tradesmen ring the bell. If I'd known what the woman standing on the other side of the door was going to drag me into, I would never have invited her in.

I put the chain across and opened the door, peering through the little gap. The woman standing on the doorstep was dressed oddly, even for our Bohemian part of London. Her outfit consisted mostly of leather. Black and a deep, mossy green. She looked like a bike messenger. Or, rather, she would have looked like a bike messenger had it not been for the exquisite cross-lacing and stitching all over the fitted jacket. I was half-expecting her to offer me a flyer for a fetish club when she spoke.

"Caroline? Please let me in. I need to talk to you about David."

"Sorry? You are?"

"I will tell you inside. Please," she said. "You must let me in. I have been watching David. He has made a terrible mistake."

So I let her in. Simple as that. She was shorter than me and slightly built. I felt confident. I was still somehow managing to do one Thai boxing class a week. God knows how, but it was my only escape from work. I mean, apart from David, obviously.

We went through to the sitting room. She watched me drinking and actually licked her lips. They were very red. Suddenly I realised she was waiting for me to offer her a glass.

"I'm so sorry," I said. "Where are my manners. Would you like a glass? It's nothing special, I'm afraid."

"That would be lovely. Thank you."

She accepted the glass I poured her and drained it. Then held it out straight-armed in front of her for a refill. The girl could drink, I gave her that. I refilled her glass, and mine, since I had a funny feeling she'd keep asking for refills till the bottle was gone.

"So, your name?" I said, again.

"Ariane. Listen to me: what I have to tell you will sound very strange. I dare say you will be seized with an urge to throw me out, but resist it: David has ventured into very dangerous territory. This will be shocking to you, so why don't you just listen while I tell you a story. Save your questions for the end. How would that be?"

I nodded, dumbly.

"So. I will tell you my tale and if, at the end, you wish me to leave, then I will leave. But you'd better resign yourself to never seeing David again. Let's see now, what is the best way to tell you this story, given that I feel sure you will initially doubt its veracity, if not my sanity.

"Caroline, you are familiar, I think, with the theory

of evolution? Spontaneous mutations that confer a small survival advantage become embedded in a species' DNA through the process known as natural selection. A bird with a longer beak can eat difficult-to-reach insects and is able to survive for longer and breed more often. A monkey with a displaced thumb finds it can grip twigs to use as tools. A predator develops a taste for a food source no other predator touches – it has a niche it can exploit to grow strong and numerous."

"Yes, I know about Darwin," I said. "But you said you had news of David. What is it?"

"He has been talking to a very dangerous woman. A woman who has the power to destroy him utterly, and you alongside him. You must prevent him working for her."

"What on Earth are you talking about? He has a perfectly good job already – with a charity. He's a scientist – he doesn't have conversations with dangerous women – or men, for that matter. The most dangerous person he ever comes into contact with is the woman who issues replacement ID badges."

She tutted impatiently, like one of those awful businessmen-turned-magistrates.

"You have heard of the one percent? The super-rich? The global citizens?"

I nodded again.

"There is a group within the one percent. About one in a hundred, in fact. They have evolved. They belong to a different species. They are all members of seven very old families. They run corporations now. In Manhattan, Moscow, Frankfurt, Tokyo, Beijing, Sao Paulo and London. They are the ultimate non-domiciles. For centuries, they have been accumulating wealth and power. But their food sources are becoming harder to access. They used to feed out in the nowhere regions of the world – in India, Africa, Latin America, the Chinese interior, the eastern Russian republics. But now that everybody has a smartphone, it's getting harder for them to operate below the radar. So they're looking closer to home. In fact, they're preying on the people who don't have a home. Street people, addicts, prostitutes, vagrants, runaways: all those who have fallen through the net. The police don't care, the public don't see them, the tourist authorities wish them gone. And the O-One have free reign to hunt at night."

"I'm sorry. But what are you talking about? What species? And what do you mean prey and hunt? And did you say the O-One?"

"One percent of one percent, Caroline – it's what they call themselves. Like in maths, you know? Point zero one percent. They prey on humans."

"But they *are* humans. You said they were the super-rich. I know not everyone likes or admires them, but they're actually not a different species. Look, would you please just come out and say whatever it is you came here to say and then I think you'd better leave."

"Very well. Have you heard of Peta Velds?"

"Of course. Came from nowhere. Youngest female CEO in the history of ever. Runs a massive global company, listed on the London and New York Stock Exchanges."

"Very good. So, Velds Industries are starting to look at the link between solar radiation and cell mutation. She has asked David to go to work for her. Do you know what he is working on now?"

"Of course I do. David is searching for the precise mechanism by which solar radiation causes melanoma – that's skin cancer. And he's brilliant," I said. Why did I feel so defensive with this woman? "He's a genius. If anyone can find that link David can."

"Caroline, I know he is brilliant. And so does Velds. But she does not hire him to cure cancer. She has her eye on another cellular mutation altogether."

"This is crazy!" I said. It was like talking to a child. Her logic was impeccable even if the world it described was clearly a delusion. I wondered if she'd discharged herself from a mental hospital. There were a couple within a few miles of our house.

"No. Not crazy. True!" she shouted. Then she spotted my crossword. I do them to relax. "You like anagrams?" she said.

"They're easy. I always do them first."

"OK, so. An anagram. Peta Velds."

I grabbed my pencil and a legal pad from my case and arranged the letters of her name in a circle. I found a couple straight away: Past Delve and Saved Pelt. I showed them to her.

"No. Look."

She took the pencil from me and wrote down a name.

VLAD ȚEPEȘ

"Does that name mean anything to you, Caroline?"

"Vlad Tepes? Honestly? No."

"Not 'Teeps', you say it 'Shepeth'. It was a soubriquet – a nickname, you would say, though a rather unpleasant one. It means, 'Impaler'. You have heard of Vlad the Impaler, I trust?"

I had to admit that I had. It's one of the gruesome stories you pick up in a history lesson and never forget.

"So. You know something at least. Imagine a field studded with 20,000 corpses, men, women and children, impaled on sharpened wooden stakes driven into the ground, some still alive, screaming as they slide slowly down over the tips of the oiled spikes. A man dines alone, in the centre of that carnage, at a table set with fine linen and silver, dabbing his lips and picking his teeth. That man was an ancestor of Peta Velds."

I'd had enough. I asked her to leave and, reluctantly, she complied. But before she left, she turned to me and looked me intently in the eye.

"This business is not over, Caroline. We will meet again. Soon."

3

CAROLINE MURRAY'S JOURNAL, 26TH AUGUST 2010

It isn't usual for me to be home before David. I'm a barrister and long days in court or chambers mean it's frequently nine or later before I dump my case in our hallway and kick my shoes off. Neither of us is much of a cook, and of the two of us, David is better with the microwave, so I ordered some Chinese and sloshed red wine into a glass and went through to the sitting room. I was pondering a difficult clue when David literally burst through the front door. I know, I'm a lawyer, words are my stock in trade. So, he didn't literally 'burst' through the front door, but he came in fast and loud and he had a wild-eyed look that usually makes me think he needs to up his meds. He is somewhat prone to mood swings and takes a little purple capsule before bed that ensures he doesn't take off, no matter how excited he gets about this new idea or that new formula.

"Caro," he shouted. "You'll never guess what happened today."

I said had he been given the Nobel Prize. My deadpan humour fell on deaf ears.

"No, nitwit. A job."

"You have a job," I said.

"No. A new job. A better job. An incredible job!"

I told him to slow down. I needed a decent night's sleep. I had a big case the next day and I didn't fancy talking him down off the ceiling at three o'clock.

"OK, calm down and tell me. What job?"

He took a deep, shuddering breath and let it out through flapping lips, making him sound like a horse.

"Have you heard of Velds Industries?" he said. My heart sank. Of course I had. From Ariane Van Helsing if nobody else. "Well, they're starting to look at the link between solar radiation and cell mutation. Skin cancer!"

Ariane had said he'd been offered a job. And she was right. But I still thought, as she'd predicted, that she was the mad one. I should explain. David is a brilliant man. We met when we were both at Cambridge. He took a double starred first in physics and computational biology while I had to be content with a 2.1 in law. Oh, and he did a PhD in a year and a half while I was doing my training. It won the Harcourt Medal. He works for one of the big medical charities researching treatments for skin cancer. It's all very technical but it's something to do with UV radiation and gene therapy. Or something. Anyway, he's a genius. With all that that entails.

"Let me guess. You saw an ad in *New Scientist* and they hired you."

"No. Yes. I mean, it's better than that. Peta Velds called me. *The* Peta Velds. She called me, Caro. Personally. She's spoken to our CEO and told him she'd give him a huge great big grant if he'd let her have me and a couple of people on my team to work directly for her."

"Wait, wait, wait. Peta Velds, the CEO of Velds

industries, gets on the phone and personally offers you a new job?"

"Crazy, right?"

"Someone's crazy, darling, but I'm not sure its Peta Velds. She's worth billions. I don't think she'd go around doing her own recruitment, do you? Her HR director's secretary probably has a secretary. Are you sure it wasn't someone winding you up?"

"No! Look, I know it sounds a little, weird. And before you ask, I'm not off my meds. I went to see her. Today. She rang me at around nine and when I looked out of the window there was a big black car on the kerb waiting for me. I went down and the chauffeur guy took me across town to the City. Up in the lift to the 25th floor of their building."

"Oh, yes, The Point. Stupid bloody name for a building. Why can't they just called it Velds Tower and have done with it?"

"I don't know, maybe she likes cones, maybe it's the pencil point she used to write her first business plan. It's not important. She said she'd been following my career. Since Cambridge. She was in the audience when I won The Harcourt. She showed me a file with all my articles and research papers. She had them all."

"OK. So she's a skin cancer groupie with a thing for borderline bipolar research scientists with brains the size of planets. Then what?"

"Then she laid it out for me. She wants me to work on a related field. It's still cell mutation, but something to do with light sensitivity. I think she's onto something, Caro. She's done a ton of research. Ran me through this PowerPoint presentation, had about a hundred slides in it. There's a definite link between melanoma, UV and this condition she's been working on. They've got a whole division just focusing on it called Velds Solar Solutions."

He grabbed me by the arms at this point. His eyes were shining and there were little webs of froth collecting in the corners of his mouth: all the signs he was about to go into orbit.

"Look, darling," I said. "Just wait one second. Have a slurp of this."

I put my wine glass to his lips and pushed it up so he had to drink or get it all down his front. He emptied it impatiently.

"OK, I'm sorry. Let's sit down. I know I'm hyper but this is just incredible. Imagine if the Lord Chief Justice just rang you one day and said, 'Oh, hi, Caroline, this is Freddie Laing, I want you to sit on the High Court'. Well, it's like that for me."

I had to laugh. David's a brilliant man, but his level of knowledge of the law or how my job really works is touchingly tiny.

"So, you get to stay in your same old lab in London but now you're working for Velds Industries?"

His eyes fell at this point and the smile, which had been widening to the point I thought his head might split in half, disappeared altogether.

"Here's the thing, Caro. She's moving the lab."

"Moving it? Where to?"

"Norfolk."

"Norfolk?"

I think I may actually have screamed that last word. I'm afraid it was a bit too much for me. I love David dearly but he just forgets that other people have careers and dreams of their own. Mine never included working in the flatlands of the many-fingered.

"I know it's a long way from London but I've thought

about it. We discussed it, me and Peta. There are people with legal problems up there too. They steal from each other and get murdered from time to time. I've Googled it. There are courts. There's even a Crown Court in Norwich."

"Oh, you and Peta have it all mapped out, do you?" I admit to snapping at him. "Well, newsflash, David. I *can't* move to Norwich. And even if I could, I wouldn't. Our chambers are on the rise. We're getting some major criminal cases now and our chief clerk seems to have an in with the Director of Public Prosecutions. I could be taking silk next year and after that, who knows? But I'm not going to achieve anything stuck out there. You must see that, darling, surely?"

I knew my voice had taken on a petulant tone. I suppress it in court but it just leaks out at home sometimes.

Now it was David's turn to act the child. He folded his arms and actually glared at me.

"I've taken the job," he said flatly. "She's tripled my salary, Caro, and given me an open-ended research budget. Do you know how often these sorts of chances come along?"

"No, I don't. But what about us? How often does something as good as this come along, David? I thought you loved me."

"I do love you, you know that. But I, I just can't let this one go by. If I read that some other scientist had snagged the job, I'd kill myself. I've already got close a couple of times to finding the way UV and gamma radiation cause these cell mutations, but with Peta's money I could do it in five years. Maybe less."

"Peta? You call her Peta now? Jesus, David, you only

met her this morning and now you're calling one of the richest women in the world by her Christian name."

"She insisted. And what else am I supposed to call her, Miss Velds?"

"But what about me?" I said. Now I really sounded like a spoilt child. But I was at a loss. We'd only been engaged for a couple of months and I thought we'd be planning our wedding. Now my fiancé was announcing he was moving to Norwich.

"Well, to be honest, how much do we really see each other in the week as it is? You come home late, we snatch a bite together and then you're in your study till God knows when, two or three in the morning, reading briefs. We barely see each other as it is. I can't remember the last time we had sex."

"Oh, yes, and it all comes back to that doesn't it? Sex. So if I shagged you a bit more often you're saying you'd stay in London with me, is that it?"

"No! Look, I'm sorry. I just meant, I don't know, would it be so bad if we lived apart during the week and stayed together at weekends? Peta said a house would come with the job as a signing-on bonus. A house, Caro! A signing-on bonus. I'm not a footballer for God's sake. Normally you get your own mug in the kitchen and a free mousemat with some pharmaceutical company's logo on it."

"Wait. She's giving you a house?"

"Yes, that's what I said. Whatever I like. Said money doesn't matter to her. She just wants me and my planet-sized brain to come and work with her on curing skin cancer."

"Hold on a second, David," I finally said, as the details began to sink in. "This woman, this mega-rich CEO, Peta Velds, who runs one of the biggest and most profitable companies in the world, comes to you and offers you triple money, all the shiny toys a science geek could possibly want, and a house. To cure skin cancer. Where's the profit? What's in it for her?"

"I knew you'd ask that. I did, too. Asked her, I mean. She says she has money coming in from her other divisions so fast her main problem is shielding it from the taxman. This is all done through the Velds Foundation. It's charitable. Tax-deductible. Plus I think she wouldn't mind, you know, some public recognition."

I had nowhere left to attack from. Maybe with more time I could have exposed some hole in his plan. But right now, I was tired. The wine wasn't helping. So after the doorbell rang, mercifully interrupting what threatened to turn into a full-blown row, we ate the food and then went to bed. We had sex: I thought it was worth a shot. But even that wasn't much good and we turned the lights off and went to sleep. It took me ages but for once, David was sound asleep within a couple of minutes, dreaming no doubt of Peta-bloody-Velds.

The next couple of weeks passed in a rush. I had a couple of cases that kept me in chambers, court or my upstairs study almost round the clock: a rape-murder and a conspiracy to defraud. David was right: we didn't see much of each other during the week. Or even at the weekend, sometimes, if I'm brutally honest. Then, one day, he was gone.

He packed his stuff into a couple of suitcases. Although his brain is big, his need for material possessions, especially clothes, is small. And he caught the train up to Norwich. Just like that. Most of his books are – were – at his lab. I assume Velds arranged to have them shipped out to Norwich too. I came home that evening and the flat was empty. I turned on some music

– Vivaldi – just to fill the silence but it just made it feel lonelier than ever. We'd agreed to keep our weekday communications to text or email. David hates using the phone and I couldn't face those disjointed conversations you have on the phone with someone who doesn't like talking that way. You could be the most in love people since Romeo and Juliet but all you can talk about is the weather or how you spilled tea on your suit.

4

EMAILS FROM DAVID HARKER TO CAROLINE MURRAY, 17TH SEPTEMBER - 9TH OCTOBER 2010

From: David
To: Caroline
Subject: Hey you
Date: 17 September 2010

Hi Caro,

I've settled in OK. I haven't had a chance to look at houses and anyway, there's too much to do at the lab. Peta (I know you hate me using her Christian name, but as I said, what else can I call her?) works ridiculous hours and expects us all to keep pace with her. She pulls all-nighters all the time and I end up discussing gene therapy and cell mutation till dawn!

She wasn't entirely honest about the lab, either. I mean I still have an open-ended research budget and all the toys I want but she'd already had it designed and built when I got here. It's not a problem though cos it's state of the art. Vacuum extraction using turbo molecular pumps for example. Did you know they can create vacuums that have fewer particles in them than outer space? How cool is that!

I miss you and I'm sorry I won't be able to come down to London for a few weeks — but Peta says once we have some initial results I can take some time off.

I love you.

David xxx

———

From: David
To: Caroline
Subject: Something is off here
Date: 24 September 2010

Hi Caro,

I had a very odd experience last night at work.

Peta was away on business and I was more or less alone here. I think there's a security guy somewhere but mostly it's just me and the radio in my private office after the others have gone home. Anyway, I had a batch of data running on the computer so there was nothing to do for a couple of hours. I went for a wander around the building and I found myself down in the basement. Don't ask me why, I just saw the door beside the lifts and went down the stairs on a whim. Boredom, maybe?

The point is, there's a whole floor down there with lighting and storerooms and some kind of massive power source. There was a bright-blue light coming from under one of the doors. I could hear voices. It sounded like Peta and there were two men. They were arguing about me. One of the men said that he thought they should, well it sounded like feed on me but it can't have been. Pay heed maybe? Then Peta shouted at him and said what would be the point of that and she hadn't picked me out to solve and then she used some weird language I've never heard before. Sort of East European-sounding but not. It sounded like Na-dash-via-tame. Then the other man said they'd lived with it for thousands of years and maybe they should just carry on that way. She went ballistic and started screaming in this weird fucked up language. Jesus, Caro, it sounded like the worst ever curse you could imagine. Then they all went quiet and I thought maybe they'd heard me. I just got round the corner before the door opened. I ran up the stairs and was in my lab for maybe 20 seconds before she came in.

She said her business trip had been cut short and then she just sent me away. Told me she wouldn't be needing me the next day.

Here's the thing, Caro. I said I fancied going into Norwich to get a bite to eat. You see I've been living here — at the facility. There's a bedroom for me here just like a hotel. And this woman brings me my meals so I don't have to cook. I mean it's great because I can just focus on my work but anyway, I said I fancied eating out and she just told me she couldn't permit it.

She said what if I was in an accident or got mugged? She would never forgive herself and I owed it to humanity to solve the cancer link. So I stayed. But it was weird. That argument. I'm going to have a little prod around tomorrow — she's never around in the daytime so I'm pretty sure I can find out what's going on.

Love you.
David xxx

————

From: David
To: Caroline
Subject: Get me out
Date: 2 October 2010

Hi Caro,

This is bad. You have to come and get me. Everything's gone really bad. I tried to leave the facility yesterday and all the doors were locked. I'm basically a prisoner here. I even tried tweeting for help but they've got this firewall here that blocks all the social media sites. She can't suppress mobile service though so I'm sending you this in the hopes it gets to you.

Peta was here last night with these three girls — well, women but you know, young. And pretty. *Really* pretty. Long hair like models and these incredible red lips. They were all giggling about something and speaking in that weird language. But the worst thing is, they had this bag with them – one of those really expensive ones they sell in airports with the gold letters all over it. The bag was moving, Caro, and oh God there was a sound coming out of it. Like a baby crying. It must have been a toy or some kind of app or something, but it was just horrible.

I wasn't supposed to be there but I was in the basement again – that's when I saw them. They took the bag into the room with the blue light. Then I listened at the door and there was this really disgusting sound. Like someone sucking up soup. I had to go. I just ran back to my room. That's where I am now.

I don't know whether I've been overworking or what but I need a break, Caro. Really badly. I've started having panic attacks too and I'm not supposed to on my meds.

Please come and get me. Tell Peta you need me to do some wedding planning or something.

I love you.

David xxx

———

From: David
To: Caroline
Subject: Us
Date: 9 October 2010

Dear Caroline,

Please ignore that last email. I was definitely overdoing it. You know how I get with work sometimes.

Look. I don't know how to tell you this, and I know it's cowardly to do it by email. But I think we should call off the engagement. I can't cope with being engaged and working these hours for Peta. She is onto something massive here and I need to focus. In fact, to be honest, I think it's best if we just, you know, call it off altogether. Us, I mean.

I'm not the best you could do and I know that guy in your chambers has a thing for you. So I want you to know I'm giving you my blessing to go for a truly happy life.

I have to go. Please don't answer this as Peta has asked for my phone after I send this. Says I am too easily distracted.

Goodbye.

David x

[DRAFT POST] RAMBLINGS OF A FREE-REVVING MIND – DAVID HARKER'S BLOG, 9TH OCTOBER 2010

I know Caroline thinks I am immune to the charms of other women. It's true I find it difficult to respond appropriately to sexual overtures (SO). In fact, the real problem is, I am not altogether sure when a woman is making an SO. Flirting is not an activity I am comfortable with. The papers are full of sexual harassment cases, especially in academia, and I for one do not want to get myself embroiled in one of those. So I tend to back away or play dumb. And now Peta is, I am fairly sure, making SOs to me. At least, I think she is. Maybe I should call them SOS, because that's how they make me feel.

This morning, for example. I was shaving and when I looked up from the basin, Peta was watching me. Just standing there in the doorway to the bathroom. I know it's her building, and she was good enough to include a self-contained apartment for me inside its walls, but that's the point, isn't it? That it's self-contained, I mean. It's a container for me, myself. She has boundary issues, I think. Anyway, I jumped when I saw her in the mirror and cut myself. Then it got really, definitely into some kind of SO situation. Her eyelids drooped for a second then she sort of glided across the floor towards me and bent over me (did I mention she's very tall?) to lick up the blood. I swear she let out a moan as she did it and what was really weird is that the skin on my cheek went numb. I couldn't feel anything for at least twenty minutes after it happened.

Then she just stroked my other cheek and told me to be more careful, before swanning off without a backward glance.

CAROLINE MURRAY'S JOURNAL, 10TH OCTOBER 2010

David's last email made me think he must have come off his meds. First he gets it into his head that Peta Velds was a baby-eating monster. I suspect Ariane must have got to him somehow. Then he dumps me by email. He'd never do that. Not in a million years. Not in a billion. Getting married was his idea in the first place. I decided to write to Peta Velds suggesting I visit him to make sure he was OK. I'd explain he's very sensitive to stress (and definitely *not* mention his bipolar disorder). Then I was going to take a few days off work. One of the silks in chambers owed me a favour. I'd peed into a cup for her when she had to submit to a random drug screening – she'd been at a festival the previous weekend and was frightened hers would be full of "happy pill" as she called it. Ecstasy, I assume. So I got her to take on my caseload and wrote to Peta Velds.

EMAILS BETWEEN CAROLINE MURRAY AND PETA VELDS, 10TH OCTOBER 2010

From: Caroline Murray
To: Peta Velds
Subject: David Harker
Date: 10 October 2010

Dear Ms Velds,

My name is Caroline Murray. Has David mentioned me to you? I hope he has, as we are engaged.

I have received a number of emails from David that suggest to me he is suffering from stress. You may not know this, given the somewhat rapid process through which you hired him, but he is somewhat prone to overworking once an idea has seized him, and, if not managed carefully, his drive can lead him into habits that are injurious to his health. I refer to going without sleep, not eating properly, and, perhaps of greatest concern to me, and I hope you, suffering from occasional distorted beliefs about the way other people think or feel about him.

I should like to pay him a visit. Partly to reassure myself as to his general health, and partly to reconnect him with the world outside his laboratory, to which, I understand, you have more or less confined him.

David is a genius. I understand that is why you hired him in the first place. You must know that such men are rare, like certain species of orchids. And, just like those much sought-after plants, they need the greatest attention paying to their wellbeing, lest they fail to bloom at all.

I plan to travel to Norfolk the day after tomorrow. Please confirm that this is convenient to you.

Kind regards,

Caroline Murray LLD Cantab

———

From: Peta Velds
To: Caroline Murray
Subject: Re: David Harker
Date: 10 October 2010

Dear Caroline,

Thank you for your email concerning David. Of course, I know all about you. David talked of very little else for the first few days he was here.

I am not sure where you have picked up this idea that his health is suffering while he works for me. He is putting in long hours, that much is true; and he displays the fervency of the genius faced with a challenge that stretches every fibre of his great mind. A mind, incidentally, before which the rest of us mere mortals can only genuflect.

David is engaged in great work here, Caroline, and interruptions are a hindrance to his progress. However, I suppose I should make an exception in your case. Our address:

Velds Solar Solutions

New Road

Great Yarmouth

Our facility lies on the South side of the road between two bends in the River Bure – we are hard to miss. You will see what I mean when you arrive.

It is a long drive from London, and as I have meetings all day I suggest you arrive at six p.m.

Kind regards,

Peta Velds

8

CAROLINE MURRAY'S JOURNAL 11TH OCTOBER 2010

I have to say that, right from the start, I didn't like Peta Velds. Something about the tone of her email just rubbed me up the wrong way. She managed in those few words to suggest that I knew my own fiancé less well than she did and that by displaying a normal human compassion I was disrupting his work. The first thing I needed to do was to find a decent hotel in Great Yarmouth and book a room. As I quickly discovered, the first part of that task was virtually impossible. I settled for a room in one of those ghastly Ye Olde Coaching Inne places that at least promised wifi in every room along with the usual amenities. In fact, two rooms, as I had persuaded my best friend, Lucinda Easterbrook, to come along. I said it would be like Thelma and Louise – "a girls' road-trip" is how I put it. She's up for anything; she's an actress and rather likes spontaneity. I collected her from her place in Pimlico at 11.00 a.m. She was standing on the pavement with her bag and looked, well, actressy. Black velvet coat, purple knitted scarf wound round her throat and a rather dashing black fedora keeping her abundant hair in place.

Lucy has always had a bit of a crush on David. He doesn't know it, being oblivious to such things, and she doesn't care that I do. So when I said we'd be going up to visit his new lab, she was terribly excited. She was patting and twirling those tresses of hers all the way up to Norfolk.

About one thing, Peta Velds was right. The drive from London was long. And arduous. I don't mind driving, though I would hardly put it on my list of favourite ways to spend five hours on a Friday. I also discovered something else. Picking a car for its suitability for London driving, London parking and London looks brings with it certain drawbacks when one is faced with a few hundred miles of high-speed cruising. Audrey made, I'm afraid to say, somewhat heavy weather of it; her little engine sounded almost frantic at any speed above 50 and we had to turn the music up to cover it.

Have you been to Norfolk? Yes or no? Either way, I hope you journeyed by train. The drive was excruciating. Mile after mile of featureless dual carriageway up the A12, a road I imagine was designed by a team of sadists working in conjunction with a group of Philistines. How else to explain the atrocious road surface, whose unremitting acoustic torture is leavened by not so much as a single interesting feature to look at as one grinds out the miles on one's journey to the Mystic East. No streetlamps, of course, so that as the sky darkened, we had to rely on Audrey's rather pathetic headlights, another feature that the designers obviously felt would mostly serve an aesthetic purpose.

Am I being a little harsh? I suppose so. There was a pretty church in Blythburgh, lit from beneath by yellow floodlights, which provided a moment's pleasure. And a marsh through which we drove on a straight stretch of road that afforded views across to the sea at Southwold with its own church and lighthouse. But from then on, I am afraid, the approach to the Norfolk county boundary was as dull as ditchwater. Dishwater? No, ditchwater. I digress. On through Lowestoft and then we arrived in Great Yarmouth.

No doubt in the summer, Great Yarmouth is a pretty town. This was October. The sky was a depressing mixture of wet slate and bruised flesh – a dark, greyish purple that presaged something bad in the weather department. I wanted to press on and get to David's lab but my bladder, forgive me, was urging me to stop. We found a place to leave Audrey that didn't look as though the local wildlife would key her and went in search of a cup of coffee and, more importantly, a loo.

We found both. A lovely little independent café called Cortado – I abhor the chains and would cheerfully wipe every last one of them off the face of the Earth. Like Peta Velds they're a symbol of globalisation and the creeping homogenisation of our culture. You could venture inside one of those temples to corporate caffeine and have no idea whether you were in Mumbai or Manchester. Not for me, thank you.

Having freshened up, as our American cousins call it, we returned to our table to enjoy surprisingly good lattes and scones. Well, I had a scone. Lucy said she was "trying to keep my figure for a part I'm up for", though I suspect she imagined looking just that little bit slimmer for David. Silly girl! We were the only customers and the proprietress came over to chat. Normally I find such advances as welcome as a not guilty verdict to prosecuting counsel. But I'd had enough of my own company, and Lucinda's endless chatter was beginning to grate. If I am honest, I was a little nervous about my meeting with Peta Velds. She took a quick look at Lucy and decided I was in charge.

"Up here on business, love?" she asked me. I suppose it was my outfit. I don't really do casual so even though I wasn't working, I'd dressed conservatively, in a navy trouser suit and a white silk blouse.

"Not exactly," I replied. "I'm visiting my fiancé. He works at Velds Solar Solutions."

"Oh, does he now? He's one of them scientists, is he? He wants to be a bit careful working up there for that Peta Vells or whatever she calls herself."

"Oh, why is that?"

"Well you probably don't get our local news down there in London. But there've been a couple of problems over at that there laboratory of hers. People getting ill."

"Ill? What kind of ill? Accidents, you mean?"

"Nobody knows, do they?" My sister-in-law's boy, Ian. He works up there as a lab technician. Night shift. Thought he'd got his dream job, what with his A-levels and that. He's always loved science, so when he got offered it, well, he was over the moon, he was."

"What happened?"

"Oh, it was all right at first. Good wage, nice people, and he hardly ever saw Ms Vells, just these two blokes what look after her while she's staying over. Suits and dark glasses most of the time, he said. One was in charge of security, well you can't blame her for that I suppose, not if she's finding a cure for cancer. But the other one, well, he was some sort of lawyer, Ian said. Made him sign something on his first day about not telling nobody what he was working on."

Lucy had already grown bored with the conversation and was checking her phone.

"A little heavy-handed perhaps," I said. "But it's standard practice for many industrial firms nowadays. To keep their intellectual property protected."

"Well, I don't know about any intellectual property. What I do know is how Ian started coming down with little bugs after a couple of weeks there. You know, fluey things. No energy. Had to go to bed for a day or two. We thought it might be viruses they was breeding but he said they wasn't doing anything like that – it was all cells and stuff. But viruses is cells, aren't they?"

I forgave her execrable grammar in favour of learning more of the story.

"Go on," I said, though she needed little encouragement by this point and even brought me a fresh coffee, "on the 'ouse", as she put it.

"Well, one day, he comes home to his Mum and Dad's, he lives at home still, you see, and complains he's not feeling right. And Dawn, she's my sister-in-law, she told me he looked so pale. She put him to bed, but he was worse that evening. So they calls the doctor. And the doctor come out and when she saw him she said he was anaemic. Anaemic! That family is strong as carthorses, always have been. If you saw Ian, you'd say he was a policeman or a builder, not a scientist. He's that well built. Anyway, he got better after a week of bed-rest and went back to work. But then—"

She stopped talking. Her voice had thickened and I could tell she was close to tears. I offered her a tissue but she shook her head and fished one out of her sleeve.

"He only managed another day before the accident. They said he was too weak and shouldn't have gone back to work. He slipped, apparently, gashed his neck on one of them flasks they use, lost a lot of blood. They took him to hospital. The A&E? But he got some sort of infection."

The poor woman was crying properly now, and her face had gone blotchy. I made the right noises, though to be honest I am never terribly comfortable around other people's emotions. She managed to get herself under control again and finished her story.

"He only lasted another day, poor lamb. One of them super-bugs they called it. That's what the coroner said. MRSA, is it? But I know who's really to blame. That bloody Vells woman, that's who! So mind yourself up there at that laboratory of hers, my darling, because others have gone down with that virus what our Ian had."

The mention of the poor man's name set her off in another paroxysm and I felt unable to offer any more sympathy so I patted her on the shoulder, placed a ten-pound note under my saucer and tapped Lucy on the arm to rouse her from Facebook or whatever she'd been absorbed in. We left the café. We planned to drive back the following morning after dinner with David. Lucy decided she'd rather not meet the great Peta Velds after all. I think she has a chip on her shoulder about rich people, but in any case, she said she'd check in and then read her script "in a bloody great big bubble-bath" till I came back with David.

I left Great Yarmouth by way of Fullers Hill, then made my way back to the A47 – Acle New Road. I was very close now and switched off the satnav in favour of my eyes. I have always found those devices rather infantilising, since one always used to manage to find one's way to new places without them. Although on trips to Crown Courts in the quainter parts of the UK, I must confess they do have their uses. As it turned out, I needn't have worried. The road was – is – a strip of tarmac laid across one of the most boring landscapes I have ever endured. Mile after mile of flat, featureless grassland – marsh, perhaps, I don't know – and then, I saw it: a low building surrounded by a dim pool of pink light from a handful of streetlamps – those tall ones you see in supermarket carparks. It was painted in receding shades of blue as one neared the roof, giving the effect of a landscape disappearing from view in the distance. No windows that I could see – oh, how depressing, I thought instantly – but a sign indicating that The Harker Laboratory, Velds Solar Solutions was approaching 55 yards on the right.

Well, David had kept that quiet. I began to wonder whether there was more to his relationship with Peta Velds than he had led me to believe. Don't get me wrong, David is a sweet man, and I know he loves me, and I, him; but he is less worldly than other men, and barely notices when women come onto him. Which believe me, they do. His curls and blue eyes may have something to do with it, but I prefer to believe it's the combination of his intellect and an innocence they find so irresistible. Only last year I more or less had to prise him from the grasp of a drunken particle physicist at a conference in Copenhagen. She said she was just trying to get an insight into his work with solar radiation, but I suspect her motives were somewhat less pure. Especially as she had enough buttons undone that he could have fallen into her cleavage and never climbed out again.

I parked Audrey in the row of spaces marked Visitor Parking just outside the main doors. I reversed in: I can park efficiently and well and always prefer to leave straightaway I have finished a meeting. The building was set amongst that particular type of planting that characterises out-of-town business parks and retail centres: lots of sharp-leaved Mediterranean plants set in shingle, as if the landscapers were embarrassed to be designing a garden in the middle of England. There was a loud hum emanating from the side of the building behind some yuccas – a huge air vent protected by a spiral wire cover.

I went inside and approached the reception desk. It was manned – and I used that word advisedly – by a most curious-looking fellow. Very short and quite fat; unkempt appearance, wearing a disgusting, ratty old jumper that looked to have been hand-knitted, and not by anyone possessed of much talent in that department. He wore pebble-lensed glasses made almost opaque by a greasy film over the glass. God knows how he could see out of them. Beyond the glasses were eyes of a burning intensity, a very deep blue, almost purple, under unkempt eyebrows that tangled and grew in all directions at once. The backs of his hands were tattooed with script; I couldn't read it as I looked down at them, but it wasn't English – and executed in that old font called Black Letter, like a Gothic manuscript. And his fingernails. My God, they were filthy. Long, ragged things like talons and completely black beneath as if he'd been working in the garden. Why a woman like Peta Velds had hired this monstrously ugly creature to greet her guests, I couldn't imagine for a second, but here he was, and here I was too, seeking an appointment with his mistress.

He looked up at me with those burning eyes and growled at me.

"You are Caroline Murray. Ms Velds is expecting you. Sign here. Wait there." He pointed to a low leather sofa by a coffee table piled high with magazines and books then pushed a leather-bound visitors' book at me. I jotted down my name, Audrey's registration number and P. Velds in the column headed, "Visiting". As I did so, I noticed a few small specks of white on the surface of the reception counter. They looked like sugar crystals. Curioser and curioser. Then I took a seat, supposing as I did so that they mustn't get very many visitors if he could so confidently identify me before I had even spoken. While I waited, I flicked idly through one of the magazines. It was a dense medico-scientific journal called *Cell*. I gave up trying to understand anything written between its covers and considered, instead, how I would approach the looming conversation with Peta Velds. I supposed I might begin by expressing my gratitude on David's behalf for her having named the whole facility after him. I know David – if he noticed at all it wouldn't have crossed his mind that gratitude was in order. He probably just thought it would make it easier to find his way to work. One less thing to remember.

Apart from the somewhat odious – and odorous – did I mention he had a funny smell, of wet earth, about him? – receptionist, I was alone. I looked all around. Just a white-painted space decorated with the usual bland corporate art that says, "We have culture, as well as money". It was quite silent, too. The man at reception merely sat inside his little enclosure, staring into space. If there were scientists they were presumably well tucked away, and to judge from my journey here, there was certainly nothing worth venturing outside for. I hadn't even seen a bench or grassy area on which one might eat lunch on a sunny day.

I felt something, a fly, perhaps, land on my neck and put my hand up to dislodge it. Then a woman's voice, cultured, East European, maybe, startled me. It came from right behind me. I whirled in my seat and there stood, I assumed, Peta Velds.

"You must be Caroline. Please, come this way. You must be thirsty after your trip from London."

Her accent was hard to place. Russia to Mayfair, by way of MTV, I'd say, if I had to guess.

She held out a hand to shake. It was cold to the touch. She must have circulation problems, I thought. Her skin felt strange. Not sweaty, like some of those awful no-win-no-fee solicitors, but not dry either. A slippery sensation, like silk running through your fingers. Not unpleasant, far from it. But unsettling. I sensed something else, too. Immense strength. There was just something about the way the muscles and tendons of her fingers enfolded mine. I do believe that, had she wanted to, she could have crushed my hand inside hers until every single bone was broken. And her appearance. My goodness!

In my line of work, I meet many people whose looks and demeanour render them quite unremarkable; all the more ironic given the crimes of which they stand accused and, when I am victorious, are convicted. I have faced, in court, a child-killer who looked like a bank clerk. A man with the bland good looks of an American TV sitcom star who beat his wife to death with a fire iron, then chopped her body up into pieces before disposing of them at the council tip in black bin liners. A pair of people traffickers – a man and a woman – who brought young girls into London and sold them into the sex trade, who looked as if they might spend their leisure time growing prize dahlias or breeding poodles. Yet here was a bona fide one-percenter, a tycoon, a philanthropist. She had even contributed to an anthology of poems for a

children's charity. I had seen it the previous Christmas in
the review section of the paper and nearly puked at the
ersatz sentiment these "celebrities" managed to cram
into their introductions to their selections. And she
looked, well, what did she look like? She looked
dangerous.

Her brow was high and entirely smooth – Botox, I
assumed. A high hairline, with dark brown, almost black,
hair swept back from her face. Her eyes were set wide
apart creating a disturbing effect of being looked at by
two people at once; they were grey, perfectly elliptical.
She had one of the hardest, most direct stares I have
even met, in or out of the courtroom, though this may
have been a side-effect of her not seeming to need to
blink. And her mouth! Full lips accentuated still further
with a lipstick of the deepest red. As she smiled at me she
revealed a mouthful of tiny white teeth, almost like a
child's. The effect was unsettling: a Victorian porcelain
doll, grown up and made real. I am not a short woman –
I'm five eight in my bare feet, plus I had changed in the
car into a pair of heels, so I was my court-dominating
5'11" – but she loomed over me. She was wearing a pair
of impossibly high stilettos – black patent Prada – that
must have taken her height to over six feet.

I followed her into the lift behind the reception desk.
It was very small – no bigger than a downstairs
cloakroom. I hate confined spaces, especially when I am
with other people. I like to keep a big space around me.
Now I found myself standing almost shoulder to
shoulder with Peta Velds. To look at a woman like that,
you would expect her to be wearing Chanel No. 5 or
some other expensive perfume. May I be candid?
She stank.

Last Christmas, we found a dead fox in the field

beyond David's parents' garden. It was writhing with maggots. Their dog, Rufus, rolled in it, and despite repeated shampooings, he still smelled of carrion: a sickly sweet odour mixed with something earthy and meaty. The smell coming off Peta Velds was like that, masked by a heavy, musky scent. I tried to breathe through my mouth. She turned and looked at my parted lips.

"You don't like my perfume."

It was a statement, not a question, but I felt compelled to reply, to apologise, caught out in a social faux pas.

"No, no, it's just, you know, in the lift. It's lovely. What is it?"

"Roja," she pronounced the name with a rough exhalation as she pressed her tongue against the roof of her mouth. "Parfum de la Nuit. It is supposed to release your inhibitions. Maybe I will give you a spray in my office."

"It's OK," I said. "I tend to stick to boring old L'Air du Temps, I'm afraid."

"No matter. Though experimentation is a good thing, you know. Sometimes."

I watched the floor buttons light up in turn. The lift was agonisingly slow and I could feel sweat prickling in my armpits. I assumed her office would be on the fourth floor. Just one to go and I would be out of the little box and the miasma of Peta Velds's body odour. Then, with a loud bang and a screech from somewhere above us, the lift jolted and stopped. The light went out, too.

"I will kill those maintenance men," she said. It should have sounded like anyone's normal, exasperated expression of dismay when something mechanical fails. From Peta Velds's carmine lips, it sounded as plain and fact-driven as a weather forecast. A declaration of intent. "Please, stay calm. I will call Renfield."

"Renfield? Is that the maintenance company? How long will they take to get here? Are they based near here?" I could hear the panic in my voice, but I didn't care whether she found me amusing, ridiculous or both. I was struggling to hold my anxiety in check and I doubted I could for more than a few minutes. My heart was starting to beat harder and I could hear a rushing in my ears.

"No. Renfield is my factotum. You met him when you signed in. He can go to the basement and restart the machinery from the control cupboard. Now, be quiet please, while I call him."

I stifled a scream as her elbow nudged my side when she brought her phone out. The bright glow from the screen illuminated her face. For a second, I could have sworn she was licking her lips. She swiped and tapped to bring up his number and then spoke.

"Renfield. The lift has malfunctioned. Please would you work your magic in the basement?" She paused. "We'll see. Later. But for now, the lift. I have Miss Murray with me and I feel she would prefer not to spend too much more time trapped in this coffin." She laughed, then, a silly, girlish sound, and ended the call. "So, Caroline, what shall we do to pass the time?"

"Could you put your phone back on, please?" I said. "The dark. It's not my favourite thing."

"Oh, I think my phone has not enough charge. Don't worry. Here, hold my hand."

Now, that I really didn't want to do, but I felt I had backed myself into a corner. Literally, as well as figuratively. I felt her hand slide around mine and squeeze. I admit, I am not really much of a tactile person. With David, it's OK, because I know him, but I hate all this public kissing and arm-patting that seems de rigueur nowadays. I'm sure some of my friends have noticed and do it excessively, just to watch me squirm. I overheard a QC in chambers last year saying she thought I must have learned how to greet a friend from a book. She was correct. Well, not a book: a course. I went on a weekend seminar called, "Let Your Body Speak For You". A dreadful experience from start to finish, led by this awful American woman called Misty or Sunshine: some meteorological name, anyway. She kept telling us to embrace our bodies' ability to communicate. To be honest I had no idea how to do it but I did get to practise kissing "in the European manner", as Breezy called it, and all those other physical rituals of social intercourse that flummox me, even as I attempt to perform them correctly. I reciprocated her grip, feeling faintly like a couple of girl guides telling ghost stories in the tent with the lights out.

"Caroline. While we wait, let me tell you a story. Would you like that? It is my story."

Quite frankly, at that point, I would have cheerfully screamed until I fainted, rather than stand still holding another woman's hand while waiting for my incipient panic attack to arrive, but what choice did I have?

"OK, fine. But I do wish your Mr. Renfield would hurry up. It's getting hot in here."

It *was* hot, and her charnel-house aroma was choking me.

"So. Perhaps you have been wondering about my name?" She continued without waiting for my answer. "Velds is a corruption of an old Wallachian name – Feldsalen. It means field of scarlet. My family were aristocrats. We ruled an area of over 2,000 square kilometres in an area that is now torn between Bulgaria, Serbia and the Carpathian Mountains. You know this part of the world at all?"

I confessed that I didn't. Such travelling as I do tends to be France or Italy. Holidays, and the very, very occasional trip to the Costa del Sol if I am defending one of the old "tan and tats" brigade.

"Well, it is rich in history. My family were good rulers. Kind to the peasants who farmed our fields and grazed their livestock on our pastureland. They were patrons of the arts, too. Music has always been a passion of the Feldsalens and we sponsored the first symphony orchestra in Wallachia. They played for the Hapsburg Emperors on more than one occasion. But all that changed in 1503.

"Our traditional enemies were the Ottomans: Muslims from the south. In that year, they surged northwards and deposed a relative of mine. Our lands were seized for a time by the Ottomans and we were forced to seek exile with other families loyal to the Wallachian princes. But we were not to be separated from our land for long. In a bloody battle called the Night of Terror, we were resurgent, recapturing our castle and executing the leader of the Ottomans in that part of Wallachia, Mehmet the Hawk. Our family name stood for the red background of our coat of arms, but after that night, the field of scarlet was understood to refer to the battleground. The following day, 10,000 corpses littered the field and their blood had stained the earth.

"Since that time, we have prospered and never again were we torn away from our land. You see, Caroline, land is like blood. It is what makes us a family. It is what connects us to our forbears. You do see that, don't you?

The Feldsalen name underwent a series of transformations until in the late 18th Century we adopted a simpler, easier to pronounce version: Velds. This change coincided with the rise of the Dutch East India Company, which, as I am sure you know, dominated the Asian spice trade for almost 200 years. I can assure you, a Dutch-sounding surname was a boon in those years and we established ourselves as one of the wealthiest families in Europe until the unfortunate demise of the company in 1800. More corruption, I'm afraid, though financial rather than linguistic.

"Then, we expanded our interests in the burgeoning world of industrialisation and technology. Ah, it was a good time to be alive, Caroline, let me assure you of that. We worked with Thomas Edison, with Rockefeller, with Brunel, with J.P. Morgan: all were our partners in business ventures that brought wealth and influence.

"Even war could not slow our ascent. In both the Great War and the Second; Korea and then Vietnam; and on into the Middle East, the Velds name was pre-eminent. Our munitions experts designed and manufactured some of the best and most successful killing machines of the Twentieth Century. Oh, our name was not on the rifles or the bullets, the gas canisters or the napalm shells: we had many subsidiaries by then. But it was Velds money, Velds expertise, Velds insights that led to those engines of war being developed at all. Our chief accountant once calculated that two in every three deaths in wartime since 1905 were caused by a Velds product. Impressive, no?"

I had been given an opportunity to speak and found I was unable to. Normally, eloquence is not something with which I struggle. It is one of the pre-requisites of my profession and I was preternaturally good at extempore argument even before taking up the law. My parents always said I would be an actress or a lawyer.

"From an economic perspective," I finally stuttered out, "undoubtedly, yes. But is it really something to be proud of? That your family's munitions have led to so much killing? So much injury? So many maimed soldiers – and civilians?"

"Of course to be proud is good! Did we start those wars? No. Was it a Velds who murdered the Archduke Ferdinand? No. Anyway, he was a distant cousin of mine, so of course not. Did we send American troops into South East Asia to chase away Communists? No again. Was it a Velds who spent the 1990s trying to remove one leader in favour of another all over Africa and the Middle East? No again. I seem to remember it was presidents and prime ministers. Councils of ministers. Committees. Governments and their security agents. How could a traditional old European family of aristocrats lead to global mass murder? We simply traded. Built relationships. Offered help. And shall I tell you something else? We were rewarded for it. Not just the money; that was merely their end of the bargain. But with honours, too. In my home, I have photographs of my family with Lincoln, Churchill, Stalin, Eisenhower, Kennedy. With the crowned heads of half the kingdoms of Europe. They showered us with honours. Orders of this, crosses of that: distinguished, meritorious, valorous and true. No, Caroline, the Velds name is synonymous with honour, not death. People die all the time. Everybody dies, in the end. The means of their passing is less important than the way that they lived. So a Velds bullet or child's toy at the top of a staircase; the heroic or the banal: it matters not."

"But to trade in death. Your profits are linked to

conflict. More young men killed means more return on investment for your shareholders. Surely you must agree that your family's business needs wars to stay profitable?"

"Perhaps. But, there were wars before there was Velds Industries. We are an old family, Caroline, but we did not count Attila the Hun among our customers. Or Genghis Khan. Or Alexander the Great. Or Nero, Caligula, Julius Caesar or Marcus Aurelius. I dare say, were we to quit the defence industry tomorrow, Peace on Earth would not be the headline on the following day's news."

I was furious. I was being bested in debate by an industrialist. I should have been winning. It was my training. I tried again.

"Perhaps not. But can you sleep at night knowing that so many people lie dead on battlefields having been killed by a weapon or a shell bearing your name?"

"I do not sleep at night. I prefer to work then. But my conscience is clear Caroline. Is yours? Do you know where your pension funds invest your money? I can tell you right now, every major pension fund in the world has millions invested in Velds Industries stock. And your profession. Do you sleep at night, knowing you are defending rapists, child-killers, murderers?"

"That's completely different. For a start, I am not defending rapists, child-killers or murderers, only people accused of those crimes. One of the fundamental principles underpinning Anglo Saxon law is the concept that one is innocent until proven guilty. Therefore, I defend innocent people. Second, we take cases on the taxi-rank principle – the next case to the next lawyer. No choice in the matter. I merely serve the law."

"Oh, I think that is just a little sanctimonious, don't you? Are you telling me you have never sat in a client conference and known, in your heart, that the person facing you was a monster? That blood was on their hands? Your job is to find loopholes in the law, weaknesses in your opponents' case, feeble witnesses or anxious police officers, and exploit them ruthlessly. Is that not so?"

I wanted to say no. To rage against her teasing tone as she picked apart my arguments. But the trouble was, she was besting me. Only the previous month I had sat in a room in a police station with an obese man with rotting teeth who was accused of multiple rapes. The evidence against him was overwhelming. There was no doubt in my mind that he was guilty. I could tell that he was relishing every moment of the discussion. His eyes kept sliding over my front and despite the fact I was wearing my robes, with a high, white wing collar and barrister bands at my throat, I felt he could see right through them. I would cheerfully have locked him up myself, without a trial, and lobbed the key into the Thames. But I was his defence counsel and it was my job to get him off. And, I am ashamed to say, I did. Two of the police officers who'd investigated his case had screwed up the chain of custody on a pair of women's underwear he'd kept as a trophy. The prosecuting counsel was new to his job and fluffed a couple of cross-examinations. I presented evidence of his levels of fitness that would make his supposedly chasing one of his victims for 300 yards along a residential road a medical impossibility. The jury found him not guilty. Afterwards, the foreman, a young guy, a student, I think, from one of the better universities, came up to me outside Court.

"We all thought he'd done it," he said. "But we followed the judge's instructions. You were so good in there we had no option. How can you live with yourself? I couldn't."

Then he turned on his heel and walked off into the sunshine. I drank rather more red wine that night than was good for me and went to sleep screaming into my pillow.

Even in the dark, I could tell Peta Velds was smiling. Her voice had a lilting, mocking quality. She squeezed my hand tighter then released it.

"Poor Caroline. Don't mind me. You're right. My family is terrible. Some of the things we have done would make your blood run cold in your veins. But that is why we are here in this Godforsaken place. We are researching skin cancer and cell mutations brought on by UV radiation. My family's foundation is pouring millions into David's research. Your fiancé is a genius. He works so hard for us. I know you are worried about him so it is my duty to reassure you that he is fine."

I opened my mouth to speak, when with a hum, the lights went back on the lift. A loud bang came from somewhere in the shaft above us and then it jolted into motion again. I released a breath I had been holding and blinked in the light. I turned to face Peta Velds, noticing as I did that she was covering her mouth.

"I hope you can do that, Ms Velds. I really do."

The lift rocked to a halt and the doors slid open. At last we had reached her office – and breathable air.

My relief was short lived.

The lift has stopped about three feet lower than the floor level. In front of us was a sharp-edged steel beam – the edge of the office floor where it intersected with the lift-shaft. Below it was smooth concrete.

"How tiresome," she said. "No matter. You look fit, Caroline. Climb out. I will steady you."

I am fit. And strong. I used to row at Cambridge and the other girls mocked me for my shoulders. They were all powerful rowers but I was easily the best – to my occasional chagrin. When buying robes for court, I still have what one outfitter in Chancery Lane called, "square shoulders, like a man's".

So I placed my hands flat on the cold steel edge of her office floor and hauled myself onto the carpet. As I got a knee planted on the floor, I felt Peta Velds put her hands on my hips and hold me. She shoved, hard, and I virtually flew into the room, landing in a splayed crouch that made me glad I was wearing a trouser suit. How she managed it I don't know, but she was out of the lift and standing by me, pulling me to my feet almost at the same moment. Then, as if to deride me for my undignified entrance into the room, the lift smoothly completed its journey, the doors gliding shut with a whisper of bearings somewhere inside the mechanism.

Waiting for us was a man dressed in a dinner suit. He was holding a long dagger.

9

MINUTES OF MEETING BETWEEN PETA VELDS AND CAROLINE MURRAY LLD (TAKEN BY J.S. LE FANU, GENERAL COUNSEL, VELDS INDUSTRIES) 11TH OCTOBER 2010

I had been opening post for Peta when she arrived with her guest, one Caroline Murray, a barrister of Roxburgh Chambers, Middle Temple. Their arrival was a little unorthodox: the lift was playing up and they had to clamber out onto the floor like mountaineers. I introduced myself. Caroline Murray appeared flushed and touched her throat several times as we sat around the meeting table. The reddening crept steadily down her neck and spread towards her ears. I noticed that Peta was quite unable to keep her eyes away from the darkening skin at Miss Murray's throat. These are my shorthand notes, transcribed and copied to Caroline Murray for her records.

PV: I am sorry you have had such a long journey to reassure yourself as to your fiancé's health. And for the malfunctioning elevator.

CM: [laughing] That's perfectly OK. Just a little hiccup. But I would really like to see David. He is at work today, I assume? As you have taken his phone away, I can't contact him.

PV: David is at work, why wouldn't he be? And as to the phone, I do not permit any of my scientific team to have phones here. The work in which they are engaged is secret, and I am afraid nowadays there are just too many temptations to share things on social media. They have all signed contracts and non-disclosure agreements drafted by Mr Le Fanu, so there really shouldn't be a problem. They are well remunerated to compensate them for my unorthodox approach – yes, Caroline, you may raise your eyebrows all you want; I know my approach is out of the common way. As I say, David is downstairs. I shall ask him to come and join us.

CM: Can't we go to him? I'd love to see his lab.

PV: Impossible. The laboratory is top secret. Out of bounds to anybody without security clearance. Unless your name is on Mr Stoker's list, I'm afraid a visit is out of the question.

CM: And Mr Stoker would be?

PV: My Head of Security. He and Mr le Fanu work closely to ensure our work here is protected physically, virtually and legally. I will not tolerate any breaches. Excuse me one moment.

[Ms Velds crosses room to desk intercom and asks Dr Harker to join her. She tells him to take the stairs.]

CM: While we wait for David, I'd like to ask you about something I heard in Great Yarmouth. Apparently there have been accidents, and a viral infection of some sort. Is that true? Are people falling ill? Is there something about David's work that is dangerous?

PV: Goodness me, Caroline. What a lot of questions. In any large lab there will be health and safety incidents from time to time. But a virus? No. Ridiculous gossip from those peasants in the town. I provide jobs, which, believe me, are in short supply in these parts. I look after them when they are ill, or pregnant. People get ill everywhere. There is no virus here. A guard fell awkwardly and did sustain an injury. But his untimely demise was due to incompetence at the local hospital, not anything that occurred here. They should model their hygiene protocols on ours: they would have far fewer iatrogenic deaths if they did.

CM: It's a little unfair to suggest that deaths from superbug infections are caused by doctors, Ms Velds. They do their best with limited resources.

PV: That's as may be. And please call me Peta. In any eventuality, our health and safety practices are out of the top drawer. You may inspect the report from the Health & Safety Executive inspector who audited the lab at the start of this project. She found nothing to complain about, did she Mr Le Fanu?

JSLF: I seem to remember she left us smiling.

[The door to the stairs opens. Dr David Harker enters]

DH: Caro! What are you doing here? I thought my email was clear. It's over.

CM: David, please sit down and talk to me. It was your last email that made me decide to come up here to see you. It was so out of character. I simply can't believe you meant it. I thought it must be stress.

DH: I'm not stressed. I enjoy it here. Peta gives me

everything I could possibly need. For my work, I mean. Don't you Peta?

PV: I try, David. I try.

CM: What's that on your neck? The plaster. Have you hurt yourself?

DH: It's nothing. I got stung by a wasp. It got a bit infected.

CM: A wasp? It's October, David. There aren't any wasps. Look, what's going on? You're acting decidedly oddly. And why won't you look at me? What's wrong, darling?

DH: It was in a mask. We wear them when we're working with radioactive isotopes. It must have hibernated or something. Like the big one that stung your Dad's finger inside his gardening glove a few years back. When was that? January? Anyway, I'm fine. Look, I really think this was a mistake. I have to go. We're about to run a gamma radiation flood test on rat skin cells. I wish you hadn't come. Peta, can I go now?

PV: I don't see that I can stop you, Dr Harker.

[Dr Harker leaves by stairs.]

PV: Satisfied, Ms Murray? It is not David's health that bothers you at all, is it? But rather his rejection of you as a lover. I sympathise. For a woman like you, a brilliant and attractive husband would have been quite a trophy.

CM: What do you mean, a woman like me? I am wealthy, successful and with excellent prospects in the legal profession. By this time next year there is every chance I shall be a QC.

PV: Which is what men dream of, yes, of course.

"Oh, I want to marry a woman who is better paid and better qualified than I." How little you know of male psychology, Caroline. Forgive me, Sheridan, but you would agree with me, I am sure. The human male wishes to marry an attractive female who will bear him many strong children – preferably sons. Why do you suppose they fixate on our breasts? It is because they bestow life on those heirs they yearn for. You are, and please, I only say this in a spirit of candour, not the best a man like David Harker could secure for his brood mare. He has always been the subject of attentions from the opposite sex. At conferences, symposia, and so on. It is only his innocence and dedication to his work that blind him to their advances, I am sure you must have noticed that.

CM: I think I've had enough of this, Ms Velds. I don't know which century you think you're living in but times have moved on. David and I were very happily engaged – and shall be again. I'm leaving. You will hear from me again.

PV: Oh, I don't doubt it, Caroline. I don't doubt it.

[Miss Murray leaves by stairs.]

10

CAROLINE MURRAY'S JOURNAL, 12TH OCTOBER 2010

After that disastrous meeting with Peta Velds and her General Counsel, I feel utterly deflated. David seemed fine in himself, he just didn't want to be in the same room with me. I mean, he wasn't hyper, or depressed, just massively unbothered and eager to get away. But that was strange, wasn't it? We are still engaged. I've resolved to do some digging on Peta Velds and to try to figure out what sort of a hold she has on David. Lucy and I had a somewhat dispiriting dinner at the pub and we both went to bed at about 10.00 p.m.

Lucy kissed me good night in the hallway between our two doors. I tried not to hold myself rigidly but to reciprocate the hug, as I'd learnt on the seminar. She has her faults but she is a sweet thing at heart and she knows how physical contact is difficult for me.

"Relax, darling," she whispered in my ear. "Breathe."

Then she was gone, shutting her door behind her with a reminder that we were due to leave for London at nine sharp and not to oversleep. I got undressed for bed, removed my makeup and cleaned my teeth. As I got into my pyjamas I caught a glimpse of myself in the wardrobe's mirrored door and wondered. Was David getting second best marrying me? He's always said he loved me from the moment we first met and it's true I have never doubted him for a moment, but I know there are women far better looking then I am who move in the same circles as he does. You'd think all those science-y types with their white coats and thick glasses would be a plug ugly bunch. But I've met a couple of his colleagues at Christmas parties and my goodness they scrub up well. Apart from the randy Dane, there were a couple of interns last year who I swear were there because they'd missed the door marked "models". All tanned legs, minidresses and long blonde hair. In comparison I felt decidedly frumpy in my lawyer's standby mufti of navy linen dress and pearls. Nothing to be done about it, I reflected with a sigh, and climbed into bed. I knew I should be reading witness statements so as not to fall too far behind in my cases, and had brought a stack with me. The trouble was, I couldn't concentrate on work. All I could think about was ghastly Peta Velds and her imperious manner. That and the creeps she had hired to protect her. So I turned to a thriller I'd bought at a service station on the drive up, something easy to get through with a lurid cover illustration and the author's name in red metallic capitals. I read for an hour or so then, when I felt sleep mercifully tugging at my eyelids, and my consciousness, I laid it on the night stand and closed my eyes.

I have no idea how long it took me to fall asleep, but it seemed no sooner had I closed my eyes than I was wide awake. I checked the time on my phone. It was just after 2.00 a.m. I wasn't sure what had broken my sleep but my heart was pounding fiercely, I was breathing rapidly and shallowly and I was covered in a sweat. My first thought was that I was having a panic attack. I switched on the bedside light and scrabbled in my handbag for my Rescue Remedy. A couple of sprays onto my tongue and a few slow breaths and I began to regain some semblance of normal functioning. Then I heard a faint sound from across the hallway and my pulse jumped again. It came from the direction of Lucy's room and I realised I had heard it in my sleep and that was what had roused me.

I pulled on the cheap towelling dressing gown that hung on the back of the bedroom door, stepped into the matching slippers and opened the door onto the corridor. It was pitch-black: pubs are legally required to have night lights if they take guests but I supposed the bulb had blown. The noise came again, a low moan and a sharp indrawn sigh of breath. It made me feel distinctly uncomfortable as it had an undeniable sexual quality to it. But something else. Beneath the sigh, there was an edge to the sound, as if someone were in pain. I say someone because the voice sounded nothing like Lucy's. Yet I knew she was alone. She is not averse to an occasional pickup – I think it goes with her professional territory – but I had kissed her goodnight not four hours earlier and unless she had returned to the prowl in downtown Great Yarmouth, that was how she should still have been.

I crossed the yard of blue carpet, wondering as I did why so many provincial hotels have the same fleur de lys pattern, and knocked at Lucy's door.

"Luce. Are you OK? I heard something," I said, trying to pitch my voice loud enough to carry into the room but quiet enough not to wake any other guests.

There was no answer. Perhaps, I thought, she'd been

having a nightmare. I turned to go back to my own room, and as I did so, I stepped on something that crunched underfoot. It sounded like glass — from the light bulb, I wondered. That's when I heard it again. Out here in the corridor it was clearer, and there was a definite pleading note to the cry.

I turned and knocked harder on the door. There was no reply and I was properly scared by now. I tried the knob but she had locked the door. I rattled it and the door shook in its frame, the twisted and blackened Elizabethan timbers having long ago fallen out of alignment. So I did what the hero in my thrillers would have done. I turned the knob fully clockwise to disengage the latch, stepped as far from the door as I could and then slammed myself against it, using those rower's shoulders of mine. With a loud, crunching crack, the latch tore through the flimsy wood of the frame and I fell into the room. The sight that greeted me will haunt me for ever.

Lucy lay on the bed on her back, no nightie or pyjamas, moaning faintly, arms flung out to either side, breathing heavily and still emitting those sad little moans of pleasure or pain – it was hard to tell which. Kneeling over her, also naked, was a young woman: she appeared to be sucking at Lucy's breast. As I stumbled into the room, she whirled round, leaping from Lucy's prostrate form to land on all fours. Her hands were bent into claws that dug into the wooden floorboards. Hissing at me, she scuttled sideways towards the window. Her mouth was wide open, almost as if her lower jaw had broken from its hinge, and two long needle-like fangs descended from her upper gums, somehow behind her regular teeth. They were dripping with blood and some translucent substance, and the mixture of fluids ran down her chin and dropped to the floor in long strings.

The muscles of her arms were like thick ropes beneath her skin and with one long limb she wrenched the sash window open and swung herself out. I was torn between wanting to watch where she went and going to Lucy. In the end I'm afraid my curiosity won out, and I rushed to the window and looked down. The girl was crawling straight down the wall, head first. Her arms and legs were braced against each other and she used the tension in the muscles to lock herself tight to the surface of the wall, pushing fingers and toes into the cracks where the mortar had fallen away from the bricks. She detached her arms as she reached the ground and simply walked away from the base of the wall on her hands, like an acrobat, before righting herself with a spring. Glaring balefully back at me with red-rimmed eyes, she ran lightly away into the shadows at the side of the road and was lost from view.

Now I turned to my friend. I knelt by the bed and cradled Lucy's head in my arm. Her left breast had two small punctures, one each side of the nipple, which was swollen and very red. The punctures were bleeding – a steady flow that I attempted to staunch with a wodge of tissues I grabbed from the box on her bedside table and pressed down firmly over the wound. The pressure made her cry out and she opened her eyes.

"Oh, Caro. I had a nightmare. Such a dreadful one. I was dying. Bleeding. From my – oh!"

She looked down, following my inadvertent eye movement, and saw my hand pressed over her chest with the tissues, which were already turning red as the blood soaked through.

"You weren't dreaming, Luce. There was someone here, a girl. She attacked you."

"Oh, God, Caro, it felt so utterly odd. There was no pain, not exactly anyway. It was, you know, arousing. But I felt something horrid was happening at the same time. How bad is it?"

She peered down at my hand and I gently lifted it away along with the bloody tissues. The punctures hadn't clotted at all and blood started flowing freely the moment I released the pressure. They weren't large at all, hardly bigger than a typed O, but the blood just wouldn't stop. I wiped it away with some more tissues and got Lucy to press down on the holes with her index and middle fingers.

"What am I going to do, Caro? I can't lie here all night like this. I don't want to bleed to death from my boob. And who was she? What was she doing here? And how did she get into my room?"

Her voice was rising and I didn't have any answers.

"She must have climbed in through the window," I said. "Maybe she was a druggie. Or, I don't know, a member of one of those weird cults that set initiation tests. I prosecuted a case last year where this married couple were running a sex cult from their suburban semi. It was really just a perverted swingers' club but they'd devised all these rituals and tests and one of those involved blood drinking. They got sent down for five years each."

"But what about me? I'm bleeding and it won't stop."

"I can find out where the nearest A&E is if you like? Take you there."

"What? And haul my poor bleeding boob out and tell some leering consultant I've been sucked by a bloody

66

sex-pest? No, thank you very bloody much! I told you Norfolk was full of weirdos, Caro, but you had to have your road trip, didn't you?"

Then she burst into tears. I didn't blame her. She's always ready with the waterworks and usually it's part of the ever-fascinating Lucinda Easterbrook One-Woman Show. But tonight I felt she had every right to cry – and to blame me, if I'm totally honest. I had cajoled her into coming with the promise of seeing David – a promise I'd not kept. Which was another problem.

"Come on," I said. "I've got an idea. You'll have to put something on and come into my room."

She pulled on a thin grey vest with spaghetti straps, and a pair of knickers, then replaced her fingers over the wounds, and together we left her room, wedging the door shut into the cracked frame. Amazingly, nobody had come upstairs to investigate. Then I remembered that the landlady had said they were quiet except for us and, "seein' as 'ow the old man and me is sound sleepers, you can have a party in your room if you really want to". I sat Lucy on the edge of the bath and rootled about in my sponge bag. Right at the bottom I found what I was looking for. A little blue plastic cylinder with faded and scratched print on it: my faithful styptic pencil. I "borrowed" it from David when we first moved in together. They're magic at stopping bleeding if you cut your leg – or worse – shaving. The only drawback is they sting like crazy. Lucy saw it and her eyes widened as she realised what it was.

"Oh, no, Caro. Please tell me you're not going to do what I think you are."

"Sorry, Luce, but I can't think of anything else. I know what you mean about A&E but we have to stop that bleeding. I mean it's not gushing or anything, but it is still coming out."

"OK. But I'm going to scream. I used one on my armpit once and I shrieked so loud the stage manager came in to my dressing room, said he thought I'd been stabbed. The dirty bastard just wanted to catch me in my undies, if you ask me. But anyway, mustn't keep you from your task, Doctor Murray. Go on then."

I gently pulled the straps off her shoulders and dragged the vest down around her middle. Then she took a deep breath, let it out through her teeth, squeezed her eyes shut and gripped the edge of the bath with her free hand. I gently lifted her other hand away from her breast, which was still bleeding from the punctures, though it did seem as if it had slowed a little. I wetted the tip of the sandpapery white stick in a drip of water in the sink and pushed it against one of the holes. Through her clenched teeth, Lucy let out a suppressed squeal of pain. Then I moved it to the other hole and repeated the process. I dabbed away the blood and was relieved to see that the flow had slowed further. It was more of a trickle now and after another application of the styptic pencil, it stopped altogether. Poor Lucy was squeezing tears out between her crinkled eyelids and I watched as a single drop slid to the end of her long dark eyelashes and dropped onto her vest, which turned from pale to dark grey.

The punctures had eventually stopped bleeding, and although the skin around her nipple was crusted with a mixture of drying blood and the salty residue from the styptic pencil, it otherwise looked fine. No swelling, and the discolouration where Lucy's assailant had sucked blood to the skin surface as well as out through the punctures had faded. I picked a makeup remover pad from the plastic sleeve in my cosmetics bag and made her hold it in place over the punctures. Then I secured it with a couple of clear plasters that I always keep in my sponge bag, along with paracetamol and anti-indigestion tablets. Careful not to dislodge the improvised dressing, or cause Lucy any more pain, I eased the vest back up and replaced the thin straps over her shoulders.

"There," I said. "Good as new."

"Thanks, mate," she said, gingerly pressing where the pad showed through the material of her vest. "Do you really think she was just some crackhead or tweaker looking for kicks?"

"Tweaker? Where do you pick up this language, Luce?"

She laughed. A good sign. Not a hysterical noise either, a proper, earthy Lucy Easterbrook special. The one that has the male talkshow hosts falling over themselves to serve up another easy question. "So, Lucinda, Oh, OK...So, Lucy, what made you accept this part? How did you find it working with a notoriously demanding director?"

"The question is, Caro, why are you surprised? Everyone knows about tweakers since Breaking Bad. Hello? Meth addicts? You must have run across a few in court?"

The conversation turned to nicknames for druggies and I inwardly breathed a sigh of relief. We were going to be fine. I poured us both a brandy, another essential component of my travel kit, which we drank from the tea cup – "tea and coffee facility's in all rooms" – and the cling-filmed plastic tumbler in the bathroom.

I checked the time: 3.00 a.m. We needed to sleep. Lucy read my mind and turned to me. She held my hands in her lap and leaned close to me. "Please can I sleep in here tonight?" she said.

"Of course. Come on, it'll be like Guides."

We climbed under the duvet and she cuddled up behind me. Was her attacker really a drugged-up cult member or rural swinger? I wanted, desperately, to believe that. The trouble was, I couldn't close my eyes without seeing that horrible distorted mouth, or the naked woman crawling down the outside of the building. Shock, I decided. I'd probably not fully woken up and fitted an admittedly scary event into a surreal narrative stimulated by Ariane's ravings of a few days earlier. With this alternative explanation jumbling around in my brain, I fell asleep to the sound of Lucy's snores in my right ear. It seemed like only seconds before my phone alarm went off at seven.

11

DIARY OF AN ACTRESS: THE LIFE OF LUCINDA EASTERBROOK, 12TH OCTOBER 2010

I am NEVER going back to bloody Norfolk! First I didn't even get to see David. Then, some crazy tweaker attacked me in my hotel room and bit me on the boob! She's still sore! I don't think Caro was best pleased by her meeting with Peta Velds, either. The woman has poor David virtually locked up in his lab like the Count of Monte Cristo. We discussed all sorts of mad plans on the drive back to civilisation. I genuinely think Caro wants to pull him out of there dressed in black ninja gear. Her, obviously, not David. I'm finding it hard to concentrate for more than a few seconds. I think my assailant – Caro's word, not mine – must have give me an infection when she bit me. I have a ringing in my ears and my mouth tastes funny – coppery, like when you bite your tongue.

I've been constantly hungry too – even after we stopped for lunch. I had a burger and Caro laughed when I asked for it rare. The silly little thing behind the counter just stared at me. And the oddest thing: for a split second I wanted to bite her. It was an urge, almost sexual. It started in my belly like a squirming thing trying to get out, like snakes wriggling around inside me. And I just wanted to lean across the brushed steel counter, grab her round the neck and bite her till she bled. Then it was gone. Caro was giving me one of her looks, all wide, questioning eyes and pursed lips. She asked me about it in the car.

"What was all that about?" she said.

"What was all what about?"

"With that poor girl who served us? You looked at her like she'd beaten you to a part in a film."

"Nothing! I just wish these places would be a little more flexible and not serve their meat cooked to shoe-leather."

Now it's late. But I'm not sleepy. In fact, I think I'm going to go out. Caro would be horrified; she's convinced I'll be mugged if I leave the flat after seven. But I feel itchy all over. And hungry.

12

[DRAFT POST] RAMBLINGS OF A FREE-REVVING MIND – DAVID HARKER'S BLOG, 12TH OCTOBER 2010

Now I'm free of interruption from Caroline I can get on with what I'm doing. Peta Velds is the perfect employer. She gives me the money and equipment I ask for then leaves me alone. I find her single-mindedness impressive. At first I wasn't sure about being kept in the laboratory but now I see it's for the best. There are too many distractions out there and anyway, as Peta says, plenty of people would rather see us shut down. Cancer charities make millions in donations, but as Peta says, how much of the money really goes to scientists and how much is just spent on marketing and gala dinners for major donors? Then there's the medical profession. If, no, when we find a cure for skin cancer, that puts a lot of rich and powerful people out of a job. Will they stand by and let us do it? Obviously not!

Peta makes sure I have everything I need for my personal life as well as my work. I have a small apartment within the facility here and she herself has a private dining room. She invited me there last night to talk over my work and what we can achieve together.

The food was amazing. I had a rare steak – really amazing flavour, too. I asked her what the cut was. She just gave me this enigmatic smile and said it was a cut from "the old country". Actually what she said was, "We butcher our beasts differently where my people come from". It doesn't matter – the flavour was really intense. Peta didn't eat anything. I thought it was a bit strange and I asked her if she wouldn't be joining me. She said her condition means she has to have a special diet. I asked her what condition.

Peta suffers from a rare chromosomal disorder called Reiser-Strick Syndrome. It affects one in ten thousand people, but that's still 7,000 sufferers worldwide. Sufferers can't tolerate direct exposure to sunlight. It cause rapid fatal cancerous mutations in their skin cells. She referred to sufferers as her "family", I guess it's a way of coping and maybe of sharing information that could lead to a cure. Kind of crowd-sourcing. Plus she's got the wealth and the connections to see it through.

Does it matter if she has a personal angle for funding my research? No! Why should it? It just makes her a more motivated patron.

13

POLICE REPORT, REPORTING OFFICER PC H. SINGH, 5643, PIMLICO PS, MET. POLICE, 3.17 A.M. 14TH OCTOBER 2010

On patrol on Embankment with PC R. Mayhew, heard groaning under bench. Investigated. Found a male, aged approximately 50, covered in cardboard, most likely vagrant. Refused to give name.

Male was bleeding profusely from wound to right side of neck. Stopped bleeding by applying manual pressure and called ambulance.

Male told PC Mayhew and I that he had been offered a hot meal by a female. His words, "a real looker". Then without warning, female had attacked him, lifting him bodily from bench and dropping him over the back, where female proceeded to bite him on neck.

At this point it became apparent victim was drunk or on drugs, as he started spinning us a tale about how she was drinking his blood "like a f***ing vampire": victim's words quoted directly.

Ambulance arrived within five minutes and victim was handed over to paramedics for treatment. Only other point of note: paramedics said this was the second homeless person they'd picked up with neck wound in past few days.

14

LONDON AMBULANCE SERVICE NHS TRUST, PATIENT TRANSFER REPORT, 15TH OCTOBER 2010

Unit G54
Paramedics: J Hudson, P Baker
Date/time: 15th October 2010; 03.25.
Destination hospital: St Bartholomew's

Description of patient's injuries/condition

Patient is white male, age 25-30. Unconscious at scene.

Severe trauma to neck on both sides; deep lacerations through skin, fascia and muscle. Jugular vein and carotid artery shredded; haemorrhaging difficult to stop, applied manual pressure but ineffective – no clotting evident.

Massive blood loss assumed, as blood pressure 80/40. No blood at scene. Very little blood staining to victim's skin or clothing.

No defensive wounds on hands. No other offensive wounds.

Patient carried no ID, cash or possessions: assumed homeless.

DOA.
Death pronounced by Dr GF O'Rourke.

15

CAROLINE MURRAY'S JOURNAL, 16TH
OCTOBER 2010

After the disastrous trip to Norfolk, I was more convinced than ever that Peta Velds had some sort of hold over David. His manner when he came into her office was so different to how he is normally. And the dreadful business with that girl who attacked Lucy. While we were there, I was able to sustain the idea that she was just some local druggie out for some kicks. But looking back, I knew she wasn't even human. Not the way we think of that word. Yes, any old pervert could drink someone's blood, but the way she moved, the way she climbed down the wall. That was beyond any rationale I could come up with. I decided I needed to make contact with Ariane again. But in the end, I didn't need to: she came to me.

I arrived back at the flat to see a familiar figure waiting on the doorstep. No leather this time. Instead a long red velvet dress. Her hair was up, too and she was wearing a tiara. As I said, mad.

I didn't bother with pleasantries, I just unlocked the door and gestured for her to go in ahead of me. Once I had dumped my bag and kicked my shoes off I poured two glasses of wine, handed one to her and then flopped into a chair.

"You look nice," I said. "Fancy dress party?"

"Dinner. With the Crown Prince of Temesvár. His title is only honorary these days but the old ways are a comfort. I came as soon as I knew you were returning from Norfolk."

"Wait. Are you having me watched?"

"'Protected' is the word I would choose, Caroline. And, since you ask, yes, I am."

"This is outrageous. I should call the police. I don't even know your full name. Who are you?"

I felt my nerves fizzing in my stomach and I could sense my blush starting. I swigged some of the wine. She took a big breath and let it out in a sigh.

"My name, Caroline, is Van Helsing."

"What? Wait a minute. As in Bram Stoker, Dracula, all that?"

She nodded, sipping now, and looking at me steadily over the rim of the glass.

"Abraham Van Helsing was my great-great-grandfather."

"OK," I said, standing up. "I think you'd better leave, now. This was obviously all a huge mistake on my part."

"Sit down," she said, sharply, and I felt my legs fold under me as if I was a wet behind the ears junior barrister being rebuked by a County Court judge.

I tried to find a way to articulate the thoughts that were swirling around in my head. It was hard. I had let a madwoman into my flat and now I was apparently powerless to get her out again.

She leaned across the gap between us and laid her hand gently on my knee. It was warm.

"We talked about evolution last time we met, you remember? So, the distant ancestors of the O-One evolved. Into vampires."

"I beg your pardon? You're telling me these, these, people are vampires?"

I do believe I laughed at this point, probably more from tension than anything funny. The woman was clearly delusional and now I was pouring wine for her in my sitting room.

"Yes, Caroline. They are. Night hunters. They gradually disappeared from view as their aversion to sunlight metamorphosed into a fatal reaction. That's when they began to hunt at night, when their victims were sleeping. As nocturnal predators they could move more easily among us and as they did so they passed from the world of reality into the world of myth, of story. The vampires developed into seven main families. They run themselves like corporations. Or criminal gangs. And there are seven equally old families who have pledged to find and destroy them. We call ourselves cutters."

"Should I ask why?" I said, dabbing at the corners of my eyes, wanting and simultaneously not wanting to hear the answer.

"Can't you guess? We sever the vampires' bloodlines. If you can destroy the mother of the family the others die – there is a link between them we don't understand. But the children can only live while the mother does."

"Don't they just breed more?" I said. Looking back I can't believe how easily I started to believe in Ariane's world, but the way she looked at me without blinking, without a telltale kink at the corner of her mouth, was very convincing.

"They don't breed. Something about the ancient mutation that changed them from human to vampire interfered with their ability to reproduce. They live far, far longer than you or I will but they can only sustain themselves by recruiting new members of their families."

"And you fight them? The cutters?"

"Fight them, and kill them. We are pledged to eradicate them from the face of the Earth; they are an abomination against God's creation. We have developed weapons that work against them, and we research them, monitor their activities around the world. Now, the vampires cannot tolerate sunlight for more than a few seconds. The UV radiation destroys the cells of their circulatory system. They literally burst with blood. So Peta Velds wants to find a way to re-engineer their DNA to prevent it happening. It gives them double the hunting time and frees them to move among us during the day once more. This is why she hired David."

I could feel my neck heating up and I touched my throat. Sometimes I can literally feel the blood under the skin. Ariane Van Helsing sat perfectly still, watching me.

"Caroline. I am sorry to burden you with all this new and unsettling information, but there are things you must know. Dracula was real. Oh, not that silly book. I will come to that in a moment. But the man was real. His name was Vlad Drăcul. His family name was Drăculea. He was married, he had children. As I told you before, he also had an extreme thirst for blood. Vlad Drăcul was Vlad Țepeș. Nowadays he would be called a psychopath and a mass murderer. But you must understand, in the 15th Century, rulers could do whatever they wanted, provided they were strong enough to retain power. You have only to look at your own country's history to see the truth of it. Slayings, torture, mass burnings of heretics, child murders, imprisonment without trial, wars, massacres: this is the history of humankind.

"But I met Peta Velds. She told me all about her family. They weren't called Ţepeş or Drăculea, they were called Feldsalen. It means—"

"'Field of Scarlet', yes I know. She has been peddling that lie for centuries. It is a convenient myth that distances all but the most dedicated researcher from her true history. Did she tell you about the slaying of Mehmet the Hawk?"

"Yes. It did sound a little over the top, but as you said yourself, this was the 15th Century. I suppose 10,000 dead in a battle wasn't all that unusual, was it?"

"Not at all. In fact, it was a modest death toll compared to some other conflicts. Why, on the first day of the Battle of the Somme, the British Fourth Army alone lost 19,240 men. Nobody knows the exact figure for the cumulative death toll but it ran to hundreds of thousands. And the O-One were there, though they did not call themselves that at the time. And did Peta Velds tell you what happened at the battle where The Hawk was slain?"

"She just said that it was a bloody battle and the earth was stained red – hence the confusion over the name."

"Oh, the earth was stained red, Caroline. Because Vlad Ţepeş devised one of his cruelest ever punishments. The death toll from the fighting itself was only 500. His soldiers were tactically and strategically superior and outnumbered the Ottomans. Mehmet was captured almost immediately by a group of turncoats who were loyal to Ţepeş and at that point, his troops surrendered, for a loss of just 500. The next day Ţepeş had the 9,500 men tied to stakes, head down. He cut off Mehmet's right arm and bound the hand around the hilt of his own sword. Then he walked amongst the screaming men and slit their throats using the blade carried in their dead leader's hand. It was a humiliation as well as a painful way to die. When he tired of the task, he had one of the Ottomans untied and promised him his freedom if he would take over. Through sheer terror, or perhaps because he had lost his mind, the man complied. So it went on, for many long hours, with one Ottoman succeeding the next as they fell, exhausted from the work. At the end of the day, there were 9,900 dead Ottoman soldiers, emptied of blood, already a feast for the crows.

"But what about the 100 who helped?" I asked, though I doubted they had lived out their days as farmers.

"He berated them for their cowardice and their disloyalty to their fellows. Then he made them swallow their swords. He invented the punishment on the spot. He had them tied to stakes, then he would push the tip of each Ottoman's sword down into his throat. They used curved weapons, scimitars – and so as the blade travelled down through the man's abdomen, it would eventually emerge through his gut or his genital area.

"But if he was a vampire, how come he could do all this? I thought you told me they couldn't go out in the daytime?"

"Not exactly. I said in sunlight. That year, there was a massive volcanic eruption in the South China Sea – Mount Orarua. Contemporary accounts described a pillar of fire that stretched to the heavens. It deposited a cloud of dust into the Earth's atmosphere that blotted out the sun for two years. During that time Mehmet the Hawk attacked, perhaps suspecting the lack of sun would disorientate or in some other way hinder his enemy. In fact, it granted Țepeș the freedom to command his troops personally during the day.

"There is only one image of Vlad Țepeș out of doors – a famous and rather nasty woodcut. Other than that, there are a couple of formal portraits only. The reason is obvious. He only ventured out in the night hours, except for that momentous battle.

"But I get ahead of myself. I said I would explain about the book, Dracula. Bram Stoker was fascinated by vampire lore, as you probably know. He was part of a decadent group of aristocrats and intellectuals with too much imagination and too much time on their hands. They included Lord Byron and also Mary Shelley, who would go on to create Frankenstein. The mother presiding over the Dracul family in the 19th Century went by the name Ellen Pierce. She turned Stoker and set him to work writing Dracula. By introducing vampires as a staple of Gothic fiction, she threw the spotlight off their true nature and made them figures of childish frights, to be read for pleasure under the bedclothes, while their real-life counterparts were abroad, and feeding.

"When you say, 'turned', do you mean what I think you mean?"

"She fed on him, but did not drain him. The vampire produces two substances that are adaptations to their way of life. The first is an anticoagulant. You know this word?"

I nodded.

"So, it prevents the victim's blood from clotting. They inject it through their fangs into the wound. The second is a micro-organism, a parasite, that co-evolved with the vampires themselves. It lives in their saliva and contains copies of their DNA with which it infects their victims. In this way they can reproduce themselves. I have studied this parasite and named it *lamia multigena* – vampire brood. The vampires attack in two ways: purely for feeding, in which case they simply drain their prey dry and the *lamia multigena* dies along with the victim; and for reproduction, in which case they take enough blood to weaken the person on whom they feed, allowing the parasite to gain a foothold. In the latter case, the parasite restores normal-seeming physical function, but leaves the victim vulnerable to suggestion. They live on to serve the vampires, eventually mutating under the continuing genetic engineering conducted by the *lamia multigena* at the sub-cellular level. The new host's mitochondrial DNA becomes transformed and their humanity is stripped away from them in the course of a few months."

"Wait. You just said for reproduction. You mean they don't reproduce sexually?"

"Correct. They are libidinous creatures, certainly – the old tales of incubi and succubi are true. But as I said, along with the mutation that led to their taking a darker path to *Homo sapiens*, they also lost the ability to reproduce sexually – a defect in their DNA. Perhaps God was trying to limit their spread, who knows? But the parasites ensured their vile race continued to proliferate among us."

I was almost convinced until some shred of rationality in my overburdened brain fought back. I accused her of confecting a monstrous tale because she was mentally unhinged, or a spy for a rival of Peta Velds. Or just another groupie of David's. That's when she offered to show me proof that vampires existed. And I, wanting her out of my home, agreed to go with her to her house in Bloomsbury.

I had to find a way to end this ridiculous conversation. I had a case to prepare for and, frankly, she was starting to worry me. I thought she might accuse me of being one and try to stake me or hit me with a crucifix or whatever they do.

"Look," I said. "Just for the sake of argument, let's say I believe you about vampires. Which I don't by the way. Prove it. Starting with your nonsensical story about Peta Velds."

"You want me to prove that Peta Velds is the direct descendant of Vlad Țepeș? That will be difficult. We would have to travel to Poland to consult libraries."

"No. Forget her family tree. Prove vampires exist. Because otherwise I think you'd better leave. David's only mistake was leaving me here in London, but that will change once we're married."

"Proof. Spoken like a true lawyer. Always there must be evidence, yes? Very well. But you must give me some time. A couple of days. Then if I call for you, will you come with me? We will find something to show you that I am sure you will find persuasive."

"Wait. One, who's 'we'? Two, come with you where?"

"We are the people who stand between Velds and humanity in England. Myself and my assistants. I have three. They maintain weapons, do research for me and tend to wounds. You must come with me to our premises."

"Premises where?" I said.

"We have a facility in Bloomsbury. An old building. It was bequeathed to us in the 18th Century."

I suppose my curiosity got the better of me, and I

agreed. I thought I could spare a couple of hours over the next few days and then I could leave this ridiculous woman to her gothic fantasies in Bloomsbury and head back to our flat alone. And I was right. The problem was, by then it was too late to go back to my case. David was in trouble.

16

HUNT BOOK OF ARIANE VAN HELSING, 17TH OCTOBER 2010

Caroline asked me for proof of the existence of vampires. I can't blame her. If you are not brought up in the tradition, if you are not either a member of the O-One or the cutter families, then why would you believe? They have spent centuries devising smokescreens, ruses, camouflage: how else could they survive among us for so long undetected? Their masterstroke was that idiot Stoker. He and his gothic obsessions. That stupid book spawned, such an apt word, an entire industry of fictional creatures and completely obscured the true nature of the lamia. And as for that ridiculous notion that a crucifix is some sort of protection: do those fools truly believe that the lamia, a separate species for a hundred thousand years, would suddenly become allergic to a religious symbol created only two thousand years ago? Why? Why not a star of David, or a mandala? No, the only reliable weapons to destroy those hellish creatures are willow, wild garlic and sunlight. And, of course, a sharp steel blade.

So, she wanted proof; I needed to provide it. Not

documentary evidence, either. Even though Caroline is a lawyer and must, of necessity, trust books, documents, precedents and written testimony, I felt that what she really wanted was physical evidence. A member of the O-One, in other words. I convened a meeting of my Chapter: Tomas Martinsson, Shimon Gregorius and Lily Bax. I told them we needed to capture a lamia. Keep it alive until we could bring Caroline to Bloomsbury to witness its existence. Then we could dispose of it and start Caroline's education. Lily spoke first.

"They are easy enough to find, but when did we ever catch one alive? The risks are too great. We should take Miss Murray on a hunt and let her see one that way. It would be more convincing in any case."

"I disagree," Shimon said. He always argues with Lily and she rolled her eyes. "Seeing us destroy a lamia might be too much for her sanity. Remember that episode ten years ago? That man is still in a psychiatric hospital. I visit him every year and he is still a wreck."

"But to capture one. How would we do it?" she said.

"Easy. We track one back to its lair. Wait till sunrise, then—"

"Yes? Then what? Exactly? They don't go home to sleep, or had you forgotten? They are still dangerous."

I intervened before they could begin a proper argument.

"Tomas, you haven't said anything. What is your opinion?"

"I agree with Shimon. To witness a kill would put too great a strain on someone not accustomed to such sights. And mere writings would likely not be the type of proof Caroline is looking for. So, we need to take a lamia alive. I suggest we hunt at night, when the vermin are abroad, and lay a trap."

"What kind of trap?" Lily said.

"My great-grandfather used to hunt tigers in India with a maharajah. Not from the backs of elephants — that was for rich Americans and British royalty. They used to tether a goat in a clearing, then wait in hiding. As night fell, the goat would begin to bleat in fear for its life — very sensibly, given that a Bengal tiger was on the prowl. Those beasts measured three metres from nose to tail: their fangs were ten centimetres long. The sound and smell would attract predators, but they scared the lesser animals away by throwing stones. They were waiting for a tiger. When the beast arrived, he would be cautious. He would circle the clearing, keeping to the shadows. They were in a tree, smeared with elephant dung to mask their smell. When he was sure there was no danger, the tiger would attack. And so would my great-grandfather and the maharajah."

"What did they attack it with?" Shimon said.

"Bloody big rifles, of course! What did you think? Penknives?"

The laughter broke the tension and we started to plan how we might replicate the hunt tactics of the elder Martinsson.

"The first thing we need is the goat," I said. "Any suggestions?"

"A homeless? They like them," Lily said.

"No. Too dangerous," Shimon said. "We're pledged to save lives, not to put them at risk to satisfy the curiosity of sceptical lawyers."

"What then?" Tomas said. "It must be living, so a corpse is out of the question."

"One of us," Shimon said. "We are used to them and can defend ourselves."

"It's a good idea, Shimon," I said. "Are you volunteering?"

"I can think of better ways to spend the evening, but, yes, if that is what it will take, I will do it. I can find some old clothes, leave off shaving for a few days. A nick from my knife to release the scent and bring a lamia out into the open, then you three can spring the trap."

Tomas laughed.

"Wait, wait! You're too old and too fat, old man. I'll do it."

Shimon grunted and made as if to swat Tomas. But I could see he saw the sense of having Tomas exposed. He is definitely stronger and fitter than Shimon.

"Which brings me to the next challenge. How do we take it alive," I said.

"A net?" Tomas said.

"And how would we transport it?"

"A crate?" This was Lily.

"The lamia are too strong," Shimon said. "It would tear its way out. Only steel can contain them and that would be too heavy and unwieldy to work with."

"I have it!" Lily said, a wide smile on her normally glum visage. "A dog-guard."

"What do you mean, dog guard?" Tomas said.

"We make a grille in the workshop for the back of the car, bolt it in place, then net the lamia and throw it in. We can transport it safely back to the house then take it down to the basement with braided steel hawsers. Three of us on the lamia and one with a crossbow to keep it docile."

"And there's the cage in the basement," Shimon said. "Maybe cutters *did* capture lamia in the old days. Maybe that's what it's for. We just need to clear out the supplies and oil the hinges and lock and it's ready to receive a guest."

"Then it's settled," I said.

"But where will we stage the hunt?" Lily said. "This is likely to be a noisy affair and the central London nests are too close to thoroughfares. We should attract attention almost before we had begun."

"I know of a nest near Richmond Park," Tomas said. "They close it to traffic at night so it will be quiet. They hunt in those towns along the Thames: Chiswick, Kew, Richmond, Teddington. Their house is on one of those roads that lead to a gate into the park. I have watched it many a time. They are recently turned, less well-versed in our tactics. We should be able to lure one out to the park and take it without too much trouble."

After that, we spent some time defining specific roles and steps to capturing the lamia. Then Lily went away to begin work on her "dog guard", Tomas and Shimon left to buy supplies and I retired to my study. I wanted to learn all I could about David Harker and his research.

The following day, we travelled to Richmond, a pleasant enough drive, even though the traffic getting to the Great West Road was the usual London mixture of jams, minor accidents and swearing cyclists. We parked at the house of one of our backers and opened the rear hatch of the car. On the floor we spread out the elements of our capture kit: a net, nothing magical about it, just thick blue nylon that would defeat even an enraged lamia; three crossbows with underslung quivers of willow-wood quarrels – because these are still dangerous creatures and if necessary I had authorised the others to kill it; three braided steel hawsers fitted with running loops; and, key to the plan, a two-million candlepower spotlamp. We intended to isolate the lamia in its beam, disorientating it for long enough to approach and net it. The bulb emitted no UV light so we would not kill the lamia, but we felt – hoped, if I am honest – that the sheer brightness would fool it for a few seconds, which is all we thought we needed.

We took the kit inside to meet our backer. Ralph is an old friend. Too old now, really, for he is 93; though he is in good health, if a little deaf. He lost his wife to the lamia in 1983 and I attended her funeral. As he stood, alone, at the graveside, I approached him and explained who I was and what had really happened to Mary. At first he thrust me away from him, but I was persistent and eventually persuaded him to listen to me. He'd not been convinced by the autopsy report of massive blood-loss caused by knife wounds and as I spoke, I could see a light of belief flicker then catch behind his eyes. Since then, he has been a friend to the cutters, providing money, resources and shelter when we needed it. Ralph used to be a police officer. He also introduced me to some senior officers he played golf with. Explained who I was. To my great surprise I was not laughed out of their homes. They kept records of unexplainable deaths. Not "unexplained", one female commander was at pains to point out; those were simply murders nobody could divine a reason for. "Unexplainable," she said. "Off. Weird. Baffling. Corpses drained of blood, for example. There's a room deep under Scotland Yard lined with filing cabinets stretching back to the very first days of the Metropolitan Police Service. They're stuffed with all kinds of cases we never want the public – or the media – to know about."

So, Ralph has always helped us, and when I called him to explain what we were up to, he opened his house to us and told us he'd do anything to help. He left the back door open and met us in his kitchen. He hugged me first, then Lily, then Shimon, then Tomas. Sometimes I think he feels we're the children he never had.

"What do you need, Ariane?" he said.

"A way out of the park after they lock the gates."

"That's easy. My garden backs onto the park. There's a dirty great fence that separates my land from theirs, but guess what?" He leaned closer, looking around rather theatrically. "I had my builder put a gate in. Nice combination lock and some barbed wire along the top to keep the riff-raff out, but it's your way in. I'll leave it unlocked and you can bring that, thing, back through the garden and round the side of the house to your car."

After a coffee and some sandwiches to fortify us, we entered the park. Normally, when we hunt, our search is for a suitable killing ground. This was different. We needed somewhere the public might conceivably stray that offered cover for three of us and a clearing for the goat. Yes, this is how we had come to think of Tomas: bait for the lamia.

He was dressed very much in character: old clothes from a charity shop, still with that smell of sweat you can never erase, covered with a stinky brown raincoat – we forbore from asking him where he'd found it, though I had a shrewd idea. He'd been out on his own a couple of nights previously and I suspect he'd found it on a lamia's kill. His stubble and unkempt hair completed the picture, and he'd purchased a half-bottle of whisky in an off-licence on the way over.

"Over here," Lily called. "I've found it. It's perfect."

We had to work fast because the sun was already sliding behind the far hills. The spot was perfect, like she said. An open space of grass about 30 metres across, fringed with evergreen trees and scrubby bushes. It was in a hollow, well hidden from the path. The local council had dispensed with park rangers in a recent round of budget cuts so once the gates were locked, from the outside, we'd be on our own.

Lily, Shimon and I hid ourselves in the trees, each armed with a crossbow. I retained the lamp for myself, Shimon carried the net. Lily's role was to cover us as we netted the lamia. Tomas walked into the centre of the clearing and sat, like some disgusting, dirty Buddha, right in the middle. He unscrewed the whisky: it was so quiet, the thin crack as the metal seal snapped was clearly audible to me. He took a small sip, then tipped a quarter of the remainder onto his coat. From my vantage point I could smell the spirit as the breeze carried its aroma over to my hide.

The sun had disappeared now and the temperature dropped almost immediately. I shivered despite my warm clothing. I had only killed lamia until that evening: our tradition does not include capturing the foul creatures, still less transporting them, alive, around London. Tomas began to sing. An old folk song from his native land. He has a beautiful, deep, mournful voice and it carried through the trees and seemed to fill the air around us. On and on went the song, through many verses. I do not speak Danish but it was clearly a song of unrequited love – what depressives those Scandinavians are.

Tomas had just started a new song, an altogether livelier tune with a chorus of "rumpa-doo-delay" or some such nonsense when there was a rustle in the bushes behind him. Not from Lily or Shimon; they occupied different hiding places. He sat up straight, or as straight as he imagined a drunk would manage and called out.

"Who's there? What do you want?"

Then, crawling out from under the bush's black leaves, came the lamia. A female. We still do not know why they prefer to hunt naked, but there she was, stalking closer to Tomas like a hairless white ape. We needed to make sure we could surround it and throw the net without scaring it off. But my heart was beating so fast: I have never lost a member of my chapter and I didn't intend to start this night. The lamia was hissing – that disgusting sound they all make before feeding. It shook its head and gaped, unhinging its lower jaw and exposing those revolting, pink, fleshy mouthparts. One more second I wanted to wait. When the fangs erect and the eyes begin to fill with blood, the lamia are at their most vulnerable.

Tomas was doing a credible acting job, scrabbling backwards on hands and heels and pleading, "No, please, no" to the lamia. He had no crossbow, though I'd insisted he carry his *salcie usturoi*-smeared hunting knife under his coat. Then I saw them. Those hideous long teeth that look as if they are made of glass.

"Now!" I shouted and hit the lamia full in the face with the beam of the lamp.

Tomas rolled away and shielded his eyes with his arm but the lamia was caught directly in its beam. It shrieked and flailed its ropy arms in front of its face, eyes squeezed shut against what I hoped was immense pain. Shimon ran towards it from his hide and threw the net over its head. The net spun into a circle as it flew and dropped to the ground around the lamia's clawed feet. With Lily covering him with her crossbow, he ran in and smashed the lamia on the temple with the butt of his crossbow. Blows, even those delivered with as much force as my 18-stone friend can manage, do very little to damage the lamia, but Shimon's knocked the lamia to the ground. I ran to join the others in the clearing, keeping the lamp fixed on the lamia's screwed up eyes. Tomas had stood up, although he was partially blinded as the beam had hit him in the eyes briefly, and was holding onto Lily's shoulder for support.

The creature was squealing and hissing – an unearthly sound that still makes the hairs on my body stand on end. I commanded it in the old tongue to be still or join its sisters in hell. I pointed the beam away from its face and it unscrewed its eyelids enough to peer up at me, taking in my crossbow and those of Lily and Shimon. Its jaw was back in place and it spoke.

"Why, cutter? Why haven't you killed me? Mother will find you and she will kill you for this. I will make sure of it."

"I have someone who wants to see the truth with her own eyes. That the daughters of Peta Velds exist. That lamia exist. Don't hold out your hopes of being saved. You are alive at my whim, and will soon be dead."

"Mother will come for me. She will sense me. I feel her coming. Run, cutter. She will take her time with you."

"Enough!" I levelled my crossbow at the creature's face. "Quiet, or I will despatch you now and find another to replace you."

The survival instinct is as strong in lamia as in humans and this final threat had the effect I sought. The lamia closed its mouth and contented itself with thrashing about in the net, though this motion succeeded only in entangling it more firmly in the blue nylon loops and knots.

It took all four of us to drag the creature back to Ralph's garden gate. He was waiting and opened it as we approached.

"Bring it through the side passage," he said. "I don't want its pollution in my house."

As we struggled with the still-twisting lamia it looked straight into Ralph's eyes. And spoke again.

"You lost your wife to us, old man. But don't worry, her blood still pulses in our veins."

Then it laughed, a breathy, coughing noise such as a dog makes when it has a bone lodged in its throat.

"You bloody——" Ralph began, shaking his fist at the thing in the net. Lily placed a restraining hand on his arm.

"Don't worry, Ralph," she said. "Mary is in Heaven and this ill-begotten thing will soon be as far from her as it is possible to be."

He contented himself with a jab from his brass-tipped walking cane then turned and went inside.

"Come and see me, Ariane," he said. "Tell me what's going on."

Then he was gone and we fell to our task of dragging and heaving the resisting lamia into the loadspace of the car using the steel hawsers. It kept its silence after insulting dear Mary's memory, though it sported a sneering smile and kept unfurling its tongue and licking all the way around its mouth. Tomas had recovered his sight by this point and slammed the hatch down, sealing the lamia inside the car after throwing a blanket over it to deter prying eyes.

An hour later we were back in Bloomsbury, parked at the back of our house. Even with three loops of braided steel wire around its neck, the lamia still exhibited great strength, but the net restricted its movements sufficiently for us to drag it through the rear entrance to the house. Negotiating the stairs to the basement was even more trying, as the creature's lunges brought its disgusting mouth within spitting distance of our faces. Eventually we settled the matter by arranging ourselves in pairs – Lily and Shimon behind it, myself and Tomas in front – and paying out the lines until they were tight. Tomas and I were at the foot of the staircase on one line, and we dragged it down the stairs with Lily and Shimon keeping their lines taut as they followed. In this way we reached the basement.

The cage stood, door wide open, ready to welcome its latest inhabitant. Tomas had greased the hinges before we left for Richmond, and fitted the largest padlock we could find from a hardware shop on Theobalds Road – stainless steel, at least five inches across and, so said the shopkeeper, "strong enough to keep a lion at bay". I prayed he was right.

Now for the most dangerous part of the operation: removing the hawsers and the net and forcing the lamia into its new home. I realised we had failed to think this aspect of the capture through. With all four of us engaged on the three hawsers, we couldn't reach a weapon and I truly believed it was only our combined strength that enabled us to hold the lamia still.

"What are we going to do?" I said.

"Let me out of these and I'll go in on my own," the lamia said. It stood quite still and held its hands over its pudenda.

"Quiet, beast," Tomas said. "I have a better idea. Lily, Shimon, enter the cage and tie off your wires onto the back bars."

They complied, then, realising what he had in mind, scooted round to the back and freed the wires again. The four of us could simply pull the lamia into the cage, maintaining tension around its neck and keeping it fixed at a safe distance between us. Now it knew it was unlikely ever to go free it began hissing and screeching, cursing us with obscenities that Vlad Ţepeş would have approved of. The net prevented its gaining any leverage with its feet and it stumbled and hopped closer and closer until it was fully inside the cage. Then Tomas and I wound our hawser into a loop until I was close enough to slam the door with a satisfyingly loud clang, and close the padlock.

We let the hawsers drop and at once the lamia ripped them over its head and began struggling out of the net. We used its anger against it, retrieving the ends of the wires and drawing them out through the bars of the cage – it does not do to give a creature as intelligent and strong as a lamia anything that it could conceivably use as a weapon or resource of any kind. As the net dropped to the ground at its feet, Tomas hooked it through the bars with a crowbar and threw it into a corner.

The capture was complete. For the first time in my career as a cutter – for the first time in my life – I had a live lamia under lock and key. As our normal approach is to hunt them down and despatch them with as much haste as possible, I found myself unaccountably drawn to the creature. What an opportunity! We could study it at our leisure, starve it to the point of weakness and perhaps even discover some new flaw in its makeup that had eluded all our predecessors.

We four stood around the cage, out of reach of those grasping hands harbouring who knew what organisms under the talons, panting from our exertion, but also looking at each other with triumph gleaming in our eyes. Then the lamia spoke to me in a quiet growl.

"She knows I am here. Mother knows. You will bring her to me just as surely as a wounded deer brings the wolf. And then, cutter, you will feel her kiss. She will take her time with you, but, yes, Mother will take your blood and she will take your soul."

"How does she know, lamia? How?"

"Don't you know? Oh, dear! The great Van Helsings, slaughterers of so many of our family, ignorant of our secret. Well, I shan't tell you, bitch. Perhaps Mother will, just before she kills you."

"She's lying," Lily said. "How could Velds know we have her? They're not telepathic, just animals."

The lamia spun in its cage and cocked its head to one side as it glared at Lily.

"I'm lying, am I? Well, I could be at that. But you will find out soon enough."

"Come on," I said, eager to leave the creature before it took control fully of the conversation. "We'll leave it here until we can bring Caroline."

Over the hissing screams of the lamia, we trudged up the stairs from the basement and I double-locked the steel-bound door from the other side. We had our proof.

17

CAROLINE MURRAY' JOURNAL, 18TH OCTOBER 2010, RECORDED ON MY PHONE AND TRANSCRIBED LATER

Caroline Murray: Ariane is taking me down the hallway to a door. It leads to the basement. I can hear a sound. Snarling. Like an animal. A dog or something. Now it's hissing and it sounds like speech but I don't know the language. I don't like the smell coming up from the basement. It smells bad. Like dustbins at the back of restaurants.

Ariane Van Helsing: Please go in, Caroline. You are safe. Nothing can hurt you on the other side of that door.

[sound of keys in locks and heavy door opening]

[CM] There are three people. Two men and a woman. They are older than me. They have grey hair, the men. The woman is not so old but she looks like them. Not English. Their eyes are very dark. They are looking at me and then at a cage. There is a big cage in the middle of the room. They've got someone in there. I don't want to look. I want to go. Please I want to go.

[AVH] You can go whenever you really want to,

Caroline, but please stay just for another few minutes just to see your proof.

[CM] It's a young woman. She is about 22, maybe, or 23. She is naked. I don't know why they are keeping her like this. Poor thing looks frightened. The woman has a sword. Long. Pointed. Old fashioned. She is pushing it through the bars at the poor thing. Why? Why are they keeping her like this? Oh! She stuck the sword into her. She's screaming. No, snarling. Hissing. She was the one making those noises. Ariane is shouting at her. Getting her to turn and look at me. No. No. I don't want to look at her face but Ariane says I must. Her face is pretty. Her eyes are blue. No, not blue. They are changing. They are filling with blood. They are red and, oh, my God!

[CM gasps, breathes rapidly]

[AVH] Caroline, calm down. You are safe. You are completely safe. You can look. She won't hurt you, can't hurt you.

[CM] Her mouth. She opened her mouth and teeth came down. They came from the roof of her mouth. Long and thin like a snake's. Stuff is dripping out of them, like spit. Stringy stuff. She's holding the bars and pressing up against them to get to me. Her tongue is out. It is very long. She smells very bad. Like Mummy's dog when we found her behind the shed. The girl smells dead. What are you carrying, Ariane? It's a bottle of wine. No. Not wine. Blood. She's pouring it out into a bowl. It's making a horrid sound. I don't want to watch. I know what's going to happen. She's putting it by the cage. The, the, thing wants the blood. It's stretching out its hand. No, not. No, her hand. She is scooping it into her mouth, slurping it like soup. It is going everywhere.

Down her neck, onto her front. She is mewling like a cat. Her nipples are erect. Oh ... no!

[CM screams]

[end of recording]

18

DIARY OF AN ACTRESS: THE LIFE OF LUCINDA EASTERBROOK, 20TH OCTOBER 2010

The strangest thing happened yesterday. Peta Velds called and said she wanted to meet me. She left me a voicemail. Me! I mean I've met the odd A-lister – it's hard not to in my line of work – but Peta Velds? Bloody hell! She said she wanted to learn more about me as she's producing a film. She said we'd go to a bar in Soho called the Lotus House.

"How will I recognise you," I said.

"Don't worry Lucinda, you won't have any trouble. I'm very noticeable."

She was right. As I came up the stairs from Leicester Square tube and onto the pavement, a woman in a black fur coat that reached all the way down to the pavement turned to face me. Really pale skin. And, if I'm honest, not that much of a looker. Tall though.

"You must be Lucinda," she said. "I always recognise those I am meeting."

The dress under her coat must have been vintage – long sleeves and full, floor-length skirt – but I could see why she wore it: the black brocade fabric highlighted her pale skin, making it seem almost translucent. She took my arm, and we walked through Leicester Square towards Gerrard Street.

We went down this tiny little alley and we came to the Lotus House. I have to say, I've been drinking in Soho-slash-Chinatown for donkey's years, and I have never even heard of the place. From the outside, it looked poky, but blimey! There must have been two hundred people in there! The noise was ferocious. It was lit by dozens and dozens of candles. And the smell! I mean, I like a little joss stick in the boudoir now and again, especially if I'm entertaining, but this was almost choking me. A waitress – pale, like Peta – showed us to a booth then returned with cocktail menus.

We ordered drinks – a Mojito for me and a Bloody Mary for Peta – and then I asked her the question that had been on my mind ever since Caro told me she'd headhunted David.

"Who's the most famous actor you've ever met?"

She laughed, showing these amazing tiny little teeth.

"Really? I am one of the most successful women in the world and you want to know about actors? Oh, Lucinda, you are a dream. Well," she lowered her voice to a whisper, leaning across the banquette to me. "You know Cady Brennan?" She actually looked left and right as if there were a chance we could be overheard. I nodded, and leaned over so she could whisper right in my ear. "I fucked him in my office last January."

I may actually have gasped. I know I did the worst-ever "surprised" face in the history of acting. Mouth wide open, eyes to match. She told me the whole story, how she had been producing a film he was in and he'd gone to see her in person about some changes he wanted to make to the script. The man has balls, I'll give him that.

Peta was rather fun, actually. She knows everyone, as you'd expect for a woman in her position, and she had this never-ending stream of anecdotes. Not at all standoffish, which she could be with her wealth. I could do a one-woman show called The Life of Peta Velds – it'd be a sellout. Ooh. Note to self: call her about that. She might even finance it. Then I remembered all that dreadful business in Norfolk and why Caro had been so excited when I said who I was meeting for drinks.

"Ask her about David," Caro said. Actually it was more of a command than a request. She was looking at me like I was one of her dreadful murderers. "I want to find out what she's got on him, because something is really wrong and I intend to get to the bottom of it." Honestly, she speaks in these dreadful clichés – it's like The Mousetrap. Anyway, friends are friends, so I asked.

"Oh, Lucinda!" Peta said, touching me on the arm for what felt like a little too long. "So many questions. Take me home and I'll tell you a story. You'll like it. I promise."

There didn't seem to be any question of paying: Peta led me towards the door without so much as asking for a bill. The Maitre D' – a dumpy little guy with taut, red, shiny skin – beamed at Peta as he held the door open.

"So nice to see you again, Miss Velds," he said as we left, "I see you have a new conquest."

As we turned onto Shaftesbury Avenue, dodging a squealing gaggle of knee-socked Japanese schoolgirls, a big black car stopped right beside us. The rear door opened on its own and Peta motioned for me to get in.

"It's mine," she said. Her chauffeur-driven limo, no less.

The seats were made of a wonderfully soft, supple leather, stained a deep shade of red. I leaned back and closed my eyes, suddenly bone-tired. Peta leaned across and began to nuzzle my neck. She smelled like wet stone. She murmured to me, nonsense words, and I felt myself drifting away, from her, from the car even. It was so relaxing. I could hear traffic noises and sense colour and light from the cars and shop windows but had no sense of time passing. I shut my eyes and felt the world spin, and it's not as though I can't hold my drink. A heaviness had settled on me and I could only lean against Peta as she stroked my neck. She was whispering to me but I couldn't understand. Then she said something I could make out.

"Here we are," she breathed right in my ear. "My house."

How long we'd been driving for I don't know. But we were in a very expensive street. Muswell Hill, perhaps, or Crouch End. Hampstead, maybe. Tall trees lined both sides of the street, and the houses were set so far back from the road that I couldn't see them, only more trees, huge double gates and, occasionally, a tall black lamppost, its bulb casting a sad yellow pool of light onto the pavement that bled away to darkness after just a few feet.

Peta reached down between us and pressed the red button to release me from my seatbelt. The black strap of the belt snaked into a slot beside my left ear. The driver came round and opened the door for us and as I climbed out I looked down at the seat I'd just vacated. In its centre was a pattern – a rose with a scroll underneath it. There was writing on the scroll. It said,

Linda & Zak

Love Burns Eternal

I was just wondering what sort of weirdo would have a luxury car with such nasty upholstery when Peta materialised by my side.

"Come in," she said. "You must be hungry."

"I am," I said. "I haven't eaten for ages."

"Me neither," she said.

Inside the house, I gasped. I have honestly never seen anywhere so beautiful. The hallway was painted a deep green, decorated with what looked like real branches of holly or yew, something evergreen, anyway. It was like being in a forest. There was a big gold-framed mirror above a table standing against the wall. I watched myself in it as Peta stood next to me and put her arm around my waist. She smiled at me in the mirror and at that moment I knew I was in love. The long, glossy tendrils of her hair seemed to squirm and shift and I watched, entranced, not turning to her but fixed on her reflection in the mirror, as two of the long tresses snaked away from her head and encircled my neck like snakes. It tickled and I laughed. Peta's smile widened.

"Let's have a drink," she said, "then we can eat." She led me into the sitting room. "What do you think, Lucinda? You're a woman of taste."

It was a long room, painted a deep red, and lined with shelves full of large, leather-bound books: the sort people usually call "tomes". A fire was already burning in the grate. Maybe she had a servant, I thought. Over the mantelpiece hung a big antique mirror. It was slightly convex, leaning out from the wall. The gold frame was moulded into crazy shapes: foliage, bunches of grapes, animals and, clinging to the very top, two grinning gargoyles.

"What would you like to drink?" Peta called from the

kitchen. I hadn't noticed her go while I'd been practising for the Antiques Roadshow.

I asked for red wine then I took in more of her baroque taste in interior décor: heavy velvet curtains puddling beneath the sash windows; a crystal vase full of deep red velvety roses; and, at the far end of the room, a grand piano. I sat and picked out the first few notes of The Lady is a Tramp. Just then Peta reappeared with the wine.

"Is that what you think of me?" She was smiling and her eyes reflected the firelight as she handed me a goblet – the only word for it – brimming with wine. "I'm afraid you'll be disappointed. I come from rather purer stock. Come and sit with me. Let me tell you about myself."

We sank into the squashy leather sofa opposite the fire and clinked glasses. As we drank she unfolded her story. She could probably have lived for six months on what some Hollywood producer would pay her for its catalogue of scheming prince-bishops, spice merchants and — frankly — murderous relatives.

As she spoke, savouring every debauched great aunt, every libertine cousin, Peta tipped her head back and closed her eyes. Blue veins showed beneath the pale skin of her throat and I realised I had this overwhelming urge to kiss her there. I pulled back. It's not that I'm a prude or even particularly straight. But there was another feeling, just beneath the first one. Like I wanted to bite her.

She opened her eyes and looked straight at me – only it felt more like through me. She took my unresisting hand and led me upstairs, past some very old, very ugly portraits – Velds ancestors, I assumed. At the top of the stairs she placed a hand in the small of my back and ushered me along the wide corridor towards a door at the far end. Light spilled from under the door across the polished wooden boards and I could hear piano music from inside the room.

"It's beautiful," I said.

"Yes, isn't it? Mozart. He wrote that piece for me."

"For you? How? Oh, you're teasing me. You mean it's your favourite. I have songs like that too. I feel the artist wrote it just for me."

She laughed, and I'm afraid I flinched a little. It was a really unpleasant rough-edged sound.

"Of course! I'm just teasing you, darling. Now, why don't you go first?"

She stood back and let me open the door. I closed my hand around the handle. It felt cold in my hand and silky to the touch. I looked down. It was a polished length of bone with a shiny hemispherical knob at one end. I looked around at Peta but she merely nodded, encouragingly.

"In you go," she breathed.

I pushed the door. It swung open quietly, the bottom edge brushing against the carpet. In the centre of the vast bedroom was a big four-poster bed, draped with gauzy material in whites, golds and reds. The music was louder now, the insistent trilling of the piano keys filling my ears. But it was what was on the bed that held my attention.

Three young women. All completely naked. All completely beautiful. They beckoned me and I complied, dumbly. I felt rather than saw Peta undress me and then I climbed onto the bed. The women embraced me, cooing and purring as they stroked me all over. One of the women placed her cold, cold hand on my breast.

Peta watched from an armchair, smoking a thin

cigarette, the blueish smoke climbing sinuously to the high ceiling.

"Watch me," she said. Then she stood up and undressed.

Faint blue lines showed through the skin of her breasts — hardly there, by the way, unlike mine — and ran beneath the taut, puckered nipples. She was standing so close I could feel her breath on my face. She pushed me back onto the bed and sat astride me; her skin was deliciously cool. The other three retreated to the corners of the bed.

She held her right hand in front of my face and I noticed a ring on her first finger that I could have sworn she hadn't been wearing earlier. She gave the jewel a twist and I heard a metallic click. Once more she held out the ring, now sprouting a tiny, needle-pointed spike. Holding my gaze, she brought her hand up to her left breast and pushed the spike gently but firmly against the skin. I knew what she wanted me to do. I knew her type. And I didn't care. Some people are into leather, rubber, role playing: she had a kind of S&M thing going. I wanted her so badly I'd have done anything right then, and anyway, I've experimented myself a bit over the years. I moved closer and began to lick up the blood. I could hear the other three hissing quietly, such an odd sound for a person to make. The blood tasted salty and I felt woozy after a couple of seconds. Then I sensed the other girls coming closer. I felt their lips on my neck.

I woke with a start and turned to look at the clock on the bedside table: 4.42 a.m. Turning to tell Peta I'd have to go, I realised I was alone in the bed. The girls had gone too. There was a note on the pillow next to me.

"Dearest Lucinda," it said. "I will be back later but you must leave while it's still dark – I have very curious neighbours. I will see you very soon. Peta."

I left Peta's house and headed in the direction of the traffic noise. It sounded like a main road so I imagined I'd find it easy to get a cab. I felt different — buzzy. I heard a loud rustle and looked around for what I assumed would be a cat or dog scavenging in a bin bag, only to see a beetle picking its way laboriously through some dry leaves. And though it was dark, flowers were almost radiating colour: luminous yellows, acid oranges, fleshy pinks. Round the next corner I almost tripped over a fox rooting in a fast food carton. But instead of running, it circled around me and, as I bent down, sniffed then licked my outstretched hand. Then I reeled back. A sudden impulse to kill the fox had flashed through me, an almost physical desire. The fox recoiled, snarling, then turned and ran.

I hurried the rest of the way to the road, my pulse banging in my ears, and hailed a cab. By the time I got home it was 5.15. I pulled my clothes off and fell into bed.

19

CAROLINE MURRAY'S JOURNAL, 28TH OCTOBER 2010

Oh. My. God. They're real. Vampires are real. I've seen one with my own eyes. Hissing and spitting like a cornered cat then lapping from a bowl of blood. Jesus, I hope the blood wasn't human. Though I wouldn't put anything past Ariane Van-Bloody-Helsing. She probably burgled a bloodbank.

As I write this, I am sitting in Ariane Van Helsing's study at the house she shares with her crew of, well, I suppose I must get used to their professional nomenclature, cutters. For God's sake, they are vampire hunters! How is this even possible? This is the 21st Century! People simply don't go around at the dead of night with sharpened stakes, plunging them into other people's hearts and saying, "there's another one gone". I mean, it's insane! Except. Except, it isn't.

Three floors below me, in a steel cage that wouldn't look out of place in a zoo, there's a young woman who Ariane claims is a vampire. Only she doesn't call them vampires. She uses the term, "lamia". Latin for vampire. What does it matter? The woman downstairs is not human. She can't be. She has fangs like a snake's. She, it, drank blood from a bowl Ariane put down on the floor.

And her body. Oh my God! I've seen girls at the gym who clearly work out too much, with their six-packs and muscly arms, but this, this thing, is beyond anything I've ever seen – even in the Olympics, those awful East Europeans. Its muscles are so sharply defined, it's as if you could see the individual fibres under the skin. Veins, too, and tendons. Apart from minimal breasts, I would say it has absolutely zero body fat. No hair, either, apart from her head. It doesn't look shaved, either. Just smooth, like porcelain.

I tried to convince myself she is just one of those poor souls who suffer from some sort of body dysmorphia disorder and repeatedly modify themselves. There was a documentary last year about a man who had transformed himself into a leopard. But of course he hadn't at all. Just tattoos, coloured contacts and some filed-down teeth. But she isn't and she doesn't. For a start, she can support her weight upside down from the roof of the cage using great curved claws that extend from her toes. And, she can dislocate her lower jaw – an absolutely revolting sight. No surgeon could produce that effect; and none would ever want to.

So this is my situation. My fiancé has been effectively kidnapped and imprisoned by a very rich, very powerful businesswoman called Peta Velds, whom I am reluctantly forced to admit is the so-called "mother" of a clan of vampires. I still gasp at the mere fact of my writing these words without being drunk. My best friend has disappeared off the face of the earth. And I have moved in with Ariane Van Helsing, who is apparently the descendant of a fictional vampire hunter in a book that turns out to be a PR stunt by Peta Velds, who, by the way, was alive and kicking – or biting – in the 19th Century. I need a drink. A large one.

But we need to rescue David. Whether he's a prisoner or not; whether this whole thing is going to turn out to be a massive "gotcha" for some reality TV show or not; whether I have gone mad without realising, or not; he is stuck in that windowless laboratory and he said he's dumped me in an email. If she tempts him off his meds the poor boy will suffer a breakdown and I can't let him go through that again; the last one nearly finished him. Nearly finished me, too, if I'm honest. So tomorrow, Ariane and I, together with Tomas, Shimon and Lily, who are actually very sweet to me, will sit down at her table and construct a plan.

I have taken leave of absence from work. Georgia, our Head of Chambers, was not best pleased but I told her it was simple: accept my application or I'd up sticks and leave for good. She knows she needs me: 23 Middle Temple have tried to lure me over to their chambers on more than one occasion and she knows that, too. So with grudging good grace she allowed me to go. I said I just needed a month. I hope I was right.

What am I going to do? David has been locked up by the literal mother of all vampires in the wilds of bloody Norfolk. I tried to call Luce but she's stopped picking up. I hope it's not because I got her attacked in that pub. I haven't told Ariane about her; I don't want that mad Dutchwoman and her crew rolling up outside Luce's flat with pitchforks and flaming torches.

This is crazy! It's like a dream. And the worst of it all is there's nobody I can talk to. I mean, I can hardly go running to the media. It would spell the end of my legal career faster than being caught doing a line on the jury box. Or social media? I know! A selfie with a sharpened stake: #ReadyForAction. No. This is just awful. All I have is Ariane and her people. I mean, they're very nice, just a bit intense.

There are three of them.

Lily Bax. She's the mechanic, the driver and the weapons specialist. Maybe 40 or so. Looks like she works out. Biceps like oranges in a sock. Sexy, though, the way she moves. Lithe. She has the bluest eyes I have ever seen - like sapphires.

Shimon Gregorius. The medic. Jewish, balding, a few gingery hairs kept in place by his skullcap. A big man, too. Well over sixteen stone. Friendly though, kept taking my hand and patting it. He used to be a psychotherapist in Israel. Then one of his patients died, drained of blood, and that's when Ariane recruited him.

Tomas Martinsson. I'm not sure exactly what he does. Apart from killing vampires, obviously. He knows his way around the Internet and does research for Ariane. We'll call him the intelligence officer for now. Absolutely drop-dead gorgeous. Tall, built out of muscle and a stylish dresser.

Plus Ariane herself. She says she's related by blood to the character in *Dracula* called Abraham Van Helsing. Who was also real. They both were, I mean. Ariane's the current head of a family of cutters based in London. My only goal at this point is to rescue David. I can't think beyond that.

20

DIARY OF AN ACTRESS: THE LIFE OF LUCINDA EASTERBROOK, 29TH OCTOBER 2010

So, what have I learned this week? One, I may have a slightly kinky, lesbian *thing* going for one of the richest women in the world. Two, she's a vampire. Three, it would appear I'm one too. Wot larks!

She texted me today. She summoned me – there really is no other word for it – to her office in the City. The building's called The Point. Bloody great tower looking down on St Paul's Cathedral.

"No need to take a cab," she said, "my driver will bring you to me."

I was so happy. After the other night, well, I began to wonder whether I'd dreamt the whole thing. Until I killed another homeless man, obviously. I'm not totally sure where this leaves my career but I suppose matineés are out! Sorry. Flippant.

Lurch, that's what I've dubbed him, like a bloody great animated cadaver with a driving licence, was standing on my doorstep at 10.00 this morning, holding a huge umbrella like a bat over his head. It was raining rather heavily and the drops were bouncing off the taut black nylon canopy. He escorted me to the car, taking care to keep the brolly down low over my head. I noticed a distinctly unpleasant tingling on my skin – perhaps it was acid rain, who knows? After a dreary ride across London, we arrived at Peta's office. I must say, the architect had let her imagination overrule her common sense. I say "her" because there was a stainless steel plaque just inside the lobby outlining the woman's philosophy of architecture. Some gobbledegook about "neo-Bauhaus within a dream framework". Translation: straight lines, lots of white paint and more steel, and a curving staircase within the atrium festooned with mythical beasts and oversized gemstones.

I think I recognised the receptionist from the other night at Peta's house. Not completely sure as she had her clothes on this time, but her green eyes were looking right through me. She flashed me a bright smile – no fangs I was relieved to see – and directed me to the lifts with a flirty instruction to "go all the way to the top".

Peta was waiting for me when the lift doors opened. She looked amazing. You wouldn't call her beautiful exactly, but she just radiates sexiness. Maybe it's that gaze of hers. I just feel like I'm the only person who matters to her. She put her hand out like a parent waiting for a child, and I took it. The difference in our height amplified the effect – I was in flats and she was sporting another pair of monster heels. There was a tiny zap of static electricity as our fingers brushed, then she enfolded my hand in hers and led me into her office.

We sat on a sofa in front of a low table.

She held both my hands in her lap and pulled me close enough that I could smell her perfume. Then she spoke. Words I will never forget.

"My daughter. My blood. Welcome to the real life. Welcome to my family."

Then she kissed me with open mouth, looking deep into my eyes. I felt those long, pointed teeth with my tongue.

I don't know where my answer came from. It felt like it had always been there, lodged somewhere in my soul.

"My Mother. My blood. Accept me. Nurture me."

She drew away and smoothed her skirt over her knees.

"Lucinda. You know what is happening to you, don't you?"

"I think so," I said.

"You are becoming like me. You are joining the O-One. The process takes a few months, during which time you will feed and grow stronger. Your body will change and so will your habits."

"How will it change?"

"Your body fat will burn away and your muscles will strengthen. Your mouth will alter. Like mine."

As she said this she opened her mouth. It kept on opening. I wasn't afraid. Which by rights I should have been. Her lower jaw sort of came adrift with a plopping sound and hinged back almost onto her neck. Those teeth like long glass needles unfolded behind her human teeth, and this sort of ring of pink tissue expanded inside her mouth like a big sucker. It should have disgusted me but it was just beautiful. Our perfect adaptation.

"Body fat? Like, my bum, you mean? Because that seriously won't be a problem."

"*All* your body fat. We are lean by design, Lucinda. Predators. When was the last time you saw a fat lioness?"

I admitted that in all the nature documentaries I've ever watched, the lionesses always looked pretty fit to me.

"Now. Daughter. There is something you can do for me. You are friends with Caroline Murray. She wishes to take David Harker back. I cannot allow this. He is too important to me, to my plans for my family."

"What do you want me to do?" I asked. I know this sounds cold, but I would have agreed to anything just to please Peta. On my own I can still feel traces of the person I used to be; in her presence I feel like a giddy teenage girl on her first date.

"I want you to find out what she is planning. She has a new friend. A woman called Ariane. Talk to Caroline. Invite her out for a drink or dinner, or to your flat for a meal. Then bring your news back to me. Now, come."

Then she unbuttoned her blouse and I felt a prickling behind my top teeth. I can't write any more. It's getting dark and the memory of what we did on her sofa has made me hungry again.

21

HUNT BOOK OF LILY BAX, 30TH OCTOBER 2010

We have been stalking one of the rarer males of the Velds family. In many ways he is magnificent. He stands almost seven feet tall. His musculature is superb, with a triangular torso dominated by massive pectorals, and lattissimus dorsi muscles like wings adorning his back. His skin is blue-black and his limbs are long and symmetrical, with thick veins protruding above the muscles. He has a way of crouching over his kills, like a falcon mantling its prey with its wings. His male parts are hairless, as with all of his kind, and he grows erect when feeding. He is very fast and dodged Shimon's bolt only a month ago. His hearing is acute, even for a lamia, and we have had to retreat beyond the range of our crossbows to avoid detection.

Yesterday we decided he could be allowed no further kills. I spent most of the day soaking crossbow bolts in *salcie usturoi*. As he emerged from their house we immediately set up our tail, all four of us taking turns to track him through the city streets. I think he suspected something but we had refined our tracking strategy in response to his heightened sensory responses. He picked up the scent of some homeless: we saw him lift his nose to the air. Then he was off, loping across the road between cars, almost floating on those long legs. He ran down a side street and then leapt a barrier into a disused carpark. There were a group of them there, homeless, not lamia: three men and a woman. Sharing a bottle of cider round a brazier. The lamia stopped behind a concrete pillar and removed his clothes. We watched as the claws on his hands and feet extended. Then that terrible yawn. Out clopped the jawbone from its hinges. Down came the fangs. Forward came that obscene funnel of tissue.

The problem with a four-person kill is that you cannot surround the target. We are all good marksmen but to miss would be to risk hitting one of our own. So we formed a crescent, each of us moving in close enough to be sure of a hit. The bloodlust deafens the lamia, we suspect it is simply the pounding of their blood in their ears, not some sensory override. It matters not.

The lamia stalked towards the homeless, arms wide, at least seven feet from talon to talon. They saw him and began hooting with laughter. I have seen similar reactions before. Often that laughter is the last sound to escape the victim's lips. One of the men waved the cider bottle at him and asked if he wanted "a wee shot of the good stuff".

I looked at Tomas, then Ariane and Shimon. We nodded and placed our fingers to our brows, lips and hearts: the old signal. Together, we fired. The four willow quarrels left our crossbows with sharp snaps, pigeon-feather flights hissing through the dank air towards their home.

His speed, his anticipation, were incredible. Not one

of our bolts hit him; he twisted and bent like a worm on a hook and left empty space where flesh should have been. They clattered harmlessly against pillars and dropped to the cold floor.

Then Ariane called out.

"Lamia! Tonight is your last on Earth!"

The lamia advanced on us, hissing loudly, flicking out his tongue. His eyes were partially filled with blood and disgusting drool was leaking from his fangs. We still had the advantage of numbers but I don't mind recording that I was frightened. Not the pang of danger we all use to sharpen our reflexes on a normal hunt. This was primal. For the first time, I thought I might succumb to the bite of the lamia.

He stopped ten feet short of us. He looked at each of us in turn, up and down, assessing us for weakness. There was no time to reload so we each drew our blade. Ariane and Tomas favour knives; Shimon and I, swords. All four weapons were anointed with *salcie usturoi* – even a glancing blow would be enough to destroy the lamia. But with his stature, even Shimon and I would have to be inside his reach to strike the fatal blow.

Before I could calculate a plan of action, Ariane took a step forward and dropped her knife on the floor. It rang out in the gloomy space, echoing off the low concrete and steel ceiling. Then she simply tilted her head to the right, exposing that long pale neck of hers. I fancy even I could hear the blood surging through the vessels in her throat.

Its eyes rolled up, fully engorged, and it sprang at her. That was its last volitional movement in this life. She sidestepped and ducked as Shimon whirled round and drove the point of his blade deep into the lamia's side. With a screech, it fell to its knees, clawing at the rent in its skin as if it would pull the poison from the wound by force. But too late. Its skin bubbled and rippled like a tide running back over pebbles, then the shuddering of its muscles began. We retreated to a safe distance and watched as splits opened up in its skin and its skull swelled. With an inhuman howl, the lamia burst open as its organs, blood vessels, body fluids and bones were obliterated by the chemical action of the *salcie usturoi*.

Shimon cleansed his blade and resheathed it under his coat. We others followed him, then turned to the boozers, still clustered around their fire, but now wide-eyed. As Ariane approached them they clutched each other. The woman started gabbling in a rusty voice, hands held palms out, like a supplicant.

"Don't, love. We ain't done nothing to you. Don't do us, too. Please. We won't say nothing. Nobody'd believe us anyway, bunch of old winos. Joff there, he thinks he sees Jesus. Local coppers just move us on, they never listen."

Arian spoke, to calm them.

"We won't hurt you. We protected you from the lamia. Have you seen others like him?"

"I have," one of the men piped up. His skin was a uniform brown-black, though whether he was that colour because God made him like that or from his unclean way of living I couldn't tell. "They're everywhere. Used to be, right, you could find a gaff to kip in for the night and only have to worry about other dossers nicking your stuff, or some pissed-up city types who get off on giving us a kickin'. Then, be about five years ago? This other lot turned up. Rich, like. Nice clothes. They'd offer you money and a bed for the night. Well, it's tempting innit? I mean, the younger ones, well, they sussed it out straight off. Sex trade, innit? But beggars can't be choosers, know what I mean? They don't care anyway. Most of them is strung out on crack, or heroin or they're just huffin' into them crisp bags. Trouble is, they never came back."

"Five years ago," I said. "You've done well to survive that long on the streets."

He puffed his chest out. "Know what I'm doing, don't I? That's the secret, knowing what you're doing."

"And you do."

"And I do. But they've changed. Used to be the young ones only. Well, that's who I'd pick. I mean, you got a bit of cash and a taste for rough trade, you're not going to want to go home with old wrecks like Molly or Joff or me, are you?"

"Changed how?" Ariane said.

"They started doing us out in the open, didn't they? Last six months, I seen 'em take three of us. What happens is, they come out of the shadows, stark-bollock naked, sorry ladies, and they're seriously fuckin' weird. You saw him, that one just now. Like him, they are, all muscly with them claws and those horrible mouths of theirs. Females are worse then the males, somehow, I mean, it's wrong, innit? A woman should be nurturing like your Mum, not bleeding you dry till you're just a husk?"

"Do the police ever come around?" Tomas said. "Asking about them? About anyone else?"

"The police? Do me a favour! There's cuts or hadn't you heard? Open a case and you got to close it haven't you? And who's going to pull lates trying to solve who murdered a dosser or a wino? Nobody, that's who. And, no, since you ask, they 'aven't been around asking after you either."

"I didn't mean us," Tomas said.

"'Course you didn't! Don't want the Old Bill cottoning on there's a bunch of vigilantes roaming the streets doing their job for them, now do we? Vampire vigilantes." He folded his arms across his scrawny chest after he said those last two words. He jerked his chin at the crossbows. "They what you use, then? To kill 'em?"

Ariane took a step closer. Reached out her hand for his. "I would like to help you. And maybe you can help us too. Are you hungry? Would you like a bath and some clean clothes?"

"I thought you'd never ask," he said, turning his hand to grab hers, then pumping it vigorously up and down.

We left his companions without a backward look. The gelatinous puddle that had been the lamia was congealing and already two rats were licking at the edge of it, their little yellow teeth bright against the dark red.

22

HUNT BOOK OF ARIANE VAN HELSING, 30TH OCTOBER 2010

We killed our biggest one yet tonight. A real brute. Unnaturally fast, and for a species already at odds with nature, an outlier. The moves I have been working on with Shimon will pay off, I am convinced. If others of its kind develop the same reflexes we will perforce have to adopt new tactics. I intend to ask Lily to develop protective gear for us. Some sort of lightweight collar. Maybe gauntlets too and something for the femoral arteries. In the meantime, we have acquired an ally from a surprising quarter.

His name is Jim. He says he prefers to keep his surname to himself. I suspect he has a background in law enforcement since he seems so confident about police procedures. Perhaps he left with a stain or two on his record. Not my business, for now, at any rate.

I intend to recruit Jim. The others are not so sure, but I feel it in him. A violence. Or a willingness at least. He could be useful. Anyone who has survived on the streets since the lamia arrived is someone I want on my side, fighting them. He can go back on the streets at night and sleep here during the day: our spy in the midst of their hunting grounds. We can disguise him again and with skin and clothes soaked in *salcie usturoi* he will come to no harm.

He is sleeping now in one of the guest rooms. Belly full of Shimon's soup and beef with dumplings. Tomorrow I will test him. See how deep his hunger runs. The lamia we captured for Caroline still waits in the basement.

23

TEXTS BETWEEN PETA VELDS AND LUCINDA EASTERBROOK, 31ST OCTOBER 2010

THE CUTTERS TOOK ONE OF MY SONS LAST NIGHT. HE HAD BEEN WITH ME FOR 17 YEARS SINCE I TOOK HIM IN MANHATTAN. HE WAS A BANKER. HE RELISHED HIS NEW LIFE AS HE DID BLOOD. WE WILL AVENGE HIM. WHAT HAVE YOU LEARNED OF CAROLINE MURRAY AND HER FRIENDS?

———

Oh, how awful for you :-(I'm afraid I haven't had a great deal of luck, really. Going through the change as I call it has left me just starving all the time. Not much time for socialising. But I will, I promise. Find stuff out, I mean. oxoxo

———

IT IS URGENT. I WANT TO KNOW THEIR

PLANS. IF YOU CANNOT SEE HER, GO TO HER FLAT. BREAK IN. CHECK HER LAPTOP. ANYTHING. DO NOT DISAPPOINT ME.

———

I would never disappoint you. You must believe me. I'll do it. Tonight. I'll call her. x

24

CAROLINE MURRAY'S JOURNAL, 1ST NOVEMBER 2010

Odd night tonight. Had dinner with Luce. My, she looks healthy. Positively glowing. Didn't eat anything though. Said she was on a detox after that business in Norfolk. Funny kind of detox if it includes the amount of wine she knocked back, but that's Luce for you. Clearly Ariane doesn't know everything about vampires – the whole "turning" thing must be superstition even if the rest of the wretched business is true. There's obviously nothing the matter with Luce, especially in the dental department! God, the way she throws her head back when she laughs you can see her tonsils, never mind her teeth. She even said she'd been on a sunbed at the hairdresser's – that accounted for the glow and pretty much scotched the idea she's one of them now.

The thing is, she seems to know an awful lot about Ariane. She was asking me all sorts of questions about her. Where she lives, what she wears, what she does all day, who her friends are. I thought it best to be discreet. I don't imagine Ariane exactly welcomes publicity. I asked Luce why she wanted to know and how she even knew about Ariane in the first place. And she said it was for a part she's up for. Some off-Broadway thing, apparently. She's auditioning for the part of one of the sisters in The Cherry Orchard. She came upon the Van Helsings in an old history book in the Royal School of Drama's library. Luce being Luce she knew nothing about Dracula, so the reference sailed right over her head. She just picked on Ariane's family because they seemed "so mysterious, so right".

Long story, short, I had to stonewall her all evening. Every time I managed to get the conversation onto more neutral matters, and believe me, for Luce, "neutral" encompasses quite the range of intimate topics, she'd drag it round to Ariane again. In the end I had to plead tiredness and left her in the restaurant. Last thing I saw before I went was her flagging down the waiter and pointing at the wine list.

25

HUNT BOOK OF ARIANE VAN HELSING, 2ND NOVEMBER 2010

Today, we sat around the table and decided what to do about David Harker. Caroline was there, of course. Her concern is the man, mine the work. He must be stopped and I do not care overmuch how we do it. It would be a relatively simple matter to send Tomas up there on his own to silence David and cut off the source of the solution. But we must try the more difficult route first.

Lily suggested a course of action that will keep everybody happy for now. We must travel to Norfolk and destroy the lab itself and all David's work. On paper, on computers, in the cloud: wherever he has recorded the result of a single experiment, we must be there to wipe the record clean. Once we have achieved that goal, we will return to London bringing David with us. The lovers can be reunited and we can continue with our programme of eradication.

One matter deserving of further consideration is whether David himself has been turned. Caroline recalled seeing plasters on his neck when she went to meet Peta Velds. His explanation sounded a little forced to me. If she has bitten him, then, inevitably, we will have to deal with him. But we will give him the benefit of the doubt. For now.

NEW YORK TIMES WEBSITE, 7TH NOVEMBER 2010

In town for a week to handle business, noted socialite and business big-hitter Peta Velds is to give the keynote speech at next weekend's skin cancer fundraiser at the Waldorf Astoria.

CAROLINE MURRAY'S JOURNAL, 7TH NOVEMBER 2010

Peta Velds is in Manhattan, to give a speech to a cancer charity. You could laugh at the irony if it wasn't so bloody terrible. But with her out of the way for a week, we have the chance we need to get David back. Tomorrow, Lily, Shimon and I will drive up to Norfolk and get David back. We also have to destroy his work and I just know that is going to kill him. He's one of those dear, sweet men who could end up working for the wrong side just because they enjoy the intellectual challenges. Now and again he needs reminding that ethics aren't just for the social scientists whom he despises.

Our plan looks so simple on paper. Enter the lab posing as Health & Safety Executive inspectors – more irony – get David to wipe the servers clean of all his experimental research, then burn the place to the ground and be back in London three days from now. I keep wanting to scream "I'm a lawyer!" and run to the police, but Ariane just keeps assuring me in that annoying voice of hers that this is not a matter for the authorities. She's probably right. I'm not sure any of the police officers I've met would give us much airtime for a story that mentioned vampires.

I've discovered one of Tomas's special abilities. He's a forger. A very, very good one. The IDs he's created for us are utterly convincing. I suspect he may not always have been playing for the white hats though he is extremely cagey when I ask him any questions about his past. Which convinces me that he has one.

While we are in Norfolk, Ariane and Tomas will travel to New York. It's so rare to see Peta Velds in public apparently that they're going to attempt to kill her while she's there. Quite how you stick a celebrity CEO with a willow-wood stake in one of the busiest cities in the world is beyond me, but then, I'm not a cutter.

28

HUNT BOOK OF ARIANE VAN HELSING, 10TH NOVEMBER 2010

We are in Manhattan. The cutter here is Frederick Arnold. It was he who destroyed Warhol: using that woman to deliver the coup de grace was a masterstroke. Frederick has agreed to work with us to take down Peta Velds. His house is a brownstone on the Lower West Side. They have been working more with firearms than we have – typical Americans! – and have developed bullets filled with *salcie usturoi* that shatter on impact. Apparently with great and instantaneous effect. We may get the chance to use them although Tomas and I remain committed to the blades and the bows for our work.

Tomorrow, Velds addresses the charity gala. We shall be waiting for her afterwards.

29

WEBSITE OF THE JUDY AND BRIAN SHAPIRO FOUNDATION FOR SKIN CANCER RESEARCH, 11TH NOVEMBER 2010

Last night, our annual fundraising gala dinner was graced with the presence of Peta Velds. Ms Velds is one of the most powerful women on the planet, and we are honoured that she made time in her busy schedule to address the donors, friends and supporters of the Foundation.

Her speech was received with a standing ovation and we reproduce it here:

Mister Mayor, Senator, honoured donors, friends:

As I look out into the audience here tonight, I see representatives from some of the greatest families in New York. Names that resonate down through the centuries, much as my own name does in what I suppose I should call, "the old country". [laughter]

I also see those whom history will crown the progenitors of great dynasties of the future. All of us here have become wealthy enough to redistribute some of our good fortune to causes dear to our hearts. And whether our fortunes are fresh-minted or inherited does not matter – we can be justifiably proud of the excellent work our gifts make possible. [applause]

Inheritance, whether of wealth, property or character, can be a difficult burden for some. In my own case, alongside the Velds fortune, I inherited something less welcome. A chromosomal abnormality called Reiser-Strick Syndrome. It has a single effect: it renders the carrier unable to tolerate sunlight, however diffuse, without suffering from a virulent cancerous mutation that destroys the very cells of which the skin is built.

This mutation led me to my interest in the work of the Foundation, and I must offer you, Judy and Brian, my sincere gratitude for the research into all skin cancers that you have so generously made possible. [applause]

Living with cancer is like living in darkness when you know the sun is shining on others; so I should like to ask you, Mayor Bloomberg, ladies and gentlemen, to raise your glasses and join me in a toast.

To standing in the sunlight.

[applause]

30

HUNT BOOK OF ARIANE VAN HELSING, 11TH NOVEMBER 2010

Disaster! Tomas is gone.

We were in position by nine o'clock last night. The dignitaries were all arriving in chauffeur-driven cars and there was a veritable jam of them around the back in a parking garage. We watched Velds arrive. Her driver was a huge, ugly brute. After she arrived, Tomas followed the limousine around the corner of the street. We discussed his attack down to the last detail. While the driver waited for his turn to drive into the parking lot, Tomas simply opened the rear door of the car, slid inside, closed the door and placed the tip of his blade under the nose of the driver. The smell was enough to ensure compliance and the lamia followed his new instructions. I watched them pull out of the queue and head down a side street – little more than an alley between two blocks. I followed on foot and when the big lamia exited the car, I was there with my crossbow.

After we cleaned off the blood from the side of the car, Tomas drove me back to the queue and we were parked and ready twenty minutes later.

All the other drivers had vanished, presumably to smoke or gossip: whatever these people do to while away the interminable hours while their charges sip champagne or listen to chamber quartets.

Our plan was beautifully simple. We would wait until all the other cars had left to collect their passengers, then we would follow, leaving a gap. We would pick up Velds from outside the building, take her down to the East River and send her back to hell.

Clearly, clapping one another on the back and praising each other's generosity of spirit takes time, and it was after midnight when the mobile phone buzzed on the dashboard of the car. The message was short. "Come now". We watched, and waited, as, one by one, the other limousines moved off round to the front of the building, a procession of glossy black beetles. Who knew how many would soon be carrying parasites as disgusting and evil as Peta Velds? Tomas texted back. "Engine trouble. Five minutes."

We waited until the parking garage was empty. Then Tomas started the car and we rolled around to the front of the building. I have always deplored these cars with their blacked-out windows – why should their occupants be invisible? But now I was grateful for them. Tomas had retrieved the driver's peaked cap and although it was several sizes too big, and somewhat wet, he padded it out with screwed up paper and wore it pulled down low over his eyes. I sat in the rear passenger seat, the one that would be furthest from the kerb when we stopped outside the front doors. My crossbow was loaded, my blade unsheathed. On Frederick's insistence, I carried a pistol loaded with the filled bullets. His armourer is a very talented woman. There was no smell of either garlic or willow acid above the leathery aroma of the car itself.

As we pulled into the kerb outside the building, I sensed something was wrong. There was nobody there. No grateful hosts waiting with the keynote speaker. And no speaker, either.

"Where is she?" Tomas asked, turning round in his seat.

Then there was a huge bang and the roof deformed inwards. Twenty rips in the headlining fabric of the car told their own story. A sinewy arm punched the glass out of the windscreen and hauled Tomas out and onto the bonnet of the car. I struggled to free my crossbow but I had been expecting her to enter the car through the door and had no clear aim between the front seats. All I could do was watch as she ripped his throat out. Then she crawled to the smashed window and looked in at me, eyes engorged, blood smeared all over the lower part of her hideously extended face.

"He tasted bad!" she hissed at me. "Maybe next time I'll come for you, cutter." Then she sprang onto the roof and was gone.

Poor Tomas. I held him as the life left his body. He looked into my eyes with that sad gaze of his and motioned for me to come closer.

"You know what you must do, Ariane," were his last words. Then he died.

The street was deserted. So I did not hesitate. I took one of my quarrels and plunged it into his heart then walked away.

Now I am alone here except for one burning question. How did Peta Velds know of our plan?

31

FACEBOOK MESSAGE FROM LUCINDA EASTERBROOK TO PETA VELDS, 12TH NOVEMBER 2010

Peta,

Did you get my last text? I told you I would be helpful to you. I found Caroline's notes for their plan to kill you and I told you. Doesn't that prove my devotion?

I'm going back tonight to have another poke around. Caroline is staying at the cutter's house so I can come and go as I please.

Lucinda

EMAIL FROM DAVID HARKER TO CAROLINE MURRAY, 13TH NOVEMBER 2010

caro its me david peta is away and I feel like ive been asleep or tripping for the last couple of months i wrote this really primitive email program on the labs mainframe its only capable of sending im afraid nobody even knows its there apart from me its a bit inelegant but on the other hand it's a hundred percent secure im using some pretty funky protocols I wont bore you with but unless you're the cia i reckon its invisible and before you start criticising my punctuation i didnt have time to code it ooh i know x there is that better x listen there is some seriously fuckedupshit going on here x its not skin cancer research at all x shes got us looking at genetic mutations that cause heliophobia you know what that is right it means fear of the sun x well not fear so much just those animals that live deep underground or at the bottom of the ocean and they like explode or die of massive cell disintegration if you expose them to sunlight x gotta go someones coming x i love you xxx

33

CAROLINE MURRAY'S JOURNAL, 14TH NOVEMBER 2010

Thank God. David's OK. Clever boy has written his own email program on the lab computer. From what I could decipher, and put together with what Ariane told me, it seems Peta Velds is using David to research a cure for her kind's inability to tolerate sunlight. Knowing him, he'll find one. Even if she's changed the terms of reference, he'll keep plugging away at the problem. It's what he does. And then one day, he'll just punch the air, yell "Eureka!" and that will be that. Vampires who can go bloody sunbathing. We have to get him back before he does it.

34

HUNT BOOK OF SHIMON GREGORIUS, 16TH NOVEMBER 2010

We travelled up to Norfolk yesterday. The weather was beautiful as it only can be in this country. Crisp, cold air, but the bluest of skies with high cirrus clouds streaking the heavens. Since her kill with Ariane the other night, Caroline has changed. She is still prone to her legalese now and then, but more and more she speaks like a huntress – like a cutter. Partly it is her love for David, though I fear that most precious of emotions will be sorely tested in the days and weeks ahead. Partly, though, there is something in her character, something buried deeply. I think the girl has a warrior in her genes.

For our mission, we needed certain supplies. A few gallons of petrol, some explosives and, perhaps most important of all, a virus. A computer virus, to be exact. I used our contacts in Moscow: there are plenty of extremely talented hackers out there who can write anything – if you pay them enough gelt! Sergei knew of a young girl, just 17, but already commanding the highest fees for her work. Sheer artistry according to Sergei. So, £50,000 and a brand new BMW and we received a thumb drive through the mail. I asked why no email and Sergei just laughed. Called me naïve and an old dinosaur. Email is for the rubes, apparently. Too easy to track and monitor. So, we have what we need to destroy David's files on the site. He will need to log on to whatever remote servers he uses for backups. Procuring the explosives and the gasoline was Lily's job. She has contacts in military circles and the construction industry, so the boot of the car is stuffed full of C4 and sloshing Jerry cans. I pray no idiot rear-ends us or we will all meet again in God's presence. Tomorrow we visit the laboratory and, I hope, rescue David.

———————

We arrived at the lab at dawn. The carpark was brightly lit but we found a shaded area near the rear corner of the building. Lily walked in through the front door, and explained to the receptionist – this Renfield character – that her car had broken down out on the main road. Caroline and I waited out of sight around the side of the building. Lily had made sure to tie her hair up, exposing that swan's neck of hers and we felt sure it would prove enough of a lure to get the man out into the open.

Sure enough, after a minute, out she came, with Renfield following on her heels. His eyes were focused on her rear, which she was swinging from side to side like a baboon in heat: I defy any man not to forget himself in its presence. My bolt entered his head through his right ear. He was dead before his fat corpse hit the ground. Caroline, Lily and I dragged the body out of sight behind a hedge – the deception didn't need to be perfect as the whole place would be ashes before too long. I retrieved the bolt and wiped it on Renfield's disgusting blue jumper before replacing it in my quiver and leaving it, and my crossbow, outside the door.

It was only once we regained the inside of the building that we realised one hugely important mistake. We had no idea where in the building we were to find David. Lily sat at the chair so recently vacated by Renfield and swung this way and that looking, I suppose, for some sort of building directory or staff telephone book.

"Here it is," she called. "The building plan. He's on the ground floor. Over there!"

She pointed to a pair of double doors away on the left of the reception area and we all ran for the door. Although Peta Velds was in New York with Le Fanu, we knew Stoker would be prowling about.

The doors led to a sort of airlock affair – a short hallway with a card-operated security door at the far end. We were expecting this. Lily slid in a dummy card connected by a ribbon of multicoloured wires to a little box of tricks Tomas had assembled before leaving for New York. There were no flashing lights or bleeps – Tomas explained those were just for the movies. Instead, after a couple of seconds, the door lock itself clicked and a red light turned green. Lily pushed the door and we were inside David's lab.

At first we couldn't see him. There were a couple of white coats tending computers and a centrifuge of spinning test-tubes like a miniature carousel such as you might find at a county fair. Both young – research students, maybe. A boy and a girl. Both looked startled as we burst in and looked towards a door at the far end of the lab. David's office, I assumed.

"Can we help you?" the boy asked. He didn't look particularly convinced when Caroline, in her best lawyer's voice, announced that we were from the Health and Safety Executive.

"We're shutting this facility down, effective immediately," she barked. "Unlicensed radioactive isotopes. Please leave with us now. Is there a David Harker working here, too?"

"Yes," the girl said. "He's in his office." She pointed at the door to which they'd directed their gaze when we arrived.

"Hold on," the boy said. "Before we do anything, I think we'd like to see some ID, please. If it's not too much trouble."

"Very well," Caroline said, her impression of a world-weary public servant a marvel to behold.

She opened her shoulder bag and retrieved a plastic ID card complete with photo, bar code and official HSE logo. Tomas had given her a rather grand job title – Senior Inspector, Toxins, Pathogens and Radioactivity – and I suspect that this, coupled with her brusqueness, was enough to convince our Doubting Thomas.

"Come on, Emily," he said. Then, to Caroline, "How long is your inspection going to take?"

"Inspection? Oh, no," she said. "You're closed. Indefinitely. Go home and wait. Breaches of the National Code on Radioactive Materials Abuse are usually on the news by tea-time, so you'll find out what's happening if you stick close to your TV."

The two scientists fled. Caroline rushed across the lab, dodging all kinds of high-tech equipment mounted on white plastic and steel benches and tore open the door to David's office. Lily and I didn't bother watching the reunion. We had work to do. Lily wedged the door open and ran back to the car to fetch the petrol and the C4. I took a screwdriver from my pocket and began removing hard disks from all the PCs I could see. These I bagged. We intended to destroy them back in London.

While I was engaged in this monotonous task, Caroline emerged from the glass cubicle with David. He was smiling broadly and holding her hand –a good sign. It meant Velds's influence over him had vanished. He was talking, gabbling, really.

"But Caro," he was saying, "how are you going to stop her? I mean, she's mega-rich and mega-powerful. You can't just—"

Then he saw me with the pile of hard drives on the table beside me.

"Hey! What are you doing?" he shouted. "Leave those alone. That's all our work. You can't—"

"Darling," Caroline said. "This is Shimon. He's helping me. There's so much I have to tell you and it's going to seem crazy but I promise you, it's for the best."

"What's for the best? What is he doing?"

I stood up and offered my hand. Instinctively, he took it and we shook. Amazing how you can derail almost anyone's train of thought with so simple a gesture.

"Hello, David," I said. "I am Shimon Gregorius. I am a vampire hunter. We need to destroy all your work, all your files, and this laboratory. Completely and utterly. My associate Lily Bax will be back shortly with gasoline and explosives."

I calculated the impact of my initial statement would cloud his mind and prevent his fully assimilating the import of my other words.

"Wait. What? You're a what? Caroline, who is this guy? Did he just say he was a vampire hunter?"

She put her hands on his shoulders and looked deeply into those eyes – such a bright blue, like my

Mother's old porcelain dinner service. She spoke slowly, and clearly, almost as if explaining something to a child.

"Yes he did say that. He, and Lily, and I, and a lady called Ariane and another man called Tomas. We are all vampire hunters. It's Peta Velds, David. She is a vampire."

His eyes widened so far I could see the white above as well as below his china-blue irises. He ran both hands through his mop of blond curls and scratched his scalp so vigorously I thought he might begin tearing his hair out.

"Ok. First of all, slap me. Hard. Otherwise I figure this is a hallucination I'm having and I should just go and lie down."

I thought Caroline would protest or use more words. But no. She drew her right hand back and delivered a resounding blow to his left cheek. The sound was amplified and reflected by all the hard surfaces in that clinical space and a red after-image blossomed on his pale skin.

"This is real, David. You have to come with us now. I can explain everything later."

I'd been working away while this little drama played out and I had gathered all but the hard drive from whatever computer David had in his office. I stowed them in the rucksack I had brought for the purpose and turned to him.

"Caroline is right, David," I said, in my best fatherly voice. "Now, what sort of machine do you have in your office? A desk-top or a laptop?"

"A laptop. I keep everything on it."

"Go and get it, please, David. And is there a server, too?"

He pointed to a grey steel cabinet, secured with a

padlock and ventilated with a grid of small holes on both sides.

"In that cupboard."

While David went to retrieve his laptop, I told Caroline to go and help Lily with the *materiel*. She left, and I severed the padlock's shackle with bolt cutters. Inside was a tower of uniform black boxes, each with a row of winking red lights along the front and the logo of a well-known Korean company. If they knew who was using their technology, I thought, they wouldn't be so keen to boast of its robustness in their advertising. "Used to exsanguinate the human race," is not much of an advertising slogan.

There were too many boxes to deal with individually, and I didn't know how much time we'd have before someone came in. Something more drastic was called for. I pulled the power cable out from the wall and cut it off where it entered the back of the assembly of servers. With my wire cutters, I stripped off the final ten centimetres of plastic insulation from the cable, exposing the copper cores. These I fed through the cooling slots at the rear of the central device until I felt them meet an obstruction. I secured the cable with duct tape. Finally, I pushed the plug home into a domestic light-timer, set the 'ON' time for ten minutes later and then plugged the timer into the wall socket and switched on the power.

David reappeared. His eyes were wary but relaxed, and he held out the laptop to me.

"This is it," he said. "Apart from the desktops and those servers, there's nothing else here. Everything else is in the cloud."

"Good," I said. "Thank you, David."

Then Lily and Caroline reappeared. Each carried two jerry cans of petrol, and the sagging rucksack on

Lily's back contained the C4. They put the cans down on the floor and the petrol sloshed heavily inside. Lily took charge. Violence on this scale is more her field of expertise than mine.

"Caroline, get everything soaked in the gas. Except yourself, obviously. Start in David's office and work your way back towards the door. David, stay close to Shimon. Do what he says."

Then she knelt by the server tower and unsnapped the catches on her rucksack.

She unwrapped the black plastic film on a package of the plastic explosive and moulded the round block into a flattish square. This she slid inside the server tower, on top of one of the boxes. She repeated the process one layer further down with a second block of explosive. She retrieved a detonator and timer from her rucksack but then she spotted my stripped power cable wires.

"Did you do this, Shimon?" she said.

"Guilty as charged."

"Excellent! But instead of trying to fry the disks with juice, we'll blow them up."

With that she pulled the plug and its timer out from the socket again – "Can't be too careful". Then she connected the wires to a slender silver cylinder the size of a cigarette, which she explained was an electric detonator, and pushed it into the oily, grey slab of C4. She replaced the plug and timer and switched on the power. I noticed a bead of sweat rolling down her temple. Never a relaxing job, working with plastique.

Caroline tossed the last of the empty jerry cans into the corner where it bounced off a desk with a hollow clang.

"Done," she called. "My God, this place stinks."

"Not half as much as it will do when the plastique

goes up," Lily said. "Now, time to leave."

I swung my rucksack loaded with hard disks onto my back, David grabbed his laptop and then all four of us ran for the door. I checked my watch. Five minutes to go. Then, disaster!

Outside the lab we came face to face with Stoker and two female lamia. He was pointing a shotgun at Caroline's chest and the two creatures separated and began advancing on us from left and right.

Lily and I drew our blades and the smell of the *salcie usturoi* drove the lamia back for a moment, hissing in that infernal manner they have. Stoker simply laughed.

"Oh, dear, mediaeval daggers soaked in a condiment against a rather nicely engineered German pump-action shotgun. You lose, I'm afraid. Now go back in there and undo whatever it is you've just done, while I wait here with Miss Murray."

"Wait!" David cried. "No! It's over, Stoker. I'm not going to solve Peta's problem. So you'd better start blasting."

"Very well," Stoker said and he racked a shell into the chamber. "But you'll have to live with your fiancée's death for the rest of your life."

He levelled the brutish looking gun and aimed at the centre of Caroline's chest. She was paralyzed with fear, eyes wide, one hand clutching her throat.

Then something strange happened.

Stoker started trembling.

Just a little at first, enough to make the fabric of his suit vibrate over his chest. Then, more violently, so that his whole torso began shivering.

He dropped the shotgun. To my great surprise, Caroline darted forward and scooped it up off the floor, before turning it to point at Stoker.

"What have you done?" he asked, as splits started appearing in the skin of his face and hands.

Lily and I knew, at least in general, and we pulled David and Caroline back to a safe distance. David answered.

"After Peta left, I came out of whatever trance she put me in. Ariane couriered me a letter explaining what was going on. And how to kill vampires. Plus a little bottle of a smelly yellow liquid. For all your cyber security, Stoker, you forgot about blokes with bike helmets turning up in reception with lab supplies. Caroline, take a look at the grip on that shotgun, just don't grab it hard."

"Clever boy!" she said. "Look Stoker. He carved a nick in it and coated the splinter with *salcie usturoi*."

Stoker's time was up and we shielded our eyes as, with a scream, he collapsed in a widening pool of his own blood that flooded out from his trouser hems and the sleeves of his jacket. As the head burst we were running for the door, the two lamia hanging back as they keened over their dead master.

"Come on!" Lily shrieked. "We don't have much time."

We reached the car in a scramble of arms and legs, piling in to the front and rear and stuffing the rucksacks wherever they would fit.

Lily jammed the key in the ignition and started the car with a roar from its engine. Her foot was flat on the accelerator. She threw it into first and screeched around in a wide circle before barreling across the tarmac for the front gates. Ahead of us, under twin pools of pinkish-yellow light, the tall gates began to close on their greased rails.

We reached them just as the distance between their

leading edges closed to the width of the car. Lily hit the space dead centre and kept her foot down as the steel gates scraped their way down the bodywork of the car. Thank God for those Swedes and their safety consciousness. I wouldn't have fancied trying the same trick in a Lada.

I swear they snapped at us like the jaws of a gigantic crocodile as we got free, before clanging shut. Lily turned left out of the access road, tyres squealing as she straightened the car onto the main road heading towards the town. As we rocketed along the road the three of us not driving looked out of the side and rear screens.

"It should have blown by now," Lily said.

"No," I said. "Those domestic timers are only accurate enough to turn lights on and off."

I was just about to explain the clockwork mechanism when there was a bright flash from the lab followed a second later by an enormous rushing, roaring boom – almost two separate sounds but running into one another. I watched as a fireball blossomed from the roof of the building – a beautiful thing if you could ignore its significance. Although, maybe if you considered what it meant it was all the more pleasing to the eye. There were a series of three or four more explosions – lab equipment, I assumed, or chemicals.

Lily slowed the car: leaving the scene of an explosion on British soil doing ninety is bound to attract the wrong type of attention. As we entered Lowestoft at a sedate thirty miles per hour, all was quiet apart from a few workers heading out from their houses to catch buses or trains or perhaps just take their pet pooch for a walk. No sirens. They would take a while to come as we hoped we had killed everyone left at the lab.

CAROLINE MURRAY'S JOURNAL, 17TH NOVEMBER 2010

I have David back. After we returned to London, the others dropped us off at the flat. Shimon said they had work to do setting another trap to catch Peta Velds. Plus they had those disks to destroy. I asked, perhaps foolishly, if they were going to "wipe" them, though I confess I had no clear idea of what that means, or even whether it's a real thing.

Shimon just laughed and said they were going to use "a bloody big hammer". Crude but effective, I suppose.

Last week, I took David to see a blood specialist in Harley Street. I thought barristers were well paid but after he presented his bill I swear I trained in the wrong profession.

David told me that Peta had indeed bitten him, and the plasters were covering up the evidence. She did it the very first night he was up there, the bitch. But here's the most amazing part of this. The results came through yesterday morning and his blood is completely free of parasites. No infections. No raised T-cell count. Nothing. She had him under some sort of hypnotic spell, but to be honest, any moderately forceful woman could probably achieve the same results with David. However, there is an interesting side angle to all the good news.

David has a rare blood disorder. Something called n-Theta-Haemoblasticity. It's asymptomatic, although it has been linked to bipolar disorder – who knew? – but it hyper-stimulates the sufferer's white blood cells. In David's case, they multiplied to 1,000 times their normal concentration. I think they just basically destroyed the parasites that came through into his bloodstream from Peta Velds's saliva.

I called Ariane, who is back from New York, though without Tomas – dreadful news. She was close to tears several times as we spoke. I told her that we, at least, had been successful, and she told me what to do with David to be absolutely sure he was "pure", as she put it. Actually, it was a rather pleasant day.

First we went for a walk in the sunshine. It was bitterly cold and I had my good coat on, but Ariane said David should expose as much of his skin as possible. We got some funny looks, I can tell you. Me in a floor-length greatcoat buttoned up to my chin and poor David in shorts and a T-shirt. But he was fine. Well, blue with cold but no exploding, thank God. Then we had to expose him to garlic oil. I booked a table at Café da Aldo in Soho and we stuffed our bellies with garlic bread and spaghetti ali e oli. The restaurant is still open and still wearing its original décor, which, by the way, I don't think has changed since about 1972. Finally, the worst test and the only bit of the day I regret.

After lunch we went to the middle of Soho square and sat on one of the benches. It was empty, apart from a couple of homeless types and they seemed far more interested in the Japanese tourists and their stupid selfie-sticks than in us. I had brought a little sharpened stick of willow wood with me that I'd cut from one of the trees in the gardens of Chiswick House.

I made David hold out his hand, palm down, and I had to push the stick into his skin until I drew blood. Brave boy just gritted his teeth but I was weeping by the end of it. That did draw blood but nothing more. No shivering, no splitting skin or any of that revolting business that happened to Stoker.

So I reported back to Ariane and she signed him A1, fit for duty. I honestly think that had I not done the tests as she'd prescribed, she would have come after him herself.

36

EMAILS BETWEEN PETA VELDS AND LUCINDA EASTERBROOK, 18TH NOVEMBER 2010

From: Peta
To: Lucinda
Subject: Vengeance

MY LUCINDA,

HAVE YOU HEARD? THAT WOMAN DESTROYED MY LAB. SHE TOOK DAVID AWAY FROM ME. AND SHE KILLED STOKER.

I WANT HER DEAD. I WANT HIM DEAD. I WANT THEM ALL DEAD. DO YOU UNDERSTAND? I AM FLYING BACK TONIGHT.

COME TO ME AT MY LONDON HOUSE TOMORROW EVENING.

PETA

From: Lucinda

To: Peta
Subject: Re: Vengeance

Oh my darling Peta,

I did hear a little something on the grapevine. I still have my sources. A boy in Caroline's chambers overheard her talking on the phone. I "persuaded" him to tell me what he'd heard.

I will come to you and together we will fix them. All.

I love you.

Lucinda x

37

[DRAFT POST] RAMBLINGS OF A FREE-REVVING MIND – DAVID HARKER'S BLOG, 20TH NOVEMBER 2010

I can't believe it. Not really. According to Caro, Peta Velds is a vampire. And Stoker. And basically everybody at the lab apart from my team. I can't deny what I saw and Caro triple-checked my meds with me: she even made me count the holes in the blister pack to prove to me I was taking them every day.

And now I have to destroy all my work. Every single test result, research note and protocol. Every simulation, every model, every iteration of every algorithm. It's just so gutting. Except, obviously, it has to go because otherwise Peta would have the key to hunting round the clock and out in broad daylight. So, yes, I see the need for it but I wish there was some way I could keep a copy. Even a hard copy. I'm sure I could refocus the work back onto skin cancer. But Caro's adamant. She says the stakes are so high we have to erase everything. Which, by the way, is not as easy as it sounds. You can't just go into Explorer and press Ctrl + Alt + Del. There are copies being created and distributed all over the place on our cloud network. I designed the system with quadruple redundancy so even if three servers went black we'd be safe.

I have a plan, though. When I was doing my PhD I made friends with a couple of Russians who were big into computational biology, but they discovered there was more money in hacking. I think they work for the Russian Government but I've never pushed them about it because sometimes it seems their clients may be a bit closer to the Dark Side.

So, I emailed Boris and Irena and they're creating a custom virus that will destroy the disk imaging software, memory infrastructure and all the files. Permanento! It's a shame, really, because I wrote it all, but I guess, you know, human race survives versus a few thousand lines of code.

They should have it ready in a week or two. Until then Caro is treating me like an invalid and feeding me up. Plus that crazy old Jewish guy, Shimon, cooks this mean roast chicken. He said on the drive to London that he already had a Russian working on a virus but I told him "better safe than sorry". Maybe we'll run both of them.

38

CAROLINE MURRAY'S JOURNAL, 21ST/22ND NOVEMBER 2010

I am now leading this insane double-life. I have tried to pick up the reins in chambers again, but to be honest my heart isn't in it anymore. I'm not sure if it ever will be again. I have a dinner tonight with an old friend. I am supposed to charm my way into his affections again, and to see if I can't persuade him to keep his cases coming Roxburgh Chambers' way.

———

The dinner with Rafe went on late, at least midnight. They were practically stacking the chairs around us. I got back to the flat at about 1.00 a.m. and I just had this sixth sense that something was up. The door was locked properly, and there wasn't any sign of damage, but I could just tell something bad was happening inside.

I more or less flew into the hall and dropped my bag and just ran upstairs. David had gone to bed and our bedroom door was closed. That was the first sign – because he always likes to leave it wide open. The light from the hall comforts him. I wrenched it open and rushed into the room and she – Lucinda – was in there. Stark naked and climbing onto the bed.

I think I screamed at her or maybe I screamed "David" – but anyway, she turned and she just, Oh, God, she growled at me. Like a dog. Her lips were drawn back and then that thing happened to her jaw. She was one of them after all. David was out of it. He was always a heavy sleeper and recently he's been taking half a sleeping pill before bed.

She kind of stalked off the bed and I know it's weird but I still had time to take in her physique. She used to be quite voluptuous but she was totally muscled, like a gym bunny. Her tits had disappeared and she just looked like an animal. Like a panther or something.

Her head was jerking back and I just watched those horrid glassy teeth lower themselves from the roof of her mouth.

"Mother is displeased with you," she said. Or hissed, rather. "Now I must take you to her."

I grabbed a pillow from my side of the bed and threw it at her. She swatted it aside but in that moment I ran back down the hall and raced down the stairs. She came scuttling after me, on all fours, screeching and whining. I had only one thought. Get to the kitchen. Ariane had warned me to be prepared to fight at any time so I'd coated the biggest kitchen knife in the block with *salcie usturoi*.

Lucy caught me just as I reached the kitchen. She clawed at my arm and ripped four great tears in my jacket. It's leather though and her nails didn't get anywhere near my skin. I twisted round and sort of tripped her and yanked my arm free at the same time. My Thai boxing teacher wouldn't have been very impressed but I bought just enough time to get to the knife block.

She reared back up at me from the floor, jack-knifing like a gymnast. Then she saw the butcher knife and stopped. She flared her nostrils as she looked at the knife then back at me.

I was crying by this time, and my nose was running. I'd nearly lost my fiancée and now my best friend was gone, turned into this hideous creature scowling at me with her whole lower jaw hanging down like a snake's. She shook her head violently, forwards and back and the jaw went back into place with a loud click. She started talking.

"Caro, join us. Let me feed on you and I can give you all this." Then she ran her hands over her body, "It feels so good. So alive." The way she was talking made me feel woozy, something about the eyes, maybe or just the sight of that wide-open maw and all that gunk dripping down from the teeth. I swear I was starting to feel it mightn't be such a bad idea when David appeared right behind her in the doorway.

"Caro? What's going on?"

Lucinda turned and I knew she'd kill David. As her thigh muscles bunched, ready to spring, I moved first.

I think the scream was to give myself the courage to do what I knew I had to. It was a horrible sound, even as I made it, all clotted with tears and snot, my voice cracking. But I did it anyway.

I drew my arm back behind me, keeping it low like Lily taught me.

Closed the gap between me and Lucinda.

Thrust the knife hard into her, below the ribs, where it would be sure to find enough soft flesh to do its work.

Lucinda whirled round to face me, tearing the blade

free, which clattered to the floor as my hand opened reflexively.

Her eyes were blood-red and wide, wide open. Her jaw slipped back into place.

"Caro!" she said. Then she shuddered mightily and turned to blood – a monstrous flood of it which slopped down in a great red tide. Just like the other ones.

I killed my best friend. No. Peta Velds killed my best friend. I must hold onto that. Ariane and the others are right. She was already lost to me when she turned up at the flat to kill David. I destroyed the sad, angry, hungry creature my best friend had become.

David just stood there, almost catatonic. His mouth was open. I think the sleeping pill was still trying hard to do its work, because he seemed almost to be sleep walking.

"Did you just—?" he said.

"Go back to bed, love," I said. "I'll explain tomorrow."

"But—"

"Go. I'll be up in a while," I said.

And bless him, he did. Just stumbled out of the kitchen and went back to bed.

It took me almost three hours to clean up the kitchen. Then I crashed out on the sofa – I didn't even have the energy to get undressed and go to bed. Besides, I didn't want to wake David. And I found something.

I don't know why I hadn't noticed them before, well, I suppose the sight of poor Lucy looking like she did was a distraction. On the floor of the hall, right outside our bedroom door, was a pile of Lucy's clothes. The usual blacks and purples. But placed absolutely centrally on the top was a phone. Some sort of bespoke thing – made of brushed silver metal and incredibly beautiful. I pocketed it. There would be time to investigate it later.

The kitchen still smelled like a butcher's shop but there was no visible sign of what had happened. I made myself a strong coffee and sat at the table. As I sipped the scalding liquid I found that I was feeling no grief for Lucy. Perhaps, deep down, I'd known already that she was lost to me. I'd persuaded myself she was OK, even through Ariane had warned me not to give in to what she called "nostalgia for the friend that was, and is no more". It sounded like a prayer, now that I come to think of it.

When David appeared, a couple of hours later, I realised I hadn't moved. Half my coffee was still there, stone-cold and greyish. He looked only slightly less bleary than he had done when he helped me finish off Lucinda. I sat him down with a cup of decaf and began, patiently, I hope, to explain what was going on.

39

[DRAFT POST] RAMBLINGS OF A FREE-REVVING MIND – DAVID HARKER'S BLOG, 23RD NOVEMBER 2010

I went to sleep in one world and woke up in another. I don't know how else to put it. Caro's been trying to tell me what's been going on but I think I just blocked it all out. It's not that hard with my condition. You just tell yourself it's your hyperactive cerebral cortex and leave it at that. But after what I saw last night, I guess I don't have a choice but to believe every word.

But I'm a scientist, for God's sake. Rational is my middle name. I don't see how any of this can be true. Caro says Ariane can explain everything much better than she can so we're going to see her and her vampire-hunting buddies later today.

If it's true – and I know it will turn out to be: Caro isn't lying, I know that – then as far as I can see, my career is over. I mean, how can you go back to fiddling around with mass-spectrometers and DNA analysis when there are those, those things creeping about London feeding off people? Jesus! I don't know how to process this. I mean, why has nobody ever gone to the police? Or the government? You can't just run a vigilante operation against bloody vampires. It's insane. And before I let myself answer that point, *it* is insane. I, on the other hand, am perfectly OK.

Caro says the phone could be important. She hasn't turned it on. Says Ariane needs to look at it first. She thinks it could be a way for us to get to Peta. Oh, my God! Peta Velds is the literal mother of all vampires. And I was working for her in Norfolk. How could I have been so blind? Was I really that simple to buy? Money and a house and I rolled over and did her bidding. Left my old job without a backward glance? No. It wasn't the money. Not really. It was the freedom she promised me. The budget. The kit. But that's all gone now, too. Blown up like a bloody great fireworks display.

It was on the news, too. The reporter said there'd been a lab explosion caused by a faulty electrical circuit. But I thought they had fire investigators. People who go on the news and talk about accelerants and all that. Plus surely C4 leaves some sort of chemical signature. They'd know it wasn't a regular lab accident. I mean the place was flattened. It looked like an atom bomb had gone off. More questions. No answers. Not yet, anyway. I'm making a list of them for Ariane later. Caroline's just got back from the shops. There's something I want to ask her.

40

CAROLINE MURRAY'S JOURNAL, 23RD NOVEMBER 2010

Well. I must confess I didn't see that one coming. I'd just got in through the front door and was about to put my shopping down on the kitchen table when David burst in looking all waggy-tailed and bright-eyed. He took the carrier bags off me.

"Cancel the wedding," he said.

"What?" I said. "What d you mean, 'cancel the wedding'? We haven't even *planned* a wedding you idiot!"

"OK, don't cancel the wedding. Just, don't let's plan one. I want to get married right away. Today if possible. We have to, Caro, you must see that."

I tried to calm him down. Put my hands on his shoulders and pressed down until he was forced to sit. But he held my hands and pulled me onto his lap so I was straddling his thighs.

He looked deeply into my eyes and I don't think I have ever seen David more serious. He delivered the following speech. He must have been rehearsing it while I was out or something.

"Caroline Murray. I love you. And I know we were

meant to be together. But with all that's happened, I realise that what matters is spending the rest of our lives with each other. I can't risk losing you to one of those things knowing that we hadn't joined ourselves fully. So let's get married without delay. Please."

So instead of talking about vampires, we spent an hour or so planning our quickie wedding. I knew my parents would be devastated, especially Mum. But right at that moment, the only person who mattered to me was the man sitting next to me as we pored over the website explaining what we'd need to do and bring, and who we'd need to notify. All fairly standard stuff and I'd collected all the documents within a further 20 minutes. However much David wanted to hop in a plane and fly to Vegas, I explained that it would be risky with Velds on the warpath and that a 35-day wait would be preferable to being carved up in the desert somewhere.

He agreed, reluctantly.

41

HUNT BOOK OF ARIANE VAN HELSING, 1ST JANUARY 2011

So. Caroline is no longer a Miss but a Mrs. Good for her. She needs a little normality in her life right now. And David is clearly besotted with her. He is a fast learner, too. From all that science, I suppose, He was resistant at first, started calling me a storyteller, but I gave him all the hard science we have done over the years, from the parasitology reports to the DNA analysis, and in the end he was convinced. Weird that lamia attempting to drain your blood not once but twice should not have proved sufficiently compelling, but a sheaf of computer printouts does the job. So. He is aware, which is good. His skills will also come in handy. He can write code, for one thing.

It was so hard losing Tomas. He and I went way back and I always thought that one day he might divine my true feelings for him. But it is too late now. Tomas is gone. For ever. He is with God. I still feel him when I am alone. I know he would want me to continue the war without him. It is my destiny, my patrimony. Great-great-grandfather Abraham would have approved of Tomas.

Now, though, I have a new team. Nobody could replace Tomas, but Jim has other attributes and skills that bring us a new way of working. We had to clean him up, inside and out, and he will always need watching whenever alcohol is about. But Shimon makes sure he goes to meetings and Lily has taken it upon herself to feed him up. Without the dirt he is rather good looking, especially those deep-brown eyes.

I was right in my initial assumptions about Jim. He was in law enforcement. But not as a regular policeman. He was Special Branch. Undercover. But he went too deep. His final mission was infiltrating an anarchist cell in London. They had well developed plans to bomb King's Cross Station. But Jim became involved with a woman. She fell pregnant and had his child. Somehow she discovered his true identity and aborted the baby. That tipped Jim over the edge and his drinking escalated. The anarchists beat him and left him for dead on the steps of Scotland Yard with a note stapled to his forehead. The note said if the "pigs" sent anyone else they would return them in separate bags.

After that Jim quit the force on medical grounds. He spiralled downwards, stopped paying his mortgage and was on the streets within six months. He hadn't lost all his survival instincts though and let himself drift into a new persona, voice and all. It is actually quite amusing now to hear this ex-Special Branch officer talking in his beautiful Queen's English and compare him to the filthy, matted creature we met in the carpark.

So, Jim is our new communications expert. He is also extremely happy with weapons. He passed his first test with flying colours – this is the expression, I think.

When we recruited Jim, we still had the female lamia locked up in the basement. She was weakened because of course we were no longer feeding her. The bowl of blood was just to convince Caroline. I took Jim down to her and gave him a crossbow.

"Kill her," I said. Not "it" – I didn't want to depersonalise the lamia. I wanted him to believe he was killing a woman, not a monster, not a species of vermin.

He hesitated, even as he aimed the crossbow. Then it did me – us – a huge favour, and screeched at him for blood. As the feeding funnel pulsed weakly in its mouth, he pulled the trigger.

"Tell me about the others," was all he said, afterwards

So we are six, where once we were four. I feel this will be our best-ever chance of defeating Peta Velds.

42

CAROLINE HARKER'S JOURNAL, 3RD JANUARY 2011

It's 10.30 p.m. we've spent most of this evening working on a plan to destroy Peta Velds. It is reassuring having Jim on the team, He's rather dishy apart from anything else, and my goodness, doesn't he know his way around fighting tactics! He and Lily have spent some time cracking the security code on the phone I retrieved when I killed Lucy. No, not Lucy. As I keep reminding myself, Peta Velds killed Lucy. I killed the creature that had taken over her poor body.

Anyway, they have unlocked it now and since Peta Velds doesn't know about Lucy, we have a way in. Because I know her way of speaking the best, I have been assigned the task of keeping lines of communications open with what I must learn to call the target. This is Jim's advice and I must say, it does help to stay focused. I never liked using her name anyway. So I send texts saying "I" am closing in on "me", as it were. The target seems not to have noticed anything amiss.

We intend to lure the target to a killing ground. More military terminology, I'm afraid. The kill team is all of us. Jim said he would always have gone in with at least three to one in his favour for a fight and as we don't know how many lamia the target will bring with her, we six are all going together. It feels fitting, somehow.

As Lucy, I am to advise the target that the other me, Caroline, is pinned down in the killing ground and that it would be best if the target did the job herself – as vengeance for the lab's being destroyed. The collective feeling is she'll go for it – being so driven by concepts of honour and revenge.

The killing ground is perfect. It's down by the river on a deserted stretch out near the Thames Barrier. The story is that I've been forced to drive Lucy there in my car so afterwards they can dump the body where the tide will take it. After all, Caroline Murray is high profile enough that her disappearance would spark a murder hunt.

Ariane has been in contact with her counterpart in New York. They were talking about guns. Apparently, he has perfected a way of firing bullets filled with *salcie usturoye*. Because we have Jim now, Ariane wants to add firepower to our crossbows. She says they're perfectly effective against individual lamia, but for a showdown with the target and who knows how many others, we need to increase our rate of fire – Jim's influence again.

He's gone off to secure some pistols and ammunition then he's going to work with Shimon to adapt the bullets. Personally, I'm happy to stick to the crossbow.

I'm going home now. I left David there with strict instructions to keep all the doors and windows locked and not to open the door to anyone. It's a bit like having a child in the house. But... oh, let's not go there.

43

HUNT BOOK OF ARIANE VAN HELSING, 4TH JANUARY 2011

I followed Caroline from our house; she ignored my advice about taking a cab and set out on foot. The hour was late, eleven or so. Although London has a well-earned reputation for 24-hour living – it has caught up with Manhattan, Tokyo, Amsterdam and Berlin – in Bloomsbury, there is less nightlife than the West End or Soho, just ten minutes' walk westward. She was still dressed for court in high-heeled buckled shoes and these were to be the cause of her troubles with the daughters of Peta Velds.

Caroline was heading for Euston Square tube station and she could have – should have – walked around the three sides of Bloomsbury Square, staying in the light from the street lamps all the way. Instead, inexplicably, she headed for the gate into the park and began to cross it diagonally. The park was unlit; bushes and trees swaying in the wind cast crazed shadows that seemed to grab at her legs as she hurried across the grass and flowerbeds to the gate on the far side.

Then, from a deep pool of shadow to her left, three daughters of Peta Velds emerged in a group. Unseen by Caroline they spread out behind her, one to her left, one to her right and one dead centre, approaching stealthily. Their arms were outstretched, fingernails extended into talons and fangs already descended from the roofs of their mouths in position for a kill. From behind them a cat yowled and the sudden discordant noise caused Caroline to whirl round. In that moment she saw them and began to run. One thing I have noticed with the lamia: they never hurry. Perhaps they are always certain of their meal.

Caroline reached the north gate of the park and grabbed for the wrought iron handle. The metal squawked in protest as she wrenched it open and headed across the road for the street that led to the tube station. This was a mistake and it placed her in even greater jeopardy than she had been in the park. The road was deserted, just a couple of parked taxis whose drivers were absent, perhaps drinking tea in an all-night café somewhere close by.

The lamia continued their relentless pursuit, not dragging their feet as the popular imagination has it, but not sprinting either. As I said, they seem all too sure that blood will be theirs if only they stay on its trail long enough. Caroline turned to look over her shoulder and screamed. A plea for help that echoed and bounced off empty office buildings and loading bays for vacant commercial premises. The creatures were gaining on her; she was running out of breath and frequent trips and stumbles were slowing her down. I knew they would not attack in the open, even at this late hour. The lamia like to feed unseen; they would drive her into a side road or alley, and that is where I would take them. Then the unthinkable happened.

As she ran across the road and reached the pavement on the far side, the heel of her left shoe jammed in a grating set into the road. Her ankle twisted and she screamed in pain as she fell to one side. The vampires twittered to each other, a hellish giggling that set my teeth on edge. Instead of speeding up, they slowed down, closing ranks until they were walking towards her three abreast in a knot of crooked claws and dripping fangs. Their breathing became audible, a panting sound as if in the throes of passion.

She was wrestling with the shoe, holding her ankle with both hands and trying desperately to free either the shoe from the iron grating or her foot itself from the imprisoning leather straps. She screamed again, pleading with them to leave her be, but, of course, they paid her no heed. Instead, they fanned out around her, keeping to a radius of perhaps seven or eight feet. I had to wait – to pick my moment. I wanted to save her, not to seal her doom. One detached herself from the others and dropped to all fours. In that animal crouch, she began circling Caroline, hissing disgustingly and running her long red tongue over the tips of her fangs, which were dripping with the anticoagulant that would keep Caroline's veins open until she was bled dry.

Caroline was pleading now, yanking her ankle and swearing at the shoe that she would not let it kill her. The two others now dropped onto hands and feet as well, and the three daughters of Peta Velds began keening: a grating high-pitched song that I have heard before but which never fails to make my blood run cold. For it foretells death. It is the ancient song of the lamia.

The lead lamia gathered itself: I could see the

muscles of its thighs bunching as it prepared to pounce. Caroline uttered a wail of the purest terror as she saw a sight very few humans have ever lived to speak of. The lamia's eyes rolled back in their sockets, revealing blood-suffused corneas of the deepest scarlet. As all three of them blindly leapt, I emerged from my hiding place and commanded them to stop using an old curse, "*Makhni se'fal dushteri na kruv. Az izprati vi'obratno vada.*"

They turned away from Caroline, as I knew they would. Death threats in the old tongue have the power to arrest the lamia, even now.

I levelled my crossbow at the lead lamia and murmured one of the old cutter prayers under my breath. "Hell calls you, filthy demon. Let the only blood you taste from this moment be your own."

I sighted on its heart and pulled the trigger. With a hiss, the willow-wood quarrel flashed across the road, catching the pinkish orange light from the streetlamp, and embedded itself in the creature's chest. As it squealed in distress, clawing at the shaft of the quarrel, the *salcie usturoi* did its deadly work. In just a few seconds, its heart had taken a lethal dose of the poison and pumped it around the body. The lamia looked at me in shock and surprise and then was destroyed. Every blood cell expanded and ruptured; the tissue forming the arteries, veins and capillaries degraded as the cells swelled and burst; and the heart itself, infernal pump, spasmed as it tried to contain the additional pressure. Then, with a shiver and a plaintive scream, the lamia arched its back, arms outstretched, mouth wracked wide in a rictus of agony – and exploded. The blood sheeted from the dying body, covering its siblings – and Caroline, too – in a red caul. They hissed and began to advance on me, fingers curled into claws, mouths lolling wide as the slime dripped from the tips of their fangs and curdled with the saliva that ran from their lower jaws.

With those terrible hissing sounds the lamia make when prevented from feeding, the two remaining creatures sprang, not at me, but sideways. Each found crevices and handholds on the walls of the old buildings facing each other across the street and began creeping higher, the talons on their hands and feet digging into the old brick. I kept them both in view even as they separated and began crawling horizontally along the walls towards me, Caroline forgotten. With relief, I noticed from the corner of my eye that she had finally wrenched her shoe free of the grating, minus the ridiculous heel, which tore off the sole with an audible pop.

"Run, Caroline," I called.

But she disobeyed me. Instead, she kicked her other foot hard against the kerb, ripping the heel off that shoe as well, so she could move with greater ease. I was impressed with her practicality; they looked expensive. She reached down into the pool of blood and slime where her erstwhile attacker had disintegrated and picked up the crossbow bolt, wiping it on her thigh. Then she advanced on the lamia from behind, keeping a safe distance. Well, I remember thinking, perhaps I have misjudged this lawyer with her regard for the proper way of doing things.

My attention was pulled rudely back to my more immediate challenge. I had been backing up carefully, keeping both remaining lamia in view to left and right. They were 12 feet off the ground now and I knew as I looked up at them that my neck was stretched and they could sense the blood flowing up and down the vessels inside. Then, silently, they dropped to the ground in a crouch, first one, then the other. The tendons and muscles in their limbs were clearly visible, almost straining in their desire to leap onto me and feed. But I have met their kind many times and so far it is I, Ariane Van Helsing, who still walks the Earth, and they who rot and scream from torments in the deepest pits of hell.

I had reloaded my crossbow by this time and was carrying it up at my right shoulder, sighting down the gleaming white shaft of the quarrel at the creatures, moving it through a 90 degree arc slowly and consistently, so neither could be sure it wouldn't receive the deadly missile in its heart. But they knew something. One quarrel, two lamia. I would not have time to reload. To slow them, I reached down with my left hand and swept the skirt of my coat aside. Strapped to my side, inside its chased steel scabbard, was a short, curved sword, forged in Bohemia in the 13th Century and whetted many, many times since then by Van Helsings. My great-great-grandfather, Abraham, wielded it in his battles with the lamia. The hilt glowed dully in the sodium streetlight, promising destruction.

"Come, lamia," I said in the old tongue. "Come and let my blade feed on you. It is thirsty and has not drunk of your kind's blood these three months."

They paused at this. The lamia have a healthy respect for cutters, as well they should. And my family has dealt with many thousands of the creatures since first we discovered their existence.

One of the two facing me seemed more confident than its sister. With a shriek that echoed off the buildings looming over us it sprang at me. So be it. I let fly the quarrel and before it had buried itself in her chest, I had danced back a couple of paces, drawing my sword as I did so. The remaining creature screeched with pain and continued to advance on me, even as her sister splashed into nothingness beside her, her remains flowing away down a drain in the gutter. Her hips twitched from side to side as she prepared to spring, like a cat. Her red lips were drawn back from her gums and the long fangs dripped. But spring she did not. With a scream of purest hatred, Caroline Murray appeared behind her and, with a sweeping downwards blow, stabbed the crossbow bolt though the evil creature's back and into its heart. Caroline staggered back and watched the lamia dissolve with a wail into a third mess of liquefaction and gore.

I ran forward and caught her as she subsided to the pavement. It was an unfortunate place to sit, and her clothes were soon soaked in blood. I was not worried about the parasites; they need to be injected into an open wound in order to multiply. But Caroline would cut a rather conspicuous figure were we to rejoin the throng on the main road. I called Lily. I told her to bring the car round to the alley. We needed to get Caroline to safety.

As we waited, a scrawny fox emerged from behind a rubbish container. I have noticed more and more of these animals around London's streets. So many night creatures, all feeding, consuming, killing, dying – this city is nothing more than a forest built of concrete, steel and glass. There is as much death, or more, here than ever there was in the days when we hunted lamia in the Old Country, among the trees and scrub of the wooded uplands.

The fox bent its head to the first pool of blood, then jerked it upwards again to look at us. Seeing we were not moving, it bent its head again, lapping at the blood, but keeping its head turned at an angle from the ground so it could keep us in its line of sight. Then it put its head up and opened its mouth. I saw sharp teeth and a long pink tongue. It pulled its mouth into a wide grimace that pulled its eyes into slits that showed white at their edges and called: a sound like a child in pain. Three of the racking cries, one after the other, rising in pitch. Then it stood still and looked towards the rubbish container. Three cubs emerged, tightly grouped, and tottered over to their mother. She yipped quietly and they seemed to take this as a signal. Hesitantly at first, then with greater enthusiasm, they drank at the edge of the pool of blood. Then all four animals scattered as bright white headlights illuminated the alley. It was Lily. Within seconds we had guided Caroline inside the car and were on the move, leaving the foxes to their evening meal.

Once we were back inside our house, I sat Caroline at the kitchen table and unstrapped her shoes.

"It's a shame," she said. "I really liked that pair."

I slung them into a corner where we had laid a sheet of thick plastic on the floor.

"Can you stand, Caroline?" I asked her. "We need to get you out of these clothes."

She complied meekly, standing perfectly still, her hands dangling at her sides, as Lily and I removed the wet trousers, jacket and blouse. Lily wrapped her in a thick white towel and took her to the bathroom.

I gathered the soaking clothes and ruined shoes and took them downstairs to the furnace. Lily joined me a few moments later, holding Caroline's underwear. We burnt the lot. It doesn't do to leave traces of the lamia near humankind. The foxes and other creatures of the night would do an adequate cleanup job on the street. The writers in the Bible who talked of the cleansing power of flames were not speaking metaphorically: *lamia multigena* are unable to survive in such temperatures and we can sever the bloodline of parasite and host alike.

"What shall we do with her?" Lily asked.

"For now, nothing. In the morning, we will talk to her and decide what needs to be done next. She'll need new clothes, too. We must act fast though. I am sure Velds will be making plans to flee, taking David with her if she can."

44

TEXT FROM CAROLINE HARKER
(POSING AS LUCINDA EASTERBROOK)
TO PETA VELDS, 5TH JANUARY 2011

Plan to kill Caroline. I catch her after work tomorrow. Do my transformation thing and force her to drive to Thames Barrier. I know a perfect spot – I filmed an ad there once. I'll text you when we're on way. You join us and finish her. Then we're free of her. Lucy x

HUNT BOOK OF ARIANE VAN HELSING, 5TH JANUARY 2011

So, it is settled. We cut the London bloodline tomorrow evening. I have waited many years for this moment. Now it is here, I feel the old familiar trepidation. Mothers are always the hardest. But we will be well armed. Shimon and Jim have struck up an unlikely but firm friendship, based, I think, on a love of weaponry and, surprisingly, chess. I see them playing late into the night after the armouring is done.

Jim referred mysteriously to "old mates" when I asked him where he had sourced the automatic pistols and ammunition he presented to me a few days ago. He wouldn't be drawn. No matter, they are fine weapons. They are heavier than I expected, but with magazines holding 17 rounds each I feel sure we can deal with the target and all who come with her.

He and Shimon have rigged up quite the ammunition factory in the basement. They have spent hour after hour drilling out the lead projectiles, filling the cavities with *salcie usturoi* and capping them with a small blob of molten lead. Altogether they have converted 102 rounds – enough for six full magazines.

So, our weaponry stands as follows:

six crossbows, each with 12 quarrels

two pistols, each with 51 rounds

two swords

four daggers

Against us we have the target and I do not know how many lamia. But our priority is the mother herself. With her gone, I suspect the others will flee and we may continue to eradicate them one by one as they disperse. Now I must sleep. Tomorrow, I will confront evil once more.

46

CAROLINE HARKER'S JOURNAL, 7TH JANUARY 2011

Yesterday was supposed to be a triumph. Ariane's victory over the target and her disgusting brood.

As planned, I sent the text to the target at 8.00 p.m. Short. Terse. As if Lucy were on the move and didn't want to waste words – or time – when she had a prisoner in the car.

The drive to the Thames Barrier was interminable. London stops being an interesting place to drive through remarkably soon after one leaves the West End. Just mile after mile of boring semi-suburban streets.

Lily accompanied me, in the seat where Lucy was supposed to be sitting. We had crossbows and daggers on the rear seat. Behind us, in that huge estate car they use, were Ariane, Shimon, David and Jim. "Tooled up" was how Jim put it. God knows what they'd have said if the police had pulled them over. Shimon and Jim with, what did he say they were, Glocks?, stuck in their waistbands, Ariane and Shimon also toting bloody great swords, and a bootful of crossbows and spare magazines.

As we negotiated the narrow lanes that led down to

the Thames, I could tell Lily was getting really tense. Or maybe not tense, exactly, but revved up. For a kill, I suppose. The killing ground was a flat patch of ancient tarmac, cracked and fractured, with Buddleia growing up through it. The moon was out and the whole scene had an unreal look to it. Hard-edged shadows gave everything a flat, two-dimensional look. There was no sign of the target or her brood. That was deliberate. We'd timed it so they would be behind us.

Lily is roughly Lucy's height and build and she'd dressed, as I'd advised, in a flowing purple cape and a floppy-brimmed hat. No question she wasn't Lucy up close, but to an approaching car, if she kept to the shadows, a passable ringer, at least for long enough for the others to spring the trap.

She and I sat in my car and waited. My heart was thumping, and no amount of breathing exercises would calm the fluttery feeling in the pit of my stomach. I'd killed twice by that time, but knowing I'd be facing an enraged mother lamia and her brood filled me with dread. Hidden along one side of the tarmac, between old shipping containers, were the other four.

Then I heard it. A car engine. A big, black Merc cruised into the centre of the killing ground and stopped. The driver cut the engine and the lights went out too.

All four doors opened simultaneously and out stepped the target plus three lamia: the driver — a male — and two females from the back seats.

Just as I was mentally congratulating Ariane and Jim for their clever plan to outwit and outnumber the target, something awful happened. There was this hideous gibbering and at least a dozen lamia dropped from the edge of a deserted warehouse on one edge of the space. I hadn't really noticed it before because it was unlit. They skittered over to join the target and the other three. So now the odds were in her favour by sixteen to six.

"Time to go," Lily said. And she pushed me to open the door. As we'd agreed, I acted scared and cringed as I stumbled upright outside the car. It was bitterly cold, and all I could hear was the slap of waves against the wooden pilings holding up the jetty that protruded from the bank into the river. That, and the hissing susurrus of the lamia's unearthly voices.

The target turned to me and as the others made to follow her, she waved them back. I could hear sounds coming from her mouth but they weren't English or any European language I'd ever heard before.

When the target was separated from the band of lamia, Lily threw off her cloak and swung her crossbow up.

"Stop there!" she cried, levelling the point of the quarrel at the target's chest.

"Yes. Demon. Stop there," Ariane shouted, emerging from the shadows of the shipping containers in a line with David, Shimon and Jim flanking her.

The target whirled round to assess this new threat and that's when Lily fired her crossbow. The quarrel hissed across the gap between her and the target but it just bounced off her and clattered harmlessly to the ground. The other lamia were clearly waiting to be told what to do because they stood still, just watching. The target turned back to Lily with a smile – just a normal one, thank God – across her face. She said nothing, but lifted the hem of her top. I was taken aback; I thought maybe she was going to flash us or something, but instead of a bra she revealed a glittery silver vest. Chain mail! I'd thought she was moving awkwardly when she got out of the car.

She put her head on one side and pouted. A mock-sad face that looked all the more horrible because we knew she'd outwitted us.

"What's the matter, Ariane? You use medieval weapons: it seemed appropriate to counter them with medieval protection."

Then she straightened up to her full height and pointed at me and Lily with one hand, from whose fingers, long, bloody talons had emerged, and Ariane and the men with the other.

"Kill them all!"

Then there was no more time for thinking.

The lamia surrounding the target ran at us. Their movements were disorientating: scuttling, slithering, springing. As if they had copied every predator that had ever killed another animal.

Instinctively, I raised my crossbow and fired at the closest creature, a female. I only grazed her shoulder, but of course it was enough. She skidded to a halt, screeched once and began that horrible quaking and shivering before she exploded in a welter of blood and tissue. Around me the others were fighting off lamia, whose clawing hands and dangling jaws were within inches of their skin.

Jim and Shimon had been busy with protection for us too: it wasn't just the target who'd hit on the idea of chainmail. From a shark-hunting website, Jim had ordered long gauntlets and other items of lightweight but virtually indestructible chain mail. Each of us wore a mail neckpiece that would protect the blood vessels and skin of our throats. Our wrists were also protected with the same material. It wasn't perfect – no armour ever can be. Even those old knights could be killed with a thrust to the groin or the armpit. But it was effective, and it gave us added confidence as we fought with the lamia.

Out of the corner of my eye, I saw Shimon shoot a lamia at close range, just as it was rearing back to strike at Ariane. She was pulling her sword from the belly of a female.

Next to me, I saw Lily decapitate a male as it sprang at her. Head and body burst separately and the noise of the splashing was audible above the clamour of the fight. We were fighting in a lake of blood, but there still seemed to be overwhelming numbers of lamia ranged against us.

Then Jim bellowed our codeword.

"Deck!"

We had rehearsed in Bloomsbury in the old ballroom, which Jim had kitted out like a mini-gym, with thick foam mats covering the old sprung wooden floor. On his command we had to go limp, instantly and let ourselves drop, no matter what we were doing or what position we were holding. He had us walking, pretending to be on the phone; sitting at tables; wrestling each other; standing on one leg; all kinds of weird and everyday activities. And every time he yelled "Deck!" we had to let ourselves fall like stones dropped from a building.

So it was this time.

We all collapsed in perfect synchrony as if a puppeteer had wearied of our antics and cut the strings. Well, not all.

Shimon and Jim remained upright. Each of them held one of the big black guns out in front of him, hands clasped as if in prayer.

With a clear field of fire, they could discharge the weapons without worrying about hitting one of us. The noise was incredible. These weren't the cracks and pops of TV or films. The guns seemed to explode each time they pulled the triggers. I covered my ears as they fired dozens of shots at the lamia.

Even though they scattered as soon as we fell, the lamia were defenceless against the guns and at least seven exploded in sprays of blood as bullets filled with *salcie usturoi* split apart inside them and released the poison into their bloodstream.

Shimon and Jim kept pulling the triggers until the guns were empty. Then they dropped them and grabbed crossbows, loaded again by those who'd been lying flat on the blood-soaked ground. Lily and I leapt to our feet and so did Ariane and David.

We looked around. There was no sign of the target or any of the other lamia. Once they're dead you can't really count them – there's nothing left to count. But I thought I'd seen enough go down that we now outnumbered them.

"Spread out," Jim said. "But stay with your partner."

He and Shimon, Ariane and David, Lily and I split up and started a search around the containers for the target. We were sure she wouldn't leave without trying to kill Ariane or me.

I was shivering. The night was cold, but I was wrapped up against the weather. This was an ancient, primal fear that was setting my muscles aquiver. Kill or be killed. Run or be eaten. For all our weaponry, for all our protection, I felt it, deep in my soul: these creatures were stronger than us. Faster than us. And far, far more dangerous than us. They'd evolved over hundred of thousands of years to do one thing: prey on humans. Why were we any different to all the countless millions of people they'd killed? Then Lily spoke, derailing my wandering train of thought.

"Up ahead, Caroline. Lamia."

I looked. Two lamia were crawling up the side of a container. As they reached the top and righted themselves, standing erect to look around for us, Lily and I raised our crossbows, aimed and fired.

Up there, the bursting was spectacularly horrid. Bright scarlet sprays in the moonlight, like showers of rubies. And I remembered what made us different.

We heard rapid firing from the two Glock pistols. Jim and Shimon must have caught more lamia. As Lily reloaded, I turned to her.

"Why have you stuck with these ancient things for so long? Why not switch to modern weapons like Frederick Arnold and his chapter in new York?"

"It is Ariane, mainly. She says they are better for urban hunting. Less noisy, less likely to draw unwanted attention. The crossbow is silent. Can you imagine loosing off shots from one of those in Soho or Covent Garden?

She had a point. London still isn't Manhattan, let alone Sao Paulo. Gunfire tends to make the news – or Twitter these days – almost as soon as it happens.

We carried on, emerging from between two containers onto a piece of scrubland that led directly down to the river. I gasped. It was a beautiful sight. Ahead of us, stretching from one bank to the other, was the Thames Barrier. Its seven piers gleamed in the moonlight: sentinels protecting London, their silver cowls like monks' hoods drawn forward over their faces.

I've learned you should never let your guard down when there are lamia about. So it proved that night. As we stood, transfixed, a lamia leapt onto Lily's back with a hideous screeching cry. She fell to the ground, trying to wrench it free, but it had dug its talons into her shoulders and hips and was clinging to her like some monstrous ape. This one had shed its clothing and those corded muscles gleamed in the moonlight as it tried to get those deadly fangs into Lily's neck. Fortunately, the mail collar worked perfectly and I saw those glassy teeth break on the metal links with an audible snap. The lamia screeched in pain and sprang backwards, hand covering its distended mouth.

I raced in, drew my blade and slashed wildly at the lamia's face. I caught it a glancing blow across the cheek, but glancing blows are enough to destroy them and the lamia knew it was dead even before it shuddered, wailed and split apart.

Lily was panting and fell to her hands and knees.

"Are you hurt, Lily?" I asked.

In the world of the cutters, that question means much, much more than, "Do I need to take you to A&E?" It demands absolute honesty and therefore absolute courage and devotion to the cutter tradition. If you answer truthfully, and admit to having been bitten, your interlocutor will kill you there and then. No more questions. She looked up at me and answered.

"It scratched me. That's all." She pulled up her top to reveal four deep scratches on the soft patch of skin between her hipbone and her ribs. They were bleeding badly, but the lamia don't transfer the parasites through their claws, only their teeth. Lily and I looked into each other's eyes and we both let out a sigh: we'd been holding our breath. The wounds would need tending, but Lily could stand, and fight, again.

There were no more lamia visible out here on the riverbank, so we turned and headed back towards the fortress of shipping containers and the killing ground inside their walls.

Then there was a shout. It was the target. I'd recognise that haughty tone anywhere. But there was something else in her voice. An unmistakable note of triumph.

"Cutters! Come here. It is time to stop fighting."

"Shit!" Lily said.

We ran towards the gap between two containers. Their corrugated steel walls seemed to close in on us as we turned sideways and squeezed ourselves out at the far end.

When we emerged, the sight I had been dreading ever since Ariane first told me about the target's true nature revealed itself to me.

She – it – was standing with her back to a container, gripping my dear David around the neck and holding him close to her like a shield. Facing her at a distance of perhaps ten metres, were Ariane, Jim and Shimon. They had their weapons raised but looked unsure. There was no way they could take the target without killing or at least seriously wounding David. Lily and I raised our bows too, but more for show than with any serious intent to shoot.

Velds had even moved her head behind David's so that for a moment it seemed as though he was the one speaking. Her voice was hypnotic.

"This ends now, cutter. You have pursued – and destroyed – my family and me for long enough. You have always presented us as vermin. As dirty things like rats or cockroaches, to be put down at will. But we are highly evolved creatures. We are Homo sapiens too. Our suffix, *lamia*? That makes us more evolved than you. Not less. More! How dare you treat us as something to be exterminated? Who gave you the right to decide that another species is to be annihilated? Your bleeding heart animal activists would be up in arms if we were dolphins or cheetahs. Why should the lamia be treated any differently?"

With that, she slid one long-taloned hand around David's neck and dexterously undid the buckles on the two leather straps holding his mail collar in place. She dropped it to the hard ground where it chinked softly.

"Your rhetoric doesn't interest me, filth," Ariane said.

Velds laughed. "Well it should. Look behind you, cutter."

We turned away from Velds and David but only in time to see two lamia holding long metal spikes rush at Jim and Shimon. They'd torn them from a security fence surrounding part of the old factory next door. We tried to aim and fire all at once, but it was already too late. As our quarrels flickered through the moonlight, the lamia plunged the triple-spiked lengths of steel into Jim and Shimon. Both men were impaled from behind and screamed as the wicked tips of the fenceposts emerged from their chests. None of us found our marks and we drew our blades now that our crossbows were useless. The two lamia bent to retrieve the Glocks and hurled them far into the middle of the Thames. Too far even to hear a splash. They chittered gleefully as they faced us again, mouths dropped open like trapdoors. With a battle cry spoken in what she calls "the old language", Ariane sprang up on the two beasts, whirling her sword around in a complicated series of movements that seemed to disorientate the lamia. In a single, continuous, slashing circle, she fetched their heads from their shoulders. They were dead before the *salcie usturoi* blew up their blood cells and reduced them to black pools on the concrete.

It was now just Ariane, Lily and me facing Velds. Her

fangs were fully erect, glistening as the moonlight caught them, pearls of saliva dripping in long strands from her lower lip.

I shouted at her. "You can't turn David. He is pure. His blood is stronger than your power to change him. You bit him before and he is still human. We tested him."

"Why do you think that?" she said.

"He told me. You bit him. But the parasites couldn't survive. His white blood cells are too strong."

David's eyes were wide with terror. He hadn't spoken at all since we'd found him in Velds's grip and I think he was almost catatonic with fear.

"Oh, I bit him all right, Caroline," she said, smiling. I bit him as I fucked him. But not with these." She ran her long tongue lasciviously over the shafts of the translucent teeth that hovered so close to my husband's skin.

Before I could say, or think, anything, she reared back and plunged her teeth into his throat. He convulsed in her arms and I could see his throat working as she fed on him. I knew what was happening. In that instant, thousands of parasites were swarming down the hollow tubes inside her fangs and into David's bloodstream. The frantic action of his stressed heart whirled them away into the major vessels and through his body, round his lungs where they would pick up vital oxygen and back into the chambers of his heart.

I gasped and sprang forward, dropping my crossbow.

Velds pulled away, and I yelled with rage and despair as blood jetted out of David's torn arteries. She laughed at me. A grating, slimy, gurgling sound as his blood ran down her throat.

She hadn't drained him. That would just have killed him and she was crueler than that. Like her hateful ancestor, Peta Velds delighted in causing pain, not merely ending life. She pushed him hard in the back and he staggered towards us, clutching his neck, where the blood, dark purple in the moonlight, ran and pulsed between his clamped fingers. I ran to him, cradling him in my arms while Lily and Ariane fired at Velds.

But it was too late. Her reflexes were lightning fast and she swatted the two crossbow bolts in midair as if they were slow-moving flies. She darted forward, making them flinch, but then sprang upwards 15 feet onto the roof of a shipping container. She looked down at us for a moment, eyes gleaming in triumph, then ran off into the darkness, her heels clanging on the tops of each new container she jumped to. Chasing her was pointless. Ariane knew it. We all knew it.

I looked down at David. He was gulping convulsively, and his muscles were twitching as the massive dose of adrenaline released in the fight pushed his body to run. But it wasn't just adrenaline that was coursing through his system. The deadly spawn of Peta Velds were in there too, already wreaking havoc on David's human DNA, beginning the inexorable process that would change him into a lamia.

He looked up into my eyes.

"Hospital, Caro. You have to get me to the hospital. A&E. It's bad: look at all this blood. Why aren't you moving?"

I just sat there, cradling his head on my lap. I was crying, and tears and mucus were running down the sides of my mouth. He was lost to me and though David didn't know what was coming, I did.

"I'm sorry, David. I can't take you. I love you, my darling. I love you."

Lily squatted beside me and put her hand in mine.

"Come, Caroline. Come with me to the car. You don't need to see this."

In a trance, I lowered David's head to the ground. He looked up at me in disbelief.

"Where are you going, Caro?" he said. "You have to get me to hospital."

I couldn't look at him. I'd have wanted to stay.

Out of the corner of my eye I saw Ariane kneel down behind David and raise his head onto her lap, just as I had only a few moments earlier. He looked up at her with pleading eyes that failed to notice the curved dagger she drew from its sheath on her left hip.

She leaned her face down to his and smiled, sorrowfully.

"Sleep now, David. She cannot harm you anymore."

I turned away and only heard the whisper of her blade as she put my David beyond the reach of Peta Velds for ever.

Lily supported me as I crumpled. I fell to my knees and howled like a wounded beast.

"Come," she said. "We must leave this place."

She led me to the car and put me in the rear seat. Then she rejoined Ariane. I assume to put David's body in the river where the turning tide would pull it out beyond the reach of humanity to find, let alone the lamia.

They came back. Lily drove us to Bloomsbury.

All the way there, we sat in silence. Only as we got out of the car in the underground carpark did Ariane turn to me and speak.

"We must stay strong. We must rebuild our chapter. We must search for the target once again."

47

HUNT BOOK OF ARIANE VAN HELSING, 8TH JANUARY 2011

After I put David beyond harm's way, we almost had to carry Caroline back to the car. To see a loved one snatched from you by a lamia is bad enough. To then see them destroyed by a cutter is worse. For me, sadly, it was not the first time. For her, tragically, it was. In any case, not all those who witness such an act survive with their minds intact. Caroline is different.

We drove back to Bloomsbury, arriving in the middle of the night, Lily at the wheel. I sat in the back with Caroline. We had lain Shimon and Jim's bodies in the loadspace and I felt their presence all the way back as a heavy weight in my chest

By the time Lily returned from parking the car, Caroline had lapsed into silence. Not the catatonia of someone struggling to make sense of an event beyond their comprehension. No. She knew enough of the lamia and their ways to be mentally prepared for the events of that night. It was her emotional readiness that was lacking. She had been with us so short a time before the ruination Peta Velds visited upon her, that all she had seen was success. Success destroying David's laboratory in Norfolk. Success rescuing her dear one from the clutches of that evil creature. Success fighting off three female lamia with me and destroying one herself. Then to have to face up to the grotesque reality we've all, as cutters, confronted. Well, she needs time to process all of it. I judged it best to let her stay with us as long as she needed. For the first few days, I expect little, and I am sure I will be rewarded with exactly that.

But what of our dead?

In each city where a cutter family operates, we have established links with priests, vicars, imams and rabbis. Not all of them. But each of the major religions has long maintained a watching brief on our activities and helps when they can. Senior figures within each tradition appoint trusted men – and women, from time to time – to work with us when we need them. They know what we do. And whilst the mythmaking around the efficacy of religious symbols against lamia is only a romantic notion dreamt up by film-makers and novelists – especially that parasite Stoker, now, thankfully, dead – they help us bury our dead. So it was that we were able to give Shimon and Jim the respect in death due to all who fight on the side of light. Shimon was a Jew and he received the appropriate rites from his people. I sat Kaddish for him along with a rabbi in north London.

I had never discussed religion with Jim. There wasn't the time, or the opportunity But he wore a small, gold crucifix beneath his undershirt and bore a tattoo of the Virgin Mary on his right shoulder blade, so we assumed he was a Catholic. Lily contacted our friend in that church and Jim, too, was interred with all due ceremony. Even though he had not received the last rites, the priest assured us that God would receive Jim into His kingdom.

He quoted Saint Thomas – Ah! Dear, sweet Tomas, how I miss you! – "Considering the omnipotence and mercy of God, no one should despair of the salvation of anyone in this life". And he told us to continue to pray for the repose of his soul.

48

TALK OF THE TOWN, THE NEW YORKER, 21ST MARCH 2011

THICKER THAN WATER

Recently, a modestly paid writer sat down with a genuine one-percenter in one of Manhattan's newest cocktail bars. Surveying the extensive drinks menu with eyes that widened progressively as they took in the prices, and grateful, therefore, that her host was paying, she selected a Vodkatini. Boring? Perhaps, given the bewildering array of classics (with or without a twist), new contenders and just plain out-there drinks on offer – Durian daiquiri anyone? Smells like a devil; tastes, apparently, like an angel. But in her experience, the fastest and most reliable way to judge the skill and potential longevity of a mixologist, and the establishment they work for, is to ask for this most traditional of all mixed drinks. Her drinking partner was Morgan Hearst, the boss of Hearst Capital, a secretive – he says, "private" – hedge fund.

Hearst opts for a Negroni. "I like the old favourites, too," he says, sipping the burnt-orange concoction from a rocks glass garnished with a fan of orange slices. "They're timeless. That holds great appeal."

The writer's Vodkatini is flawless. Grey Goose vodka, chilled down to a gloopy viscosity that suggests something engineered rather than distilled. Lillet vermouth sprayed onto the inside of the martini glass from an atomiser. And a garlic-stuffed olive skewered through its heart on a freshly cut sliver of birch wood. The writer offers her host a sip, but he wrinkles his hawk like nose and declines, preferring, he says, to stick with his Venetian classic.

Hearst is known to many for his wealth. Wealth for which the adjective "fabulous" might have been invented. Known to be ruthless in business, he's attracted his fair share of criticism, not least in Congress. But he's on the PR trail this month for a different reason. A charity, no less. Asked by the writer to explain, his eyes, notable for their long lashes and dark-brown, almost black, irises, widen with what can only be genuine enthusiasm.

"We're going to find a cure for Reiser-Strick Syndrome," he begins, leaving his interlocutor baffled. "I know," he continues, "why not go for one of the big killers? Coronary heart disease, leukaemia, cancer? Truth is, we do give to those causes, generously, I might add. But so does everybody else. They're drowning in funds. The problem isn't cash, it's the science itself. But there are these other conditions that maybe don't affect so many people, but if you suffer – or a family member, a child, perhaps, does – then they're just as bad. Only they don't get the funding. Reiser-Strick's like that. A real Cinderella condition, if you know what I mean?"

Hearst finishes his Negroni and signals the bartender for a second round, motioning to the writer to drink up.

Then he explains the condition that has attracted his attention, and opened his wallet. It's a chromosomal disorder that involves hypersensitivity to sunlight. Sufferers are under a self-imposed curfew from dawn to dusk, or must wait for days when the heavens are thoroughly obscured by cloud if they're to avoid catastrophic cellular breakdown that causes them literally to bleed to death.

"A cousin of mine from England lives with RSS," he says. "She's over here, staying with me for a while. We've decided to join forces to look for a cure."

With that, he checks his watch, a Patek-Philippe that looks as though it cost more than the writer makes in a couple good years, finishes his Negroni in a single pull, and rises from his red-velvet upholstered seat to a towering six-foot-five. He kisses the writer's hand, a surprisingly Old World gesture for a titan of the Manhattan finance scene, and departs.

The writer is left feeling mildly woozy, either from the alcohol or the gentleman's divine manners

49

HUNT BOOK OF ARIANE VAN HELSING, 19TH APRIL 2011

Velds, we think, is in New York. I have been in contact with Frederick Arnold, and he reports sightings. Not one hundred percent certain, but as he put it, "good enough to lock and load". I bade him be patient. Caroline must be involved in the destruction of Peta Velds. She has awoken from her grief, at least enough for her to kill lamia and to badger me about traveling to Manhattan to finish off what we started. I told her, yes. I also told, her, as I told Frederick, patience.

Without their "mother" close by to protect them, the lamia remaining in London have become lethargic. They must come out at night to feed still, but their reflexes and senses seem blunted. There is a psychic connection between them and Velds that has been either weakened or broken altogether. They are easy targets, and Lily, Caroline and I have despatched at least forty since David's death. Scant compensation for his loss, I know.

If Velds now resides in the bosom of the New York family, then we face a double threat. Not just her, but the ancient one who rules there. Morgan Hearst.

50

CAROLINE HARKER'S JOURNAL, 23RD MAY 2011

Ariane and I arrived in Manhattan yesterday. Frederick met us at the airport and brought us to the cutter house on the Upper West Side. The place is vast, at least five storeys. He has a big team: six men and four women. All between twenty-five and forty-five. They look as though they get good value from whichever gym membership they've taken out.

Since Peta Velds killed David, I have felt hollowed out emotionally. My memory of the days and weeks after that dreadful night is hazy. Ariane and Lily kept me fed, warm and, I think, occupied. I spent a lot of time dipping crossbow bolts in *salcie usturoi*. So much so, that whatever happens to me in this life or the hereafter, I think I shall never get that oily, garlicky stink out of my nose. They were away a lot. Reconnoitring during the day, and hunting at night. They'd come home at four or five in the morning, grim smiles on their blood-spattered faces, quivers full of red-tipped quarrels. They tell me I helped them. I can't remember.

But that was then. Somehow I have found a way to

separate out my grief at losing David from the daily necessities of living, and of tracing down that bitch, Peta Velds. Compartmentalising, I think the popular jargon has it. I am here for one thing, and one thing only. Once she is dead, nothing more than a red stain on the ground, then I will go away and grieve properly.

New York is famous for its pace, its energy, its 24-hour culture. How these confident Manhattanites would react to the presence of vampires in their midst, I can't imagine. Though having watched the antics of a couple of street performers yesterday, acting out a protracted drama involving a pith-helmeted hunter and a "savage" in leopard-skin and tiger-tooth necklace, I suppose many would just assume it was more entertainment laid on for their pleasure, watch the show, toss a few dollars into a cup and depart. But it is not just the residents who behave differently. So do the cutters.

We used pistols in our doomed attempt to kill Peta in Docklands. Ariane still prefers edged weapons. She says it's for the silence. I suspect she simply doesn't trust anything too mechanical when it comes to tackling lamia. But Frederick Arnold and his people don't merely trust them, they love them. Each of the cutters carries two about their person at all times. The Glocks that we had in London, and an assortment of other makes and models that I wearied of trying to remember after an hour with Frederick's armourer, a black woman in her thirties with a ferociously athletic build and blue-black tattoos on her shoulders. Her name is Angela, so appropriate given her lifelong mission to wipe out evil. She has adopted me and makes sure I am not left alone too often or for too long.

I asked Frederick over a bottle of wine not long after we arrived in New York, whether they had ever had any trouble with the police here. Carrying concealed weapons and so forth. He laughed.

"Where do you think we get them from?" he asked me with a grin. "The NYPD has always known about the lamia. How could they not? But for reasons of operational efficiency and public relations, they outsource the job to us. For a modest fee per kill, naturally."

"Naturally," I replied, thinking how wonderful it is that even the job of slaying vampires in America is folded into the mechanisms of private enterprise.

Tonight we are voyaging to the Bronx on a hunt. Ariane and I will accompany Frederick and three of his team. Apparently there is a small nest of lamia, four or five, who have infested a condemned apartment block. I am looking forward to it.

NYPD INCIDENT REPORT. REPORTING OFFICER A. GUZMAN 05/24/2011

CLASSIFED: TOP SECRET
FILE: PROJECT OMEGA

Transcript of action captured on cell phone by Antwan Jackson, 17.
Location: 1936 Hering Avenue, Bronx
Date: 05/24/2011
Time: 10.21 p.m.

Four African-American children, aged approximately 6-11, playing basketball. Beyond chain-link fence, four humanoid creatures approach.

Voiceover: Yo, yo! What the fuck are they?

Creatures all Caucasian. Bald. No body hair. Extreme musculature. Two male, two female. Three spring at fence and climb. Creatures hissing. Claws on fingers and toes aid climbing.

Kids on court screaming. Running for gate.

One more creature, female, appears at gate. Lower jaw dislocates. Kids stop. Run back to centre of court. Huddle together.

V/O: Get the fuck out of there, man! Those white things look evil.

Creature at gate rips it free of hinges, steps onto court. Kids screaming.

V/O: Oh, shit, oh shit, oh shit!

Creatures climbing fence reach top. All have dislocated lower jaws. Fangs and feeding funnels clearly visible.

SFX: Gunshots. At least 20. Handguns.

Three creatures on fence fall backwards, talons on feet entangled in fence links, hang upside-down. Writhe spasmodically. Explode into clouds of blood.

V/O: Fuck, man. What's happenin'?"

Creature in centre of basketball court halts. One kid (oldest-looking) picks up basketball and throws it at creature. Hits it on side of face. Shouts. "Fuck you asshole!"

Six people enter court. Spread out. All dressed in black. Silver glinting at throats and wrists. Armed with handguns.

Creature crouches, claws outstretched towards kid who threw basketball. Springs.

SFX: Gunshots. Too many to count. 50+.

Creature sprawls at kids' feet. Kids run. Creature jerking, shaking. Liquefies.

V/O: Go, go! Get out of there!

Man leaves group. Approaches A. Jackson, gun extended. Hand out. Speaks.

"Hey, kid. I'm gonna need that phone for a minute.

A. Jackson brought in for debrief at 1 Police Plaza. Told saw unlicensed movie production team. Video downloaded from phone then deleted. Mayor's office informed. Bounty of $40,000 requested, authorised & paid to F. Arnold.

52

MORGAN HEARST'S JOURNAL, 25TH MAY 2011

I lost four children last night. Idra survived the attack. Recently, Arnold and his infernal cutters have upped their game and we have taken to posting lookouts rather than letting everyone feed at the scene. She fled at the first shots. Poor thing. She felt each of her siblings' deaths as if they were her own.

Arnold surveils us. But we are not passive. Maybe in some of our other locations, the O-One have become lazy or complacent. Here, we pride ourselves on being proactive. So, we operate counter-surveillance measures against him. Each confrontation is an opportunity to gather intelligence about him and his people, their methods, their equipment, their tactics. When she was calm again, Idra gave me a description of the cutters.

Arnold was there, of course. He enjoys his work. Too much, I sometimes think. His background in the military has given him a taste for killing. A very refined taste. He was accompanied by three of his team. We have already identified them and Idra was unable to supply anything of value in relation to these three. But.

On this attack, they were joined by two strangers. Both women. From Peta's description, I recognised one. She is Ariane Van Helsing the head of the London cutters. But the other woman is unknown to me. Idra said she was tall, fit. Strong-looking. Broad shoulders. Wide hips. Both were adept with the pistols. I am having dinner with Peta this evening. I will ask her if this second woman rings any bells.

53

TASTING MENU – BANQUET IN HONOR OF PETA VELDS, DRAFT SUBMITTED BY CUSHING CATERERS, 26TH MAY 2011

Cocktails

Corpse Reviver | Bloody Mary | El Diablo | Zombie | Death Flip

———

Amuse Bouche

Espresso cups of red cell foam

———

Appetizers

Plasma jellies § Heart carpaccio | Deep-fried blood sausage

———

Entrée

"Un Homage à Vlad Țepeș"

Dessert
Mousse au sang

Liqueurs
25-year Reserve du Patron | Absinthe | Sang de la
Vierge

54

MORGAN HEARST'S JOURNAL, 26TH MAY 2011

My dinner with Peta was pleasant. Her European manners are a refreshing change from the New World "Hey Buddy-isms" we are forced to mimic. Chef excelled himself. Apparently, he saw a chocolate fountain in the window of a confectioner's in Midtown and took his inspiration from there. I told Peta about the events of last night. She was sympathetic, naturally. No family head can hear of the loss of another's children without a pang of regret. And, if we're honest, just the tiniest frisson: *Brr. They could have been my children*. But she masked the latter emotion well enough.

I told her about the women Idra had described to me. She confirmed that the first was undoubtedly Van Helsing. Her taste for black leather alone is enough to mark her out. So the bitch is hunting outside her own back yard. Well, she'll have to pay for that. I'll see to her myself. Recently I have developed a new feeding technique for those who have especially displeased me. I explained it to Peta. It seemed to delight her to judge from her smile as she dabbed at her lips.

When I described the second woman, Peta's eyes flashed so dark I thought the frenzy was going to hit her. Then they cleared. Her voice was thick with anger.

"I know who she is. Her name is Caroline Harker. She's the widow of that scientist I told you about."

"The boy genius?" I replied.

"Yes, the boy genius!" She actually snapped at me. I guess this is a personal thing. "We could have been free to hunt in daylight had she and her friends not blown my facility into atoms."

I tried to reassure her. With our money and our combined resources, we can find another geek and shower them with toys until they solve the mutation. I've even got the media on my side now. That silly cunt from The New Yorker wrote our meeting up as if I were one of the philanthropy crowd. But Peta was not to be consoled so easily.

"It's not about the money, Fred. He was different. One-of-a-kind different. Once-in-a-generation different. An Einstein of gene theory. A Hawking. A Leonardo da-fucking-Vinci!"

For her to lapse into such contemporary idiom indicates a severe loss of control. I told her we would find someone to replace him. A woman, perhaps. A Marie Curie. A Dorothy Hodgkin. A Rosalind Franklin. If a woman could get within a whisker of the structure of DNA, I said, I was sure she could find a way to help the lamia overcome their problems with sunlight.

Finally, I was rewarded with a smile.

"You Americans and your relentless optimism. So you think your can-do attitude will save us from the night?"

"Why not?" I answered. "Just give me some time. The banquet in your honour takes place in ten days' time: June 5th, to be precise. The whole New York family will be there. Every one of our children. I will announce our need for a replacement for David Harker then."

She seemed placated. At 1.00 a.m., I went to my home office to catch up on some work. Peta said she wanted a dessert. She left the house telling me not to wait up. The woman has a sense of humour, I'll give her that.

55

EMAIL FROM PETA VELDS TO LUCY EASTERBROOK, 27TH MAY 2011

To: LE
From: PV
Subject: Matters of business

My Dearest Lucy,

How are things in London? I am too far away to feel my children.

On which subject...

Morgan described to me a most entertaining method of feeding. His creativity extends beyond the accumulation of wealth, it seems. Let me describe my search for something fresh to round off my dinner with him on Friday.

I walked through the city to Central Park. Manhattan is so much livelier than London. Food abounds, even in the small hours.

I found myself in a small copse of trees, their yellow flowers grey in the moon light. And guess what. There, trysting beneath the canopy, I discovered two lovers. A real Romeo and Juliet of New York. Romeo tried to play the hero, all bluster and biceps. Over Juliet's protestations, I picked him up bodily and despatched him without even bothering to feed. Her screams were tiresome, so I simply pinched her throat, enough to put her vocal cords beyond use.

Following the method Frederick had described over dinner, I strung her up by her wrists from a high branch. A broken branch made a perfectly acceptable hook.

Then I opened the posterior tibial artery in her right foot, just above the knob of the ankle bone.

I drank her dry. While she looked down and watched.

Oh, there are people on whom I should very much like to try this technique! Two of them, happily for me, have followed me to Manhattan.

I speak of Ariane Van Helsing and Caroline Harker. Yes! They have followed me here. The impudence. The sheer arrogance! At any rate, I assume they are here for me.

I learned of their presence here from one of Morgan's children. She, Idra, is a sweet thing, though traumatised by witnessing a cutter attack here three nights ago.

Well, they may arm themselves to the teeth with Arnold's silly toys. I relish the chance to meet them again. This time, we will see who flees the scene and who stays to feed.

I must go. Send me news of my family in London.

Warm wishes,

Peta

56

CAROLINE HARKER'S JOURNAL, 28TH MAY 2011

I felt so good last week, despatching those lamia before they could attack the children playing basketball. Whatever Ariane says about them, I love the guns. I love the feeling of power they give me. Yes, killing with the blades is the established method. And perhaps, for Ariane, that carries weight. But I am not part of her tradition. Shit! Not so long ago the only tradition I was part of was the British legal tradition. Now I find myself thousands of miles away from the Inns of Court, shooting down lamia in a rundown neighbourhood playground using bullets filled with garlic oil and salicylic acid.

Frederick told us this morning that he has learned the lamia of Manhattan are planning a grand dinner in honour – honour! – of Peta Velds. It seems that even vampires need banqueting suites and a cousin of Frederick's works for the largest catering firm in New York. The caterers have apparently been asked to provide a pre-dinner drinks service for two hundred people at a swish boutique hotel called Mallory's; the client will be bringing in his own chefs and waiting staff for the banquet itself. The client is one Morgan Hearst. He is a hedge fund manager, so another member of the one percent. Just like Peta. He is also the head of the New York family, so another member of the O-One.

This could be our way in. Frederick and Ariane were doubtful when I suggested an attack. But I am confident I can win them round. Think of it! Every single vampire in New York, gathered for whatever obscene feast they have planned. Plus Peta Velds. I put forward a case for a final confrontation that could wipe out two families at once. By the end of my presentation, I could see Frederick was beginning to take me seriously.

The only problem is one of numbers. A team of eleven New York cutters, plus Ariane and me, versus two hundred lamia. We need to find a way to even up the odds in our favour. And I think I may have thought of something.

5/29/2011 3.43.17 PM
PITT'S HARDWARE
71 Bayard Street
New York, NY 10015
T: (212) 555-1962

Receipt # 876,499
Store 1
Cashier Maya

****

ITEM – QTY – PRICE
3-1/4 in. x 0.131 in. Paper-Taped
Ring Shank 304 Stainless Steel Offset
Round Head Nails 1,000 per Box

UNIT PRICE $102.99
QTY 10
SUBTOTAL $1029.90
8.875 % tax $91.40
Receipt total $1121.30
Tendered $1121.30

****

THANK YOU FOR YOUR CUSTOM.
HAVE A NICE DAY!

CAROLINE HARKER'S JOURNAL 1ST
JUNE 2011

Frederick and Ariane have agreed to the proposal I presented to them last evening. We sat up until gone two in the morning discussing practicalities. I seem to have a talent for paramilitary planning, according to Ariane. Frederick looked impressed as I sketched out my thoughts on a large whiteboard in their conference room on the ground floor.

Essentially, my plan consists of wiping out the colony of lamia in a single move. To engage 200 of the things in one-on-one combat is simply not feasible. No. I decided we needed to treat this as a battle, not a hunt.

I suggested using a bomb. One need only open a newspaper or read the BBC homepage nowadays to see evidence of the destructive power of so-called IEDs. "Well," I said, "we shall have to improvise our own explosive device."

My idea is for a three-part bomb. At its core, some sort of explosive charge. A big one. Not so big it will destroy the venue, since we will be inside too. But big enough to take out – see how I have picked up the military jargon from Frederick? – the lamia.

Now, we know they have extraordinary powers of cellular regeneration, so flesh wounds and even broken bones are apparently easily mended. I therefore proposed a second part to the bomb: a wrapping or external layer of shrapnel of some kind. After some discussion, we settled on nails. These have already been purchased. Here is the beautiful part. And yes, I realise how far I must have come if my idea of aesthetic perfection is a nail bomb.

The third part of the bomb is some sort of outer sleeve, double-walled like a wine cooler. A container, anyway. We fill it with salcie usturoi. The charge detonates. The explosion drives the nails outwards at presumably supersonic speed. They smash through the sleeve, collecting on their hot surfaces and dispersing into an airborne mist the poison that we know exterminates the lamia on contact with the smallest flesh wound. I think it's fair to say that sitting or standing in the path of an exploding fireball of three-inch nails will result in plenty of flesh wounds.

"What if some of the creatures survive?" Ariane asked. I suspect more to test I had thought of all the angles than to try to drive a hole through my plan.

"Even if one escapes the blast, they will be disorientated. I imagine a bomb makes quite a loud noise?" I asked, looking at Frederick, who smiled and nodded. "Then while they try to make sense of the carnage we have unleashed, we step in with whatever weapons we carry and send them to hell."

"Caroline," Frederick said, when I had finished. "You missed your vocation. As an attorney, you may have been good, but let me tell you, as a cutter, you're fucking amazing."

It's funny, I used to hate bad language. I think it's a hangover from my upbringing. Mummy couldn't abide swearing. But hearing Frederick praising me in such robust terms gave me, I admit, a thrill of pleasure. For a moment I could forget David and revel in my newfound role. I spent today with Con McKay. He is the engineer/fixer here. Short, dark brown, almost black hair, pale blue eyes beneath long, almost girlish black lashes. Irish ancestry screaming out from every pore. Whatever the New York cutters need, he can find it, fake it or fabricate it. Our first stop was to be Floyd Bennett Field in Brooklyn. The headquarters of the NYPD Emergency Services Unit. Con had made an appointment and drove us there in the cutters' van, a nondescript grey transit with scuffed paintwork and battered sides.

"It's not what I was expecting," I said, as he blipped the fob to unlock it in the parking garage beneath their building.

"Why? What were you expecting? The Batmobile?"

His tone was affronted and I wondered whether he was one of those men who refer to their cars as their "pride and joy". He said it with a grin though, and I guessed that perhaps the distressed exterior was merely a form of camouflage. I played along.

"Well," I said. "I just imagined for people engaged in a centuries-old struggle with vampires, you might have something a little more, you know, purposeful."

He grinned. He'd twigged I was teasing him.

He opened the rear doors and stepped back, throwing his arm wide with a courtly flourish.

"Step inside, my lady," he said.

Stepping inside was hard; there was barely any room. Just a narrow passage between two wooden racks. Each rack was divided into compartments housing reels of electrical flex, lidded plastic tubs in various colours, tools, coils of rope, and what appeared to be climbing equipment: karabiners, helmets and the like. I looked up at the roof. It seemed too close to the top of my head given the van's external dimensions. I rapped my knuckles against the bare metal. The roof thudded. I turned to look at Con, who as still smiling, if anything with the proud look of a new father.

"Go on," I said.

"Twin-walled all the way around. Four-mil steel plate. The gap's packed with roofing insulation soaked in, guess what? Our verminous friends' favourite-recipe hot sauce."

"What about up front?" I asked. "The glass isn't steel-reinforced, surely?"

"Nope. Bullet-proof. You could empty a Kalashnikov into it and anyone sitting inside could carry on sipping their latte or whatever. Step down without a scratch on them and send the fucker with the AK to meet their ancestors. Then you've got your run-flat tyres, extra armour over the battery, fuel tank, ECU and tail pipe. Shall I go on?" he finished with a smile.

I could see he was enjoying himself and decided to indulge him. Although I had dropped the pretence at teasing him. I was genuinely fascinated by now.

"Doesn't all this extra weight make it a bit sluggish?" I asked.

"It would if all we had was a stock Ford engine under the hood. But I've breathed on this baby a little. Now she's got five hundred horses under there ready to let rip if I tell them."

I confess his macho enthusiasm for "car stuff" left me perplexed for a moment and I asked him to explain.

"And when you say 'breathed', you mean..."

"Oh, sorry Caroline. OK, so in laywoman's terms, I boosted the power. Took out the original motor and dropped in a 6.8L V10–"

"Sorry," I said. "You've lost me again."

Perhaps suspecting that my enthusiasm was for what it could do rather than how it could do it, Con changed track.

"Let's say you're driving around late at night. And you come round a corner – it's a bad neighbourhood. Suddenly there're lamia every-fucking-where. This thing weighs a couple tons unmodified. Set up like I've got it, you can add another three-quarters of a ton, maybe more, depending on the payload. A couple of them jump on the roof but that's OK, they just rip their claws off trying to get through the steel and if they do they hit the insulation and it's red-shower time! So you put your foot down. Just mash that fucker to the floor. You're doing sixty before you've breathed in and out all the way. If you're feeling feisty, you just turn it around at the end of the street and come back for a second bite. Run the bastards down then get out and do them with your Glock. Or whatever you British cutters use. I heard Ariane saying how she still likes blades. That right?"

"She's old fashioned. They have their uses, but I'm a convert."

He nodded as if satisfied I wasn't clinging to outmoded equipment like some olde worlde vampire hunter out of a Hammer horror.

Having agreed between us that "Martha", as he calls the van, was the hottest and possibly deadliest thing on four wheels in the whole of the five boroughs, we climbed in and set off for Brooklyn.

This is my first time in New York, and I confess to being startled by its beauty and sheer grandeur. Con kept up a running commentary as we passed buildings and parks I was familiar with only from TV or films. The Chrysler Building is a favourite of mine: although I said I haven't visited Manhattan before, or not in person, I have books at home that celebrate its architecture. And here we were, driving down Lexington Avenue right past it. I craned my neck to try to get a better view but all too soon we had moved on. Perhaps if we can bring this business to a satisfactory conclusion, I might stay on for a while. I could take a holiday! Ha! Do cutters get paid holiday? How about dental?

We crossed the East River by way of the Brooklyn Bridge. More spectacular views of Manhattan's downtown skyscrapers behind us and Brooklyn up ahead. The sky was a bright blue, streaked here and there with white trails from jets. As we crossed the midpoint from Manhattan to Brooklyn, Con pointed to my right. I looked down. A bright yellow water taxi was passing under the span. Its sides were striped with black and white chequering like its land-based cousins.

We arrived at Floyd Bennett Field just after 11.00 a.m. It's an old naval base, Con said, and now houses the ESU's headquarters. Con showed the officer on duty at the gate a piece of ID, which clearly satisfied her because she nodded at him and opened the gates. We parked at the rear of a nondescript building at the southwestern edge of the base, just inside the security wire.

Inside we passed through security and found ourselves escorted into the office of one Captain Jerome Stensgaard, his name being affixed to the door in one of those sliding aluminium plates. Or, what do they say over here, a-LOO-minum? I judged him to be in his midfifties. Trim, though running a paunch under his immaculately cut uniform jacket. Very short, silver hair, appraising blue eyes, clean-shaven cheeks disfigured on the right side by a jagged scar that stretched in a crescent from his ear to the corner of his mouth. Rising from his chair behind a cluttered desk, he didn't look pleased to see us. His forehead was creased with, what? Worry? Displeasure? And his thin lips were clamped together into a slit.

"Con," he said, packing plenty of Eeyore-ish gloom into that single syllable.

"Jerome."

They shook hands and Jerome beckoned us to sit.

"What do you need?" Jerome asked Con. "And who's your colleague?" He turned to me. "No offence, Ma'am, but we have what you might call strict protocols for dealing with Con and his, er, crew."

"That's perfectly all right, Captain Stensgaard," I said, in my best courtroom manner. "My name is Caroline Harker. I'm a barrister, or what you would call an attorney. I am working alongside Con and his colleagues."

"Long way from home, aren't you?"

I don't think he was actively trying to be rude. It's just that I sensed he found the whole business of dealing with cutters – and, therefore, their prey – deeply unpleasant.

"I am," I answered. "Although 'home' has become significantly less attractive to me in the last few months."

Con interjected.

"Caroline lost someone to the lamia not too long ago. She's helping us fight the good fight, you could say."

Jerome's expression softened and he shrugged his broad shoulders.

"I'm sorry for your loss," he said, and I felt that he meant it, despite its being a formula they teach at police colleges all over the world nowadays.

"Yes, well, I'm dealing with it. Fighting those creatures helps. Tell me, if I may ask a question..."

Jerome spread his hands and I noticed he was missing the top joint of his left index finger.

"Fire away. Seeing as how you're on the side of righteousness."

"How is it that the New York Police Department has outsourced the hunting of the lamia to what is essentially a family-owned business? Surely the city should be paying for it. After all, isn't the ESU better resourced and equipped?"

Jerome and Con exchanged a look. Amused. Resigned. World-weary. Amazing how a few millimetres of lift to the eyebrows and the faintest curl of the lips can signal so much. I began to hear Jerome's answer even before he started speaking, so eloquent was their body language.

"You're right. We got specialist vehicles. We call them trucks. We got body armour. We got semi-automatic weapons. We got highly trained SWAT teams. We can talk jumpers off bridges, stick it to terrorists in a firefight, take down school shooters. But vampires? We get into action and you can bet within five minutes there're media choppers overhead, citizen journalists getting in the way, every damn thing. You really want to see those abominations exploding in clouds of blood on Facebook or primetime TV? I tell you," he said, clearly warming to his theme, "we went into action against those things, and it got on the Internet? Half the population of New York would get tooled up with crucifixes and sharpened stakes, and the other half would film the whole thing on their cell phones and put it all on YouTube."

"Crucifixes don't work. Only –"

"I know that!" he said, clearly exasperated with my pedantry. "But you think John Q. Public does?"

Chastened, I apologised.

"I'm sorry. Of course. You'd have to declare a state of emergency. Bad for business, bad for tourism."

"Damn straight," he said. "Especially given those things run half of Wall Street. There are people way above my pay grade, people who rely on a happy financial community to get re-elected, who feel," his mouth twisted with disgust, "that we have to find a way to live with 'em."

A penny dropped. I heard it clink between my ears.

"And when you say people who need to get re-elected, you're talking about the Mayor?"

"Sure, why not? The Mayor, congressmen and congresswomen, the DA, plenty of powerful people have skin in the game when it comes to the smooth running of Wall Street."

"But you don't," I said.

He held up his mutilated finger.

"See this?" he asked. Then drew the puckered stump along the scar on his cheek. "And this"

"What happened?" I asked.

"I was a sergeant in the ESU. The Lower Manhattan Squad: ESS 1. We got a call from colleagues in the Lower East Side. Tuesday 17th August 1997. About three in the a.m. Some winos on a deserted lot off Mulberry Street were screaming the place down. A concerned resident called it in. Said they could see the whole thing from the window of their apartment. Bunch of naked people were ripping into the winos and eating 'em. That's what the guy said.

"We turned up in the truck and those fuckers," he blushed, charmingly, "pardon me, Ma'am." I smiled and shook my head to show no offence had been given. He continued. "Anyway, those things were still there, chowing down on the winos. Six bodies lying there in a lake of blood and those disgusting," his mouth clamped tight again and I could see his jaw muscles bunching, "those fucking, evil things were just lapping it, sucking it up into those disgusting funnel things they got coming out of their mouths.

"We drew down on them and shouted the standard warning, but to be honest, I don't think there was a single man among us who thought they were going to stop. They just stopped feeding and turned to face us. They stood up straight and I don't mind telling you, I was scared. No, I was terrified. They were hissing, and kinda stalking towards us, head cocked to one side with those long teeth glinting in the moonlight. It was a hot night but I was clammy with cold. I can still picture my weapon shaking as I held it out in front of me.

"We started shooting. We had Glock 17s, Ithaca Model 37 shotguns, Colt AR-15s. A couple guys had their second weapons out, large-calibre revolvers, you know? Smitty Model 29s. Those things'll put a bear on the ground. You shoot a human being with one, they basically come apart. But the things we were shooting at, we could see we were hitting them, ripping chunks of flesh off them. But it didn't make any difference.

"We fell back, but we were cornered. Then I heard a whistling sound. Right past my ear. One of the creatures stopped moving. Looked down. It had what I thought was an arrow sticking out of its chest. It shuddered and kinda writhed, then bam! Motherfucker just burst. Like a bag of blood. It was Con and his friends. First time I met them. Three of our guys went down to the vampires, the rest of us picked up scratches, but not bites. When the cutters had finished, the lot was inches deep in blood. They cut our guys' throats before we could say or do anything. Explained what would happen if they didn't.

"Then, maybe ten minutes later, when we're all just leaning against the truck, or sitting on the ground trying to process what just happened, this all-black Caddy Escalade shows up and out jump these Men In Black types. You know, like the CIA with better tailors. They confiscate all our cell phones and tell us to get in back.

"We get driven to an office building in Midtown, somewhere on West 57th, I think. And we get debriefed. And I mean properly debriefed. None of that, 'It was tweakers in fancy dress' BS. They gave it to us straight. Told us, now we knew New York's best-kept secret, we had to keep it that way. Laid out the consequences if anything should ever leak out. And I got a new job. Get this, my official role designation is Nonconventional Threat Taskforce Liaison.

Con interrupted, though I sensed that the captain was relieved to have reached the end of his narrative.

"Jerome keeps us supplied with things we can't get from regular stores here in Manhattan. Ammunition, mostly, other bits and pieces normally off-limits to civilians; they're very generous with their time and expertise as well. Which brings me to the purpose of our visit today, J."

Looking like a man who'd just had to relive a nightmare, which I suppose he had, Jerome puffed out his cheeks and swiped a hand across his forehead, which I had noticed was beaded with sweat.

"Tell me. Bazookas loaded with garlic cloves? Miniguns adapted to fire willow wood bullets?"

"C4."

Jerome's eyes widened and his jaw pulled in and down. He folded his arms over his chest

"Say again?"

"C4. I need five M112 Demo blocks."

"Do I get to ask what for? Beyond the obvious, I mean?"

Con smiled, his blue eyes twinkling beneath those long lashes.

"It was Caroline's idea, actually. We've discovered the entire Manhattan clan of lamia are going to be in the same place at the same time a couple weeks from now. We're going to take out the fuckers en-fucking-masse."

Jerome leaned back in his chair and folded his hands behind his head. I watched as a slow smiled crept across his face. It started at his mouth and worked its way up to his eyes, which sparkled as the crows feet deepened. He let his head drift back, almost as if he were doing some kind of yoga, until all I could see was the underside of his lower jaw. Con waited and I followed his lead. He looked sideways at me and winked. Finally, Jerome eased his head forward and brought his hands down to rest them on the small patch of desk not covered with paper.

"Let me get this straight. You're going to take six and a quarter pounds of C4 and use it to blow up every single vampire in New York City? That amount of plastique'll create a big noise, a lot of destruction and a plume of smoke that'll stretch higher'n the Empire State Building. You don't think you might also blow a hole in our carefully constructed media blackout about their existence?"

Con smiled. Now it was his turn to lean forwards.

"Yeah, you're probably right. Which is why we also need you to run a little," he paused, "interference."

Jerome stared at him. The smile had almost gone, although what remained spoke volumes. The captain wanted the problem gone, I'm sure. But he knew something was coming his way he wouldn't like. He was right. Finally, he growled out a question.

"And when you say 'interference', you mean ..."

"We were thinking you could get the whole thing declared a terrorist attack. Give you an excuse to cordon off the whole block when it goes down. We'll make our excuses and leave in our van, or you could loan us one of yours, then you quarantine the whole place, send in a cleanup team and–"

Jerome's eyes were so wide I worried the eyeballs might drop out of their sockets.

"Whoa, whoa, whoa. Just slow down there a minute, OK? You know, we had a little problem with terrorists here just under ten years ago. Maybe you heard of it? Goes by the name of 9/11? Now you're suggesting we fake up another one as 'interference' for whatever vampire shitstorm you guys are planning? The Mayor will have a weapons-grade shit fit."

"So maybe it's a gas explosion," I said. "One of the big commercial ovens in the hotel kitchen has some sort of mechanical fault."

I think Jerome had forgotten I was there for a moment. He swivelled round to face me but his scowl was retreating.

"That could work," he said. "Now come with me. Let's get you guys what you need then you can be on your way and I can hunt out some Pepto Bismol." He rubbed his stomach and grimaced. "Every time I talk to you, Con, I get reflux."

59

NOTEBOOK OF ESU CAPTAIN JEROME STENSGAARD, 06/01/11

Today I did one of two things. Either I made the smartest move in my entire military and law enforcement career. Or the dumbest. Only time will tell. Which means two weeks.

So, Con McKay calls and turns up in my office with this British chick in tow. An attorney. Not bad looking. Tall, too. Would have made a great marine. We get the small talk out of the way and then he hits with me his request.

No Glocks this time. No hollow points. No surveillance gizmos or covert entry gear. No. Because that would have been far too simple, wouldn't it? All he wants – all, mind you – is five M112 demo blocks.

I take Con and his new best friend Caroline (who speaks like the Queen of England, by the way, very lah-di-dah) over to the armory. We talk to Casper Flynn over there who's on duty and inside of a minute they're yakking away about where you can get the best Guinness in the five boroughs and I have to remind them why we're here.

Casper takes us out back to the magazine. To get there we have to walk through the firearms racking and boy, poor old Con's eyes are out on stalks. He's practically drooling at the AR15s.

"Do you really need machine guns?" Caroline asks.

As she's a guest, and a Brit, where they don't give their cops guns for some crazy reason, I take the time to explain. I tell her,

"These aren't machineguns, Ma'am. They're what we call semi-automatic rifles. They fire one bullet for each time you pull the trigger. It's just you don't have to manually chamber a new bullet each time."

I didn't mention that we've actually got a request in for full-auto M16s, and I felt like I was dumbing it down calling 'rounds' 'bullets', but I figured she needed all the help she could get. I think she understood. But, hey, not my problem.

Ten minutes later, we're back in my office, Con clutching a box full of M112s to his chest like it was a newborn baby.

That crazy fucking Irishman wants to blow up all the Manhattan vamps in one go. And what's even crazier is, I believe he can do it. Whatever happens there's going to be the biggest shit-hits-fan moment in the history of the NYPD. But you know what? I think it's time. Just recently there's been too much 'rationalization'. Too many smooth-talking, Ivy-League-educated aides from the Mayor's office poking their noses into what we do out here with the cutters.

60

EMAIL FROM LILY BAX TO ARIANE VAN HELSING, 2ND JUNE 2011

From: Lily Bax
To: Ariane Van Helsing
Subject: Russia victorious

Dearest Ariane,

Since you left for Manhattan, things have been far from quiet. I have been in touch with our counterparts in Moscow.

They have sent two members of their group to help me clean out the remaining filth from London. Sergei and Yulia are very experienced fighters and together we have despatched another thirty or so lamia this week.

With Velds gone they display great lassitude. It has become child's play to wipe them out. I wouldn't say the fun's gone out of it, but certainly the adrenaline is way below its peak.

Before he died, poor Jim showed me how to convert the ammunition for the pistols to hold a few drops of *salcie usturoi.* I, in turn, showed Sergei, and he and I spent a few enjoyable hours last week manufacturing several magazines'-worth of ammunition. Sergei is Russian Orthodox and insisted on having the bullets blessed, so we walked from Bloomsbury to the Russian Orthodox Cathedral in Ennismore Gardens, day sacks weighted down with hundreds of bullets. Thankfully no police showed any interest in us, although we were carrying our identity documents as you always insist we do when armed.

The Diocesan Hierarch is 40, but looks younger. Apart from a bushy black beard, that is, which gives him the appearance of an Old Testament prophet. His name, or rather his title, is Bishop Peter of Sourozh. He met us under a grand, gold-leaf covered cupola inside the cathedral. He led us to the font, where he scooped up some of the water in a gold jug. He called it a 'ewer' – such a charming old word, don't you think?

Then he led us to a small side chapel, defended from prying eyes by a tall and ornately carved wooden screen, mounted with icons painted in jewel-like colours and decorated with more gold leaf. Once inside, he closed the little gate behind us and emptied the ewer into a large silver bowl. Sergei and I produced the bullets and Bishop Peter motioned for us to tip them into the bowl. We did so carefully, not wanting to scratch or damage the fine metalwork. (Of the bowl, I mean! The bullets will withstand a certain amount of rough treatment.) When they were all submerged, he prayed over them in Russian. Sergei bowed his head and mumbled along with the Bishop. I closed my eyes out of respect for their tradition, but I was thinking about the use we had planned for them.

Do you remember that nest of lamia over in

Richmond? The night we captured one of the females to prove to Caroline they were real? Of course you do! Well, we travelled there yesterday. During daylight hours. It was a calculated risk, but we attacked them in their house.

It was Sergei's suggestion. He said, in his rather charming English, that it was better to take them in a confined space – a crucible – he called it, than to have to chase them down in the open. He quoted what he claimed was an old Russian proverb, though from the look that sped between him and Yulia, I suspect it may have been an old Russian joke.

"A bear can't turn round in a tunnel."

As you know, we have never tried it before because they are so fast and so confident on their own territory, but with Velds gone, Sergei felt we should take our chance. After all, he said, we might not get it again.

Oh, Ariane, he was right!

We attacked from the rear of the house, breaking down the door with a sledgehammer. Wielded, I might add, by Yulia, who has a sweet soprano singing voice and a body like an Olympic shot-putter's! At her first blow, the door shivered into splinters of wood and glass.

Sergei and I were armed with pistols that he had brought into the country with him from Moscow. I asked him how he brought them through customs. He declined to answer, offering a wink and a smile instead. Had he connections with the Russian Mafia? I asked him. Again, he refrained from answering, this time tapping the side of his nose instead. Yulia, whom you would like, I think, opted for a more traditional cutter weapon. I had given them both a tour of our house, including all our stores and the armoury. She selected one of the scimitars. In her hand it looked like a child's toy, though anointed, it was as lethal as the guns Sergei and I were carrying.

The day was sunny and that would also help us with our plan to exterminate the nest. As we entered the rear of the house – a large, open-plan space with a sloping, shuttered glass roof – the first of the lamia appeared. Seeing us, it hissed and dropped its jaw. Yulia slashed through the cords holding the shutters closed and they sprang back, rolling up with a rattle that startled the creature and made it look up. Which was a mistake.

The beams of sunlight now blazing down through the glass caught it full in the face. With a squeal, it collapsed before shuddering to its death. We were standing well back but still, in that confined space, we were soaked in its blood. Another reason for preferring to attack out of doors. Five more lamia had arrived on the threshold of the room by now and we stood, facing them, bathed in that cleansing fire delivered by the sun, and laughed at them. It felt good, I tell you, good! To stand inside their lair and taunt them.

They were hissing and spitting, extending their talons and making ready to feed, but with the sun protecting us, what could they do? They looked unsure of themselves and tired, as I said earlier. Their musculature was poorly defined and their movements hesitant.

Sergei yelled an old Russian cutters' curse and then we attacked. He and I began shooting and killed four of the things, but one skittered sideways and leapt for the wall to attack round the shady side of the room. Instead it met Yulia's blade. She screamed as she swung it and fetched the creature's head from its shoulders.

We ran further in, relying on their lethargy to strengthen our advantage. The ground floor was free of them so we headed up the stairs. Despite her size, Yulia reached the first floor first and booted in the first door she came to. The woman has no fear! She strode in and within seconds had destroyed four lamia. Marching out, face spattered with their remains, she grinned at Sergei, then at me.

We heard the next lamia before we saw it. A male, it had found its way onto the ceiling and was screeching down at us while digging its talons into the soft ornamental plasterwork. It dropped down onto Yulia's shoulder and reared back before striking. Sergei and I hesitated: the pistols are not accurate enough and Yulia was already moving. We couldn't risk hitting her. We needn't have worried. While the lamia had its throat exposed, she whirled the scimitar above her head and removed the top of its skull in one powerful slash. The lamia fell backwards and exploded before it hit the ground. Yulia was by now drenched in lamia blood but if anything it seemed to have sharpened her appetite for killing.

Facing outwards in a triangle, we manoeuvred our way down the hall, kicking open doors and despatching everything within.

After half an hour, we were done. The house stank of blood. *We* stank of blood. The stairs ran with it; the floors were thick with it. So guess what? With the lamia gone, we decided to make ourselves at home. We showered there!

To celebrate, Sergei and Yulia cooked an enormous meal last night. Sergei seems to know all the places to go in London for Russian delicacies. We began with iced pepper vodka and caviar on blinis with sour cream. Then he produced a baked carp, which he served with pickled cucumbers, potato salad and Georgian champagne (I prefer the French stuff!). I confess that after the fish, my stomach was protesting, but Yulia went to the kitchen and returned with pork meatballs, seasoned with parsley, paprika, lemon and garlic. They were delicious, and I pleaded my stomach before the dessert. It was no use! We finished our meal with plums soaked in brandy and covered in dark chocolate.

It is my fervent wish, dearest Ariane, that by the time you return from Manhattan, it will be to a cleansed city. These have happened so rarely in our history that it will be the occasion for a celebration that will make the feast Sergei and Yulia prepared look like a light snack! I spent some time in the library last night after they had gone to bed. Do you know the last time cutters declared a city cleansed? 1621. Venice. Before that it was Constantinople in 1499. And before that, Baghdad in 1156. Will London join that illustrious list? I pray that it will.

I pray, also, for your success in New York.

Love and strength,

Lily

61

CAROLINE HARKER'S JOURNAL, 3RD JUNE 2011

Preparations are well underway for the banquet. From Frederick's cousin, we have learned of the timings for the evening. Sunset on the 5th falls at 8.23 p.m. That is when the guests are scheduled to arrive. The drinks service starts then. We, that is to say, Ariane, Con and I, will enter the hotel with the other waiting staff at 8.00 p.m. Con will work with Frederick's cousin to set up the bomb inside the centrepiece. I can't wait to see what they contrive, since it must be big enough to conceal a device the size of a beer barrel.

The caterers have been told to be gone by 9.30 p.m. That is when the lamia's own people will take over the kitchen to begin preparing whatever ghastly "meal" those things intend to fill their bellies with. Ariane and I will find somewhere to hide. She will have the number of the disposable phone programmed into her own; I will have it, too, as a backup. I can't imagine anything worse than our not being able to detonate the bomb because of a flat phone battery.

When we judge the lamia to be sated and least likely

to be leaving their tables, Con will dial the number and boom! Two hundred dead vampires. The rest of our team will be outside the hotel: there is a back entrance to the kitchen: we'll unlock the door and let them in. Then, together we check the ballroom and finish off any lamia who have escaped the blast. My only regret, if it can be called that, is that I won't be able to finish off Peta Velds myself. After what she did to David, I would have enjoyed watching the look on her face as she realised what was about to happen to her.

62

EMAIL FROM ARIANE VAN HELSING TO LILY BAX, 3RD JUNE 2011

From: Ariane Van Helsing
To: Lily Bax
Subject: RE: Russia victorious

Dear Lily,

Perhaps I should leave you to manage alone more often! Your success against the lamia with Sergei and Yulia fills me with optimism. I have recently dared to let myself wonder – hope, even – that we may one day achieve our historic goal: to rid the world of the lamia.

Frederick's fixer is an amusing man with Irish ancestry named Con McKay. Yesterday, I helped him assemble the bomb with which we hope to eradicate every single lamia in New York. If we succeed, that will be two cleansed cities in one year. You may be sure, the feasting will be prolonged.

Con has a workshop that would make you apply for a transfer the moment you stepped across the threshold.

Lathes, presses, bench drills, a welding rig and something he called a 3D printer. These are very rare apparently, even in industry, though he says within five years they will be within reach of ordinary people. But the cutters here have backers with deep pockets. And they have provided this machine. He can use it to manufacturer weapons, components, even specialised ammunition. All out of either plastic or metal powders. He showed me crossbow bolts, a plastic single-shot pistol undetectable by X-ray scanners, paper-thin armour strong enough to defeat knife thrusts. What he will do with it all if we are successful, I don't know. But I get ahead of myself. It's just, oh, Lily, they are so optimistic here, and their enthusiasm is infectious.

Con began by taking the C4 explosive he and Caroline brought back from the Emergency Services Unit and moulding it around a steel core. This assembly he slotted into a plastic cylinder that he produced using the 3D printer. Stage 1 complete.

Then we wrapped the cylinder with three-inch nails, 10,000 of them. They came stuck to paper bands, which made the task of attaching them to the cylinder rather easier than it would have been otherwise. At this point, the whole assembly had a distinctly Mediaeval appearance. I suspect Great-great-grandfather Abraham would have recognised it, at least in its essentials: a glinting steel tower – all sharp points and dully gleaming grey metal – the approximate size and shape of a milk churn. Con wrapped the tower in several metres of clear food wrap so that it resembled a giant cocoon. And believe me, when the monstrous butterfly inside hatches out, the lamia will truly be witnesses to the transforming power of fire and steel. Stage 2 also complete.

Finally, we filled 36 plastic bottles (they had once held

Poland Spring mineral water) with *salcie usturoi*. Together, we taped the bottles around the outside of the assembly in four rings of nine.

When the bomb was finished, Con stood back from his workbench, the better, I think, to admire his creation. It now had the dimensions of a barrel.

"That'll do the bastards, don't you think?" he asked me, that wicked twinkle back in the corner of his eye.

"It will. But tell me," I asked him, "how you intend to smuggle such a device into the hotel?"

"You like flowers, Ariane?" he asked me, grinning.

I shrugged. As you know, I have little time for fripperies, and flowers rank very close to the top in that category of entertainments.

"Not really," I said.

"Well, the lamia do. Hearst has ordered ten thousand dollars' worth of floral arrangements from the caterers. Everything red or as close to black as possible, naturally. I'm thinking the centerpiece might deliver more bang for his buck than he was expecting."

I asked him how he would detonate the bomb. He told me he intends to use an electronic detonator triggered by a simple disposable phone. He, Caroline and I will be inside dressed as waiting staff, though we will keep to the kitchen. Once the lamia are seated and, I regret to say, sated from their meal, he will set off the bomb. Despite the considerable amount of destructive power of the C4, he assures me that provided we are behind a wall, neither the explosion itself, nor the shrapnel, will harm us. I have to trust him on this. He showed me some video footage on the internet of C4 explosions of varying sizes in an attempt to reassure me, but I think I shall find a back stairway and suggest we all hide there. Anyway, once the bomb detonates, the rest of

Frederick's team will enter the hotel and join us. Any security the lamia are using will be drawn inwards away from the doors.

So, my dearest Lily, in a few days, God willing, I should be able to return to England with the news every cutter wishes for from the deepest and most sacred part of their soul: the creation of a cleansed city.

Take care,

Your friend,

Ariane

63

PETA'S SPEECH FOR WELCOME BANQUET. DRAFT DATED 4TH JUNE 2011

My dear Morgan, honoured guests, family members both old and new, thank you. As you may know, my work in England to find a cure for our aversion to sunlight received a devastating setback recently.

Aided by the fiancée of the scientist I hired – and subsequently killed – the London cutters blew up my facility, killed my head of security and destroyed every last shred of work that we had completed. They won that particular battle, but we will remind them of something my ancestor knew only too well.

[pause for emphasis]

Wars matter, battles don't.

I am here in New York with my General Counsel, J.S. Le Fanu. Many of you will know Sheridan. He was instrumental in identifying and recruiting David Harker and with his help I am sure we can find a suitable replacement.

But enough of setbacks. We have weathered storms before and look at us now. Look at our wealth. Look at our power. Those pathetic beings beyond these four walls think they reign supreme over God's earth. But are we not also created in His image? Perhaps, far from resting, He was busy on the seventh day improving on his first attempt.

Let me set out a vision for you. A few years from now, our scientific researches will bear fruit. We will have discovered a cure for the chromosomal disorder that renders us unable to tolerate sunlight. We shall mass produce it and distribute it worldwide to every member of every family. Then – oh, my brothers and sisters – then what sport we will make with the humans. Our hunting time will double overnight. Free to move among them at our leisure, we shall grow to dominate them in a way our ancestors could only dream of. And this will bring problems.

[pause for emphasis]

Yes, problems. How will we husband our cattle? We cannot afford to eat all of them! We shall need to set up breeding programmes. Build farms. Mechanise. Industrialise! Perhaps we will get the humans to help us. After all, they have proved adept at turning the Earth into a giant food-processing factory to feed their incessant cravings for meat. Perhaps we will merely steal a leaf from their book. I look to the future, and I think to myself, I'm lovin' it!

[pause for laughter]

All that lies ahead of us. There will be hard work and no doubt sacrifices along the way. But for now, we celebrate.

I would like to thank Morgan for extending such a warm welcome to me and Sheridan as we regroup and re-equip ourselves. And to all of you, my extended family. So, a toast.

To the O-One.
To our eventual victory.
And to blood.

64

CAROLINE HARKER'S JOURNAL, 5TH JUNE 2011

Ariane and I changed into our waitresses' outfits together, in her room. Ariane invited me to join her and I was a little surprised since, so far, she has always struck me as a very private person. When I was staying at the cutter house in Bloomsbury, I don't think I ever saw her in anything except her day clothes, unlike Lily who would frequently wander about in her pyjamas until noon or later. As we undressed, I understood. I had my back to her, as my own shyness about my body makes me uncomfortable. When I used to row at Cambridge, the other girls would tease me about it. I had just taken off my jeans when Ariane spoke.

"Caroline, turn around."

For a fleeting moment, I had the bizarre thought that she was going to ask me to embrace her. But no. I turned to face her. She was only wearing her knickers and bra. My eyes were immediately drawn to her chest. Four ugly, parallel scars stretched right the way across from just below her right shoulder to the soft flesh above her left hip. Without asking, I knew what they were.

"A lamia did this to me when I was sixteen," she said, in a soft voice. She traced her fingertips over the shiny white lines scraped across her otherwise flawless pale skin. "I was standing shoulder to shoulder with my father. There were three of them and two of us. It should have been an easy fight for us. But I was inexperienced. One of the lamia laid open my father's cheek. His shout of pain distracted me and I turned to see what had happened. I dropped my guard and in that moment one of the other lamia clawed me, right through my clothes."

The scars disappeared beneath the bra cup and reappeared on her ribcage, beneath the band. I tried to imagine the agony, the fear, that the sixteen-year-old Ariane must have felt.

"What happened next?" I asked.

"I screamed. My father spun round to help me and in that split-second, the creature that had slashed his face sprang onto his back and bit him. He killed it as he fell. In my fear and rage I swung my sword at the other two lamia and killed them both with a single blow. But my poor father was dying. The blood was gushing out of his neck. You know what that looks like, Caroline. And you know what our law requires the survivor to do."

I could only nod, spellbound at her story, yet also horrified at what I knew had to be its end. I asked the inevitable question, anyway.

"What did you do?"

Ariane sighed. She shrugged her shoulders and it was at once the most heartbreaking and the most eloquent expression of grief and despair I have ever seen.

"What I had to."

"I'm sorry," I said. It sounded so inadequate, however much I had tried to communicate my feelings for her and for the poor bereaved girl she became at that moment.

"We will be heavily outnumbered in there tonight," she said. "I do not want to lose you as I lost my father. As I lost Tomas. As I lost Shimon and Jim. We will wear the chain mail as we did before. They have an even stronger and lighter version here."

She pointed to her bed where a pile of silvery metal mesh lay, its folds glinting in the light. We sorted the garments out, each taking a collar, a chest piece, two wristlets and what I suppose I should call a pair of drawers each – something akin to cycling shorts, only a little looser. Black tights and long-sleeved lycra vests protected our bare skin from the metal links, and by the time we were dressed, in black trousers, baggy white shirts and red ties, I would defy anyone to notice that we were wearing the extra protection. They were not even too heavy, although for once I was glad of my muscular shoulders.

Ariane, Con and I entered Mallory's through the rear entrance at 8.00 p.m. with the rest of the drinks waiters and waitresses. We had been expecting security and were thus unarmed. This turned out to be a strategic miscalculation: no bruisers dressed in black bomber jackets were there to welcome us. But then, as Ariane said, who in their right mind would try to attack a banquet attended by 200 vampires? It would be a suicide mission. Sometimes her gallows humour can be a little too close to the truth. We each brought a small daysack with us, similar to those our colleagues were carrying. But where theirs probably contained their iPhones, makeup bags, and maybe a spare blouse or shirt, ours were packed with flasks of *salcie usturoi*.

We entered in the kitchen, a modest-sized space filled

with stainless steel cabinets, grills and ovens, fridges, freezers and all the paraphernalia you would expect in a professional kitchen. Con nodded once at Ariane, then again at me, and wandered off to a far corner. They had checked and rechecked their phones and had agreed a set of signals to use should one of them discover a problem with their device.

"We need weapons," Ariane whispered. I looked around. Chefs have their own knives, I knew that. But surely a professional kitchen would maintain a set of its own, as well? This one did. Oh, how we smiled when we saw them. Perhaps Ariane would have preferred her usual weapon, but her sword was secure at the cutter house. Frederick had promised her he would bring it for the final cleanup. As it was, I pointed at the magnetic rack.

"Take your pick," I said, with what I hoped was a suitably battle-ready smile.

What a choice! Boning knives with finely curved blades. Long cook's knives almost a foot from butt to point. Santokus with scalloped edges. Twelve-inch butcher's knives with curved blades like miniature scimitars. Heavy cleavers with solid rectangular blades that would snap bones as if they were breadsticks.

Ariane took one of the butcher knives and hefted it. She turned it in the hard light bouncing off the stainless steel worktop and nodded, grimly. I reached for a cleaver. It felt good in my hand; it had a real heft to it. I swung and I immediately realised the problem. It had such momentum I would leave myself wide open to a counterattack. I stuck it back on the rack with a snap from the magnets and pulled down a chef's knife with an eight-inch blade. Still a powerful weapon, and more than enough to send a lamia on its way, but far lighter and more manoeuvrable.

As the others busied themselves talking to the drinks guy – "mixologist", he corrected me when I asked if he was the barman – Ariane and I took our knives to a sink in the corner, away from the hubbub, and liberally anointed them with the garlic and willow oil. The catering company had issued each of us with a black apron and the pockets across the front were capacious enough for us to secrete our blades. They wouldn't fool a zealous airport security agent, or even, to be honest, a half-asleep one, but as I already said, the lamia had clearly not felt the need for such precautions.

My pulse was racing, and I had to pause to take a few long, slow breaths to try to calm myself. I had the fizz of excitement in my stomach I get when I'm about to enter the High Court, but it didn't bother me. I was there to exact retribution on Peta Velds for David's death. I felt, the only word, righteous. The lamia were due to start arriving at 8.30 p.m. It was now 8.15 p.m. Ariane and I left the kitchen. We wanted to assess the field of battle.

The ballroom was huge. Its architect had managed to find a way to support the vast space with virtually no pillars; just one, admittedly thick, marble column in each corner of the room. Going for an overblown gothic look, and showing a distinct lack of imagination, the designer had employed a limited palette of black and shades of red, with silver and gold much in evidence. He or she had even thought to stand a suit of armour at the foot of the stairs. The windows were shrouded in deep-plum velvet curtains that puddled against the floor as if bleeding onto the polished parquet blocks. Red candles in tall, floor-standing silver candlesticks flickered and danced, throwing shadows onto the walls. Gilt-framed mirrors reflected the candle flames over and over again so that the whole room appeared to be dancing with thousands of points of yellow light. The circular tables, each surrounded by ten gilt-framed, red-cushioned chairs, were dressed with red cloths. In the middle of each, a tall, black vase stood. The vases contained a dozen or more arum lilies, their conical spathes such a dark purple as to be almost black.

Then I saw the centrepiece Con had devised to conceal the bomb. It stood on the ground in the very centre of the room. The container – for vase is surely the wrong word – was a huge, red ceramic sphere almost a metre in diameter. Erupting from the opening at the top were flowers of such strangeness that for a moment I wondered whether they were plastic, the creations of a floral artist driven mad by reading too much H.P Lovecraft. The centre of the arrangement consisted of three tall green stems, each well over seven foot and as thick as my wrist, surmounted by foot-long scarlet blossoms like spiked zeppelins. Spiraling outwards from this unholy trio were dozens of orchids of a vivid, acid green, spotted with what appeared to be beads of blood. But it was the third tier of blooms that drew me in, pulling me close enough to smell and touch them. Honestly? They looked like bats. Outspread "wings" of a blackish-purple to left and right, a "head" that even appeared to possess tiny white teeth, and dozens of white and purple streamers that dangled below each surreal flower. The perfume of these exotics – honey, cloves, and the sweet, cloying smell of decay – was so heady I felt my head swim. Ariane pulled me back with an urgent hiss.

"They're arriving. Come. We have to go."

Access to the ballroom was through double doors at

one end, and also from a gracious, sweeping staircase of wrought iron that curved down from a galleried hallway on the floor above. We sprinted for the stairs and took them two at a time, knives bouncing against the front of our thighs, arriving on the balcony as the noise levels from the lobby just beyond the ballroom doors intensified. Ariane turned away from me and tried the handle of a door behind us, marked "Staff Only". It was locked. She brought out a pair of lock picks from her trouser pocket and within a few seconds had jiggled them into the keyhole and sprung the lock. Beyond was a simple storage room containing supplies of soaps, shampoos, and all the other little fripperies hotels like to use to convince us we're getting value for money when all we need is a comfortable bed and a quiet night. Ha! A quiet night would elude anyone staying at the hotel on this particular date had the management not accepted whatever obscene fee Hearst offered them to keep every single room free for the lamia.

"The drinks service finishes at nine," Ariane said. "That's what Con told me. Then they will seat themselves. We'll wait in here until ten or after, when they have filled themselves with blood, and then Con will detonate the bomb. We'll be safe in here. The angle of the blast will send any nails that don't find a home in a lamia into the hallway ceiling. And that door looks nice and solid."

Not wishing to confine ourselves to our bolt hole too early, we left the storage room, now unlocked, and made our way round the galleried hallway to the door marked with the universal green-and-white sign for the emergency stairs. We descended to the basement, having decided to try to block of any means of escape for the lamia. We had full confidence in Con's bomb itself, but when you're fighting lamia it pays to be doubly certain. They are cunning, fast and possessed of a fierce survival instinct. We couldn't risk even one of the creatures eluding the cleanup operation.

The corridor was concrete-floored, painted plain white and although clean, musty-smelling. No smart, contemporary painting on the walls here. Our footsteps rang out, echoing away down the long, straight passage. We turned a corner and found ourselves facing a fire-door closed with a push bar and flanked by large, red-and-white signs declaring, "DO NOT LOCK". Ariane locked the door with her picks, then broke them off in the keyhole. She smiled at me, a look of determination mixed with that brand of grim humour I had grown to like over the time I had known her.

We walked back to the dogleg in the corridor and were about to head back when a sound brought me up short. I shushed Ariane, who was telling me how we should approach the scene after the bomb detonated.

"If they're still moving, use your – what?" she said, a look of irritation flashing across her features.

I pointed to a door just ahead of us, on the right.

"Did you hear it?" I asked her.

"Hear what?" she answered, still frowning.

"It was like a whimper. A human voice, at any rate. I think it came from beyond that door."

I put my ear to the door and strained to hear something, anything, that would convince me I hadn't imagined it. But the room beyond was silent. I leaned back.

"Must have been nerves," I said.

"Maybe," Ariane said. "Maybe not. Knock."

"What?"

"Knock. If somebody's in there they'll answer."

She drew the butcher knife from her apron and I did the same with my own knife. And I knocked.

There was a sound on the other side of the door that might have been feet shuffling. And something else. Muffled whispers. More than one voice.

"Hello," I said, trying to pitch my voice loud enough to penetate the door but not so loud it would travel down the corridor. "Is anyone in there?"

The voice that answered me sounded very frightened. A young woman's voice. An American accent.

"Help us. Please! You have to help us. Oh my God! Quick!"

I pushed down on the handle. It was locked. I turned to Ariane, about to ask her to work her magic when I remembered she'd just snapped off her lock picks in the fire door.

I put my lips to the door.

"Can you hear me," I said.

"Yes."

"Stand back. I'm going to break the door down."

I could have used my knife but I didn't want to risk damaging the blade.

I took a step back while Ariane kept watch, looking back the way we'd come from the stairs. Then, trying my best to copy the move I'd seen in a hundred films, I lifted my right foot and kicked out as hard as I could against the door, just below the handle. The wooden door emitted a creak of protest but held firm. I tried a second time, visualising Peta Velds's face at the point of impact.

The sole of my shoe struck the same spot as before and this time, the noise was more of a splintering than a crack.

"It's breaking," the woman cried out from her side.

I decided to use my shoulder, just as I had when I broke into Lucy's room at the pub in Norfolk when she was attacked by the lamia. I hurled myself at the door, barging it with all the force I could project through my torso.

It gave. The aluminium handle was buckled and half-torn out of the wood surrounding it. One final kick and the door burst open. I stepped through, rubbing my bruised shoulder. And gasped.

Facing us, huddled in groups, were twenty or so men and women, all naked. Their faces betrayed the fear they must have been feeling. Ariane took charge.

"Listen to me. We're going to get you out of here, but right now, this room is probably the safest place you can be."

A man stepped forwards, his hands clasped over his genitals. He was young, maybe twenty five, with a straggly brown beard. I noticed he had scabs on the inside of his elbows. A junkie, I assumed.

"You can't leave us here. Those men who brought us here are going to come back. They said they'd kill us if we even tried to fight. What are they gonna do when they find the door's been kicked in?"

"What men?" Ariane asked. "What did they look like?"

I knew what she was getting at.

The man stared at her like she was mad.

"I don't know. Like, doormen, you know? Security types. Big. Tall. Shaved heads."

What he hadn't said was as revealing as what he had. These weren't lamia. They were humans. Servants like Renfield back at David's laboratory. The lamia are rich enough to find willing helpers who can disregard their evil in return for a payday. Perhaps this was why we hadn't encountered any security at he door – they were too busy bringing these poor souls into the basement.

"Listen to me," Ariane said. "If they come back, tell them the truth. Say two crazy women broke the door down. If they leave you to come and find us, it will be their ending."

A young, ginger-haired woman rushed up to us, one hand covering her breasts, the other her pubis. No needle marks but she was a skinny thing. A runaway, I wondered.

"Take me with you?" she pleaded. "I'm frightened."

Ariane placed her hands on her shoulders and fixed her with a stare. It was warm but I've seen that look before. It brooks no dissent.

"No. It's too dangerous out there."

She stepped back and addressed them all at once.

"You have to trust us. The people who had you brought here are evil. We're here to stop them hurting anyone else. Wait here for us. We'll be back."

A black man shouldered his way to the front of the small crowd. He was tall and strongly built, but his eyes had the same look of fear we'd seen in all the others.

"Listen. You busted the door down, which is great, you know. So, thanks for that. But we're not waiting here to be fucking tortured or whatever." He turned round and addressed the rest of the prisoners. "I say we go now. There's a fire door right outside that door. We can get out and call the cops."

Then Ariane did something that surprised me. She pulled him round by his shoulder and slapped him, hard, across the cheek. His eyes widened and his lips pulled back from his teeth. Before he could do or say anything, she spoke.

"Listen to me!" she shouted. To him, but I knew she

was intending her words to be heard, and understood, by the rest of them. Having silenced the mutters of dissent, she lowered her voice, though it still carried to the back of the room. "Last century, people like you were enslaved in this country. Brutally treated. Denied even your basic rights. My friend, compared to what's waiting for you upstairs, slavery would seem like a blessing."

His face contorted with anger.

"What the fuck racist shit are you talking about, you——"

"The people up there?" she interrupted, pointing at the ceiling with her knife. "They are going to bleed you dry, do you understand me? They will drink your blood and throw your drained corpses aside like so many oyster shells."

This stopped him. He blinked.

"You're crazy. They can't. Why? I mean——"

He gave up and stood silently, waiting for Ariane to explain.

I saw the others shuffling closer to hear Ariane's words.

"Look around you. What did you think was going to happen to twenty naked drifters, runaways and junkies kept prisoner in a hotel basement? Are you expecting your party outfits to arrive in carrier bags from Saks Fifth Avenue? No! You listen to me. Your lives were in danger. But now you are safe. My friends and I will deal with the people who captured you and brought you here. Whatever you hear, whatever you smell, whatever you may think is your best course of action, ignore it. Stay here. We will come and get you as soon as we can."

Over their protests, she turned and left. I walked out after her, pulling the door to behind me. I was gratified to see that none of them tried to follow us. Perhaps her tone convinced them that their salvation did indeed lie in trusting us.

We made our way back to the balcony and were just in time to shut ourselves into the storage room when we heard the double-doors below us open and the excited chatter of the lamia fill the ballroom. The scraping of chairs, laughter and shuffling of shoes on the floor sounded for all the world like any other formal party. A group of happy people ready to enjoy each other's company along with plenty of free booze and gourmet food. Only in this case, they were parasites readying themselves to fill their bellies with human blood.

The noise died down and then we heard Hearst calling for quiet. He welcomed them to what he called "this welcome feast for Peta Velds" and then introduced his guest of honour. The opening words of her speech had me and Ariane looking at each other and gaping.

"Dear Morgan, Mister Mayor, honoured guests, family members both old and new, thank you. As you may know, my work in England to find a cure for our aversion to sunlight received a devastating setback recently."

"Mister Mayor?" I mouthed at Ariane.

She shrugged. I suppose that during her career as a cutter, she has witnessed so much that the Mayor of New York's turning out to be a lamia is worthy neither of comment nor amazement.

As Peta continued speaking, Ariane nodded towards the door and whispered to me.

"Let's see what we can see."

She pulled the handle down and slowly pushed the door open. On her belly, and with her phone ready in her hand, she slithered through the gap and pulled herself across the carpet to the ornate iron railing. She looked back at me over her shoulder and beckoned me with a jerk of her head. Heart racing, I squeezed through the gap and joined her.

Beneath us, the ballroom was now filled with lamia. Twenty tables, ten to a table, looking for all the world like patrons of a charity, gathered to express their support and make their pledges. The males were in black tie, what the Americans call tuxedos, the females in elaborate dresses in black, dark-purple, bottle-green, scarlet and midnight-blue. At the furthest table, Peta Velds was standing as she addressed them. She was wearing a sheath-like dress in an iridescent silvery fabric that clung to her frame, revealing the taut musculature beneath.

In the far corner, raised up on a small, black-draped platform, stood a very expensive-looking video camera on a tripod. I could see a red light above the lens.

Peta closed her speech and raised her glass in a toast. It was filled with a red liquid and although I have seen with my own eyes just how fond the lamia are of alcohol, I knew this was blood.

"To the O-One. To our eventual victory. And to blood!" she cried and downed the contents of her glass in one.

The room echoed her toast and as one, the lamia stood, raised their own glasses and swigged the contents, many wiping their lips afterwards with the backs of their hands, which came away smeared with red.

Waiters appeared with plates of what I took to be food and began serving the lamia. Soon they had begun chatting as they speared whatever disgusting dish their chefs had prepared and conveyed the morsels to their mouths. They were not using their feeding funnels. I can only assume they can manage without them if they aren't attacking living prey.

While they were eating, the double doors below us swung open and in marched two heavyset men dressed as the young man in the basement room had described. They looked just like nightclub bouncers. They were carrying tall wooden poles set in black metal X's about half a metre across. They took them over to Peta's table and the one next to it and stood them up on the floor. I had to stifle a gasp. The poles were stakes, sharpened to a wicked point. I watched as Hearst leaned over to Peta and spoke into her ear. She smiled and nodded and raised her glass, which one of the waiters had refilled.

The burly men left, only to return a minute later with two more stakes. We watched as two by two, they brought in another sixteen. Eventually there was one stake standing beside each table. The lamia were laughing and smiling, taking photos of the stakes and posing beside them for selfies.

Hearst clapped his hands for silence. At once, the room stilled. In a deep, commanding tone that reached us as clearly as if he had been standing beside us, he addressed the 200 vampires before him.

"Brothers and sisters. You know about Peta's illustrious forbears. There is one of that magnificent line whose name is a byword for the power of the lamia. We know him as Vlad Drăculea. The humans as Vlad Țepeș."

At the mention of the Impaler's name, the assembled lamia murmured their assent. Hearst continued.

"Tonight, in honour of the Drăculea family, and its most recent head," he turned and nodded at Peta, "I have asked my chefs to prepare a course that I hope will entertain as much as it nourishes."

He leaned down and picked up a small, black device that I realised was some sort of remote control. He pointed it a white projector bolted to the ceiling. At once, the walls were covered with a huge, projected blowup of that grotesque woodcut I remembered discussing with Ariane the very time I met her.

In the foreground, Vlad Țepeș, dressed in some sort of winter robe and soft hat, sits at a dining table draped with a cloth. A large goblet and two plates, all, one assumes of silver, stand before him. In the centre of the table, on an oval platter lies, well, I dearly wish to believe it is a roast chicken. However, there is something about the way the creature is positioned, and its anatomy, that reminds one of a baby. Two loaves of bread complete the meal.

To his right, a forest of sharp-pointed stakes bears aloft his presumably recently vanquished enemies. The people appear to be alive: their eyes are open. They are impaled through the anus, the chest, upside down, the right way up. And before him, a man with an axe is chopping up still more people. Body parts are strewn around and a disembodied head stares blindly up from a pan cooking on an open fire.

The lamia cheered and applauded as they took in the details of the woodcut, made all the more vivid for being projected on fifteen-foot high walls.

As the horror of what was to become of the naked people in the basement dawned on me, I leaned closer to Ariane and whispered into her ear.

"They're recreating that ghastly woodcut."

"I know."

She looked calm, but I had to hope that internally she was as revolted as I was.

"We have to do something," I whispered. "We can't

let them murder those people. Not like that. It's inhuman."

"Of course it's inhuman! *They* are inhuman. Or had you forgotten?"

I was shocked, Was she really going to let the lamia impale twenty human beings while we looked down on the scene and did nothing? As we conducted our argument in whispers, the doors opened one more time. The men appeared beneath us, their shoulders and torsos foreshortened into black blocks beneath us. Each man carried a silver jug. They walked up to the two nearest stakes and reached up to tilt the jugs over the points. I almost wretched. They were pouring oil onto them.

"Please!" I whispered. "Text Con. Tell him to detonate it now. Or do it yourself."

By way of answer she pointed down. I realised not all the lamia were seated. Some had left their chairs to inspect the stakes. Others were table-hopping, bending at their neighbours' places to talk. Still others were approaching Peta and either kissing her or shaking her hand. Then, disaster! She gestured at the centrepiece then pointed off to one side of the room. She seemed to be saying that the huge display of flowers was obscuring her view of the furthermost stakes. Half a dozen lamia moved immediately to the red ceramic sphere and bent to encircle it with their arms. As one, they straightened their knees and lifted the whole thing clear of the floor.

They were carrying it between the tables. It was now or never. I elbowed Ariane in the ribs.

"You have to tell him. Now!" I hissed.

She nodded. Just once. But it was an eloquent movement.

She tapped out a brief message and sent it to Con.

We wriggled back into the storage room and shut the door.

Once inside Ariane spoke to me at a normal volume.

"Over there," she said, pointing at the far side of the room where folding tables had been stacked like an oversized pack of playing cards. We raced to the tables and squatted behind our makeshift barricade and I offered up a prayer that she was right about the likely trajectory of the flying nails.

"Send it, Ariane!" I said.

She shook her head.

"It's Con's bomb. He should do it."

She sent a second text to Con. It consisted of a single word.

"Now."

I closed my eyes and held my breath. I think I had it in mind to start counting. If I did, I got as far as mentally forming my lips around the number "one" before the bomb exploded with a bang that rattled the window on the far side of the storage room. I heard a kind of pattering sound like an over-energetic woodpecker. Breaking glass. Rumbles. And screams. Thank God! Lots of truly appalling screams. We'd done it. We'd wiped out the entire New York clan of lamia.

Ariane and I left the sanctuary of our improvised bomb shelter and rushed to the door. She pulled it open and I understood what the woodpecker noise had been. The side of the door facing outwards was studded with nails at random angles. Some point-inwards, some head-first. The air was filled with acrid smoke and the smell was thick and clogged my nostrils – burnt meat and a weird plasticky smell like when you leave a kitchen tool too close to a gas flame.

We leaned over the balcony. The sight that greeted

our stinging eyes was like something from a Mediaeval engraving, probably entitled, "the tortures of hell". The floor was a mess of blood and semi-liquid tissue. A few lamia were staggering around, clutching their torn faces or the stumps of severed limbs. They burst as we watched, spraying their fellows before they themselves exploded into fountains and sheets of blood. Those nails that had not found a home in a lamia had flown out in a hemisphere from the centrepiece and were now embedded in the walls, the pillars and the ceiling. The tables nearest the blast had been obliterated. Fine chips and burning splinters of wood floated in the air around us, crawling with orange sparks along their edges.

The curtains, until the blast such elegant swags of red velvet drapery were burning merrily, releasing swirls of black smoke that eddied upwards towards the spiky plasterwork ceiling.

As we looked over the edge, a shout went up. Frederick Arnold and the rest of his crew came through the double doors and spread out into the room. At once, Ariane shouted down to him.

"Fred! Look out!"

He whirled round in time to see an uninjured lamia staggering towards him, jaw hanging, teeth erect, taloned hands clawing towards his face. Up went his pistol and he shot the vile creature in the head, stepping back as it burst and already turning away, gun arm still level in front of him, ready for new targets.

Ariane told me to draw my knife. I saw that she had already pulled the butcher knife from her apron and was holding it, point uppermost, ready to despatch any lamia foolish enough to attack us.

"Did we get them all?" I asked her, flicking my gaze left and right, behind me and below, searching for Peta.

"I pray we did, but be watchful, Caro. Until we have searched this whole building we cannot relax."

Together, we ran round the balconied landing and descended the staircase together. Reaching the ground level I skidded in the blood, which was inches deep on the parquet flooring.

Frederick and his crew had spread out and most had disappeared through the emergency exit or the double doors, looking for lamia who had managed to escape the blast.

The gunfire was sporadic. I jumped at the first shots but then took each new volley as a signal that we were closer to our goal of wiping out the vermin.

The smell was appalling. A dense, meaty, coppery stink that seemed to worm its way beyond the nostrils and deep into some primitive part of the brain designed to run at the first signs of predators, or attack at the first sign of prey.

It felt good. To be the predators for once. After our abortive and disastrous confrontation with Peta in Docklands, this time I truly believed we had won.

Then came a sound that will live with me as long as I draw breath. A screech, so loud and so filled with hatred that the hairs on the back of my neck and on my arms stood on end.

I looked up, towards the source of the scream. And I saw her.

Leaning over the railing of the balcony, glaring down at me with ruby-red eyes, mouth hinged down and flashing obscenely long, translucent fangs dripping with slime, was Peta Velds, the mother of the London lamia and the murderer of my own dear, sweet David Harker.

The blast had blown her dress clean off her body, though sadly not a single nail into her flesh, which was rippling with muscle and as white as china clay, apart from the streaks, spatters and smears of lamia blood. She stood above us, talons gouging deep cuts into the wooden bannister, hissing at me, an obscenity made flesh.

I didn't even think. I ran across the ballroom, splashing through the blood, and pausing only to grab the sword from the fist of the suit of armour that had been standing guard at the foot of the stairs. It had been blown backwards by the blast and was studded with nails.

"Caro, wait!" Ariane yelled.

She mustered such command in her tone that I did stop. I turned, intending to tell her not to try to impede my progress. Peta was mine. But she didn't. She was holding a flask. Frederick or one of his crew must have given it to her. She rushed over to me and slopped the contents all over the blade before running her thumb across it and anointing my forehead with a cross.

I nodded once, then ran for the stairs. Peta was waiting for me. As I gained the upper floor she hissed once then turned and fled. She disappeared through a door, slamming it behind her.

My mind was completely clear. Yes, I was bent on extinguishing the hideous monster who had caused so much pain, so much suffering. But I was riding a wave of calm intensity. I felt my body was responding as a big cat's might, not as something I had to urge on, but rather as something carrying me with it, allowing me to focus my conscious mind on the prey ahead of me.

I threw the door wide, looking up as I went through it. I hadn't forgotten my experience with the three lamia in Bloomsbury Square the night Ariane showed me the one they'd captured. But the ceiling was clear: no clawed monstrosity hanging there like a spider waiting to drop onto me and sink its fangs into my flesh.

"Peta!" I screamed into the darkness. "Come out, you bitch! I'm here to kill you!"

She was too canny to reply and signal her location. So I ran on, down the corridor. At the far end I saw another of the fire doors. On the way, I tried each of the bedroom doors in turn, using my left hand so that my right could stay curled round the hilt of the sword. Each was locked. There was no other way out of the corridor apart from the fire door.

I approached the innocuous slab of grey-painted wood with the green-and-white sign of the little man on the stairs. My heart was pounding. I stretched out my left hand to hit the push bar and that's when the lights went off. No dramatic amplified thump. No flickering or buzzing. One moment the corridor was brightly lit, the next, utterly black. The gap in our planning was revealed in an instant. I had no torch. I felt panic creeping up on me: a cold, shivery feeling that began in my belly and spread its icy tentacles upwards to my chest and then my neck and the back of my head, before sinuously winding their way down the muscles of my arms and into my fingertips.

Then I remembered. My phone, of course! I dug it out of my hip pocket with my left hand and switched on the light. Now I had a cone of pale, bluish-white light that at least dispelled a little of the darkness, though my terror was real and still there, clawing at my reason and making me want to turn and run.

Fearing that Peta would be waiting for me on the other side of the fire door, I readied my sword, gripping the hilt so tightly my knuckles cracked. I took a step back, inhaled deeply, then lunged at the push bar and barged through, sword held in front of me so that I might impale her if she were waiting to pounce.

The landing was empty. Or empty as far as my phone's pathetic torch could show me. I took a moment to slow my breathing. Would she have gone up, or down? I knew Ariane and I had disabled the basement fire exit, but did she? *What would I do?* I asked myself. *I'm extremely agile, strong and determined. The roof!*

I inhaled deeply, trying to force oxygen into my bloodstream. The stairwell smelled of damp and mould. She called to me at that point. The sound all but froze me to the spot.

"Oh, Ca-ro-line," she sang out. "I'm wait-ing for you."

Mockery and spite dripped from those few words. I tried to think of something to shoot back but my mind was blank. She saved me the trouble.

"You made me miss my dinner," she hissed, a guttural whisper that triggered a primitive response somewhere deep in my brain. The hairs on my forearms and the back of my neck erected and a painful shiver raced over my ribs. "Now I need to get something to go."

I turned to the stairs and placed my right foot on the first step. It took an effort of will to follow it with my left, but once I'd left the safety of the landing, my legs seemed to take on a life of their own, and soon I was running up the stairs, imagining how I would take Peta Velds with my sword.

I spun round a corner and leapt for the third step on the next flight. My foot connected with the tread but it was coated in something slimy and I slipped immediately. I fell forwards, smashing my right shin into the edge of a higher step and yelling in pain. Worse than the pain, much worse, was the loss of my phone. As my hand smacked down onto the concrete step, the phone skittered out of my grasp, spinning out and down into the stairwell. I heard a distant smash as it hit the ground.

Orange afterimages from the bright, white light of its flash streaked across my retinas, but other than these unwelcome phenomena, I was blind. I pushed myself upright. My left palm slid in whatever substance Peta had slathered over the step. I wiped my hand on my bottom and carried on up, feeling my way with outstretched fingertips brushing the wall as I climbed.

Peta's voice echoed down towards me.

"That sounded painful, Caroline. Did you fall over?"

I didn't give her the satisfaction of an answer.

Gradually my eyes adjusted to the darkness of the stairwell. On every landing, an emergency light sent a few pathetic photons into the space around it, and little by little I grew accustomed to picking my way up the stairs using these light sources. I tried to keep my steps soft, straining to catch any sound of her moving towards me.

I reached another landing and had to stop to catch my breath. This one lacked the emergency light for some reason, and I stood in utter blackness. I even tested it by waving my free hand in front of my face. Nothing.

"I love the darkness," Peta whispered into my ear.

I screamed and jumped back, swinging my sword wildly in the direction of her voice. Her stink was in my nostrils and I retched.

My back slammed into the wall and I pressed myself hard against it, sword arm held out in front, though I could feel it shaking as if it might come loose at the shoulder joint.

"Stay back, beast!" I yelled, slashing left and right.

"Beast?" she whispered, from a few feet away.

"That's very harsh coming from someone who just murdered two hundred people."

I lunged with my sword towards the sound of her voice but she just laughed at me.

"David's blood tasted sweet," she said. "So did his cock."

I whirled my sword again. It struck something hard and metallic, clanging away with a vibration that sent an electric shock up my arm from wrist to elbow. The handrail.

Peta's feet scraped on the bare concrete. I tensed.

"Time for the final act, Caroline Harker," she hissed.

Her footsteps were unbelievably rapid, almost as if she were scuttling on all fours, as she left the landing, heading towards the top storey of the hotel and the roof.

I raced after her, abandoning caution, trusting that my upraised sword and burning desire to avenge David would give me the protection and the strength I needed.

Three more flights and then I arrived at the top of the staircase. I looked up, hoping to see some sort of hatchway leading to the roof, but the dim light revealed nothing but a fly-spotted ceiling. To my left was another fire door. I squared my shoulders, put out my left hand, and pushed it open. The corridor on the other side was dark. I stepped though, feeling my pulse jumping in my throat like a steel ball bearing, painful with each beat of my heart. The corridor stretched away to a door, this one clearly marked with a sign saying: ROOF ONLY.

Got you! I thought.

Then the lights snapped back on.

"Oh, thank God for that," I said, smiling with relief.

Gripping the hilt of my sword tighter, I ran down the corridor. I hit the push bar without breaking stride and almost dislocated my wrist. It was locked.

I sensed Peta, rather than heard her, as she dropped from an air conditioning duct set flush with the ceiling and obscured by a rectangle of moulded white plaster. Her talons raked down my back. I screamed from the agony of those razor-edged claws as I whirled round to face her. She sprang towards me, that hideous, fanged gape filled with puffy pink tissue. I kicked out and hit her mid-thigh, not a clean contact but enough to throw her aim off so her teeth clicked against my chainmail neckpiece. One snapped in half: I heard it go.

She reared back, hand across her wounded mouth. When she brought her hand away, I saw the broken shaft of the tooth, its splintered tip dripping with stringy slime.

She shook her head and flicked it back and forth to reseat her jaw. Then, chest heaving, she spoke in a grating voice.

"I killed your precious David. Now I'm going to kill you!"

I held my sword arm out in front of me but she swatted the blade aside as it if were nothing more than a child's wooden plaything. The sword clattered against the wall and fell to the floor.

I retreated until my back hit the fire door. She was advancing stealthily. Not hurriedly, but as a predator who is one hundred percent sure of a kill. Her tongue was flicking in and out, dancing lasciviously across those carmine lips. From her mouth a disgusting low-pitched growl was issuing. I could hear my own blood rushing in my ears as she closed the distance between us to three feet, two feet, one...

I slumped a little, letting the door bear my weight.

"Take me, then, Peta," I said. "I'm too tired to fight any more."

And I let my head fall to the side, exposing the flesh

of my neck above the chainmail collar.

She hissed out a breath and placed her taloned hands on my chest. I felt her warm breath on my skin and was almost retching at the fetid stink coming off her in waves.

Then she jerked backwards, blood-filled eyes popping wide, jaw swinging from its dislocated hinges. She choked out a single word, gurgling its two syllables through a throat rapidly filling with blood.

"Cutter!"

I shoved her away from me with the palm of my left hand. As she reeled backwards, the chef's knife I had retrieved from my apron slid free of her gut with a sucking noise.

She clutched the rent in her stomach with both hands, but the blood streaming over her belly and through her fingers was a sideshow to the main event, which we both knew was only seconds away.

I slashed her across the face, left then right, as she stumbled back. My cuts severed the skin and tendons holding her jaw in place, and the whole assembly of bone, muscle, sinew and teeth fell to the floor.

The shuddering began, then. I pointed the knife at her face.

"This is for David Harker," I said, my voice grim with triumph. Then I stabbed her through the right eye, which burst with a disgusting pop, and left the blade embedded deep in her skull.

A second later, with a scream that I know will haunt my nightmares, Peta Velds deliquesced into a bursting cloud of blood that covered me from head to foot.

Gasping, I fell back against the fire door and slid to the ground, my back sliding down the blood spattered wood.

65

HUNT BOOK OF ARIANE VAN HELSING, 6TH JUNE 2011

Between us, Frederick's crew and I finished off the lamia who had avoided the effects of the nail bomb. Only a handful survived the blast and they were so disorientated from the pressure wave and the effects of seeing so many of their kind destroyed in one go that we had no problems killing them. Outside, we could hear sirens, but as we had agreed with Captain Stensgaard, ESU officers had established a *cordon sanitaire* around the entire block. Any concerned, or merely curious, citizens wondering about the detonation and gunfire would be told that what they had heard was the sounds of a gas main explosion and the subsequent rupturing of bottles of liquid nitrogen stored for the use of the hotel's avant garde chef.

The people Caroline and I discovered in the basement were given blankets then led away by more ESU officers and taken to one of the local hospitals for assessment and treatment for shock. They hadn't seen the lamia so believed merely – merely? – that they had been taken from the streets to be the victims of a particularly nasty blood-drinking cult.

Con's bomb not only destroyed the lamia, but a sizeable part of the hotel's ground floor. The damage is not structural, so in time, it may open again, although I believe the manager and owners will have some hard questions from the good Captain to answer. I told him, when he arrived in the lobby, that Caroline and I had seen the Mayor among the guests. He grunted noncommittally. Then muttered something about maybe getting more resources now they'd be getting a human in charge.

I found Caroline slumped in the top floor corridor. She was soaked in blood from head to foot. Before her, a lake of blood has soaked into the carpet, staining the blue fibres almost black. As I arrived, she grinned at me, and it was a look of the purest triumph. A warrior's smile. Teeth bright white, blue eyes flashing in a mask of red.

"I got her," she said. "The bitch is dead. I sent her all the way to hell."

"Yes," I said. "You did."

I knelt to hug her, then I hauled her to her feet and led her downstairs, through to the van and back to the sanctuary of Frederick's house.

66

HUNT BOOK OF CAROLINE HARKER, 6TH JUNE 2011

OPENING ENTRY

Last night, we celebrated. The night turned into morning and still we were too elated to go to bed. It is 7.00 a.m. now and I write this before attempting to sleep, even for an hour or two. I am drunk, I think, though I have so much adrenaline running through my veins that I feel stone-cold sober.

Peta Velds used her dying breath to call me "Cutter". Ariane told me that as the killer of the head of a lamia clan I am entitled to use the name without having been born into a cutter family. I closed my journal yesterday. From now on, I will enter my thoughts into this book. My hunt book.

On his way out of the ballroom, Frederick retrieved the SD card from the video camera I saw on the platform. The camera itself was smashed to pieces, but the card was intact. We watched it last night. It answered my one remaining question from the night. How did

Peta escape the blast to taunt me from the balcony into chasing her?

Hearst makes his little speech about the course to come and then sits down, turning to speak to Peta. She leans towards him and laughs, displaying those undersized, little, white teeth. The burly servants are bringing in the stakes and setting them up, one beside each table.

As the final stake is erected on the far side of the ballroom, the man to Peta's right frowns, then checks his phone. I recognise him as her General Counsel from Norfolk: Le Fanu. He places a hand on Peta's forearm and speaks into her ear. The camera's mike doesn't pick up his words clearly. Except for one short sentence on which, clearly unable to contain his emotions, he raises his voice. "We've found another scientist."

She rises from her chair, turns to Hearst and excuses herself, then follows Le Fanu to the nearest pillar. The camera angle reveals how she escaped the destructive power of the bomb. You can see her in front of the veined marble column, but the centrepiece is invisible behind its bulk. Le Fanu stands to one side, gesticulating. He looks excited and is smiling as he talks.

Peta nods and takes his hands in both of hers and raises them to her lips.

The hubbub in the background rises in volume.

Peta drops his hands and says something. He walks away from her, heading back to the table.

Then the bomb detonates.

The roaring explosion is cut off at the midpoint. Presumably it destroyed some sort of audio circuit inside the camera. The video spirals crazily, showing the ceiling, then the wall, then the floor, then the view across the ballroom again, this time sideways on. When the camera comes to rest, a large, silver-grey blur obscures the lower left quarter of the screen and a more sharply-defined crack cuts across the rest of the lens in a splintered, diagonal line. A nail, we assumed, had smashed into the lens, which is also tinted by a red smear across its upper right corner.

The scene visible in the remaining part of the screen is both horrifying and deeply pleasurable to watch. Bodies are strewn across the tables, smashed and mangled almost beyond recognition. The nails, carrying their lethal slick of *salcie usturoi*, are sticking into, and out of, every visible object. Gobbets of flesh slide off chairs and candlesticks. And the blood. So much blood. One by one, the lamia shudder and explode like liquid fireworks. One creature staggers towards the camera before bursting. The resultant mess spatters the lens so thoroughly that further visuals are lost. All that remains on the video are the screams, though these dwindle quickly to a few last moaning whimpers and then silence, apart from a distant fire alarm, ringing impotently from a distant point in the hotel.

67

HUNT BOOK OF ARIANE VAN HELSING, 7TH JULY 2011

Caroline has disappeared. She has been agitated these last few weeks since she and I returned from Manhattan. I now worry that bestowing the name Cutter on her undid something in her mind. She talked incessantly of the risks of the lamia returning to London, even though Lily and I assured her this was not possible. This morning, I had arranged to have coffee with her and she didn't show up. I texted her, called and left messages, tried all the usual – and unusual – channels, but nothing. I called round to her house but there was a for sale sign up outside. Nobody answered when I rang and knocked at the front door.

68

PRIVATE NOTES OF BEN SCHRADER
MRC PSYCH – FOR POSSIBLE BOOK –
22ND AUGUST 2012

My name is Ben Schrader. I work as a consultant psychiatrist with the NHS in a large teaching hospital near Euston Station. For the past 12 months, I have been treating a very disturbed young woman named Caroline Harker, a barrister. Caroline is under my care because she was sectioned. A member of the public had reported her to police for walking into an Aston Martin showroom in Park Lane carrying a sharpened stake. She claimed to the arresting officer that she was a vampire hunter and refused to relinquish the stake. By the time they subdued her, with a Taser, I think, she had managed to plant the first couple of inches of the stake into the chest of a merchant banker discussing finance options with a salesman.

When I first met Caroline, I thought her case history quite the most remarkable I'd ever read. Delusional, of course. But fascinating nonetheless. She claimed to have been a vampire hunter.

When she was released from residential care and began attending my clinic on an outpatient basis, I saw her for an hour three times a week. I recorded all our conversations and much of what you have already read is based on our talks (she has an extraordinary ability to remember — or fabricate — verbatim dialogue). I also became interested in her carefully constructed paranoid delusions about vampires – the people she calls The O-One – and began conducting some research into vampire mythology. Caroline is eloquent and articulate, as one would expect of a barrister. From time to time she lapses into a peculiarly archaic idiom, almost as if she is voicing the thoughts of a young Victorian woman, and not a thirtysomething born in the 1980s. She is tall and has striking looks – a prominent, almost sculptural nose with sharp edges to the ridge, and a wide mouth that when she smiles transforms the plainness of her face, though nose and mouth then appear to be competing for space. An old-fashioned, rounded figure, with what my old Grandma Rosenberg would have called, "hips a baby would thank God for giving its mother". Wide, anyway.

My diagnosis was one of borderline paranoid personality disorder incorporating hallucinations and aspects of dissociative disorder, and, perhaps not surprisingly, given what she claims to have seen and done, a healthy dollop of good old-fashioned anxiety. She was hypervigilant and could become withdrawn, almost catatonic, in fact.

As to medication, I prescribed the following daily medication suite: 30mg of Paroxetine – a selective serotonin reuptake inhibitor, or SSRI, antidepressant – for the anxiety; 2 mg of Aripiprazole– an anti-psychotic – for the paranoia and the hallucinations; 20 mg of Zopiclone, a mild sleeping pill, as needed. I also prescribed 2 mg of Diazepam – Valium – not on a regular basis but to be kept by her as an emergency measure if she suffered a panic attack. A "break the glass in case of emergency" option.

She responded well both to the medication and to our sessions and I also arranged for her to speak to a colleague of mine who specialises in cognitive behavioural therapy (CBT), to counter some of the unusual thoughts and beliefs that Caroline had come to rely on.

During our sessions, Caroline consulted a book of writings that she referred to as her journal, as well as other documents. It was clear to me that this work was the product of her psychosis rather than any normal record of the daily comings and goings of a young barrister's life.

I had intended my notes on Caroline's case to form the basis of an academic paper: I am friends with one of the editors at a leading mental health journal; but I now lean towards a book-length piece, perhaps for standalone publication. Caroline's 'sources' constitute an impressive narrative, if one is minded to take them as fiction. And a chronicle of a deep, but thankfully transient, psychosis, if one chooses, as I do, to take them as an elaborate facade to mask a stress-induced nervous breakdown.

The mobile phone, the printouts of emails, the so-called "Hunt Books", the blogs and journals: they created a patchwork of distinct voices that lend verisimilitude to her fantasy of vampires running global corporations, suborning scientists, seducing actresses and generally creating mayhem in the world's capital cities.

To counter her delusional thinking, I was able to show Caroline news reports of the fire at the Harker Laboratory in Norfolk in which her husband was killed, downloaded from one of the largest global media organisation's websites. Her friend Lucinda Easterbrook is not dead. I found a press release online announcing that she had been appointed as an executive presentations coach for a company in Los Angeles owned by Velds Holdings.

It seems clear to me that Caroline suffered a psychotic break brought on by overwork and triggered by her new husband's violent death. She now agrees with me and this analytic breakthrough, coupled with a carefully managed drug treatment regime, have restored her to sanity, though one must be careful, in my profession, when bandying such layman's terms about. Nonetheless, she is healthy. I told her so today and have signed the medical papers necessary for her to be released from my care.

69

BBC NEWS WEBSITE 23RD AUGUST 2012

Breaking news: top NHS psychiatrist, Benjamin Schrader, 37, was attacked in his Harley Street consulting rooms today by a seriously disturbed female patient. Dr Schrader suffered horrific injuries to his neck and died from blood loss at the scene. Witnesses report seeing a naked woman fleeing the scene and appearing to leap onto the roof of a bus before clearing a two-foot gap to the top of a nearby building.

70

HUNT BOOK OF CAROLINE HARKER
24TH AUGUST 2012

It was a shame that Ben had to die. But there was no way I could warn him what he was getting into without ruining all the careful work I'd done in our sessions to convince him I was sane again.

I left Ben's office for the last time two days ago clutching that precious piece of paper declaring me no longer a threat to myself or society and therefore under no restrictions of movement or need to report to the hospital, social services or the police. And something else. A spare key, which I found in his desk drawer when he excused himself to visit the lavatory. I returned late that night and, with my newly acquired lock-picking skills (thank you, dear Jim) I retrieved all the files concerning my 'case'. The manuscript of Ben's book is safe with me in Bloomsbury.

Ariane and Lily are rebuilding the London chapter. With Peta gone it won't be long before a new mother appears to lead the lamia here.

And me? I have finished with my old life. I state the following for the record.

My name is Caroline Harker.

I am a Cutter.

The End

71

DRAFT PAPER FOR SUBMISSION TO NATURE MAGAZINE, 13TH MAY 2018, AUTHOR: ARIANE VAN HELSING

Proposed title: Origins, lifecycle and physiology of new species of human with notes on mythological and cultural interpretations.

Abstract (100 words): A sub-species of human being exists that I propose to call *Homo sapiens lamia*. Vampires. They evolved some 100,000 years ago ie towards the end of the Neolithic period. Their gross anatomy is identical with *Homo sapiens*, although there are certain mutations, both structural and physiological. They exist in symbiosis with a parasite that has re-engineered their DNA. The resultant hybrid feeds exclusively on human blood, and has certain evolutionary advantages over *Homo sapiens*. These include strength, up to ten times greater; longevity, ages of 375 years are not uncommon; and the ability to reproduce non-sexually. They are extremely dangerous.

Evolution of *Homo sapiens lamia*

In early prehistory, there was a group of hominids living in caves in the region of modern-day Bulgaria. Their diet, as far as we can tell from occasional bodies preserved in peat bogs, and skeletal remains from cave burials, included grains (mostly barley and a form of wild oat), small rodents (voles, shrews, mice), and water snakes, we assume from the caves themselves.

The snakes are the critical element in the evolution of *Homo sapiens lamia*. We have conducted research in Bulgaria and have discovered a species of water snake that lives many hundreds of feet underground in aquifers that feed cave systems. These snakes are blind and albino. They subsist on a species of salamander that also occupies the same environmental niche, plus the occasional rodent or bird that enters the cave system and becomes disorientated until it dies and falls into the water. We believe their senses have evolved to compensate for the lack of vision, and include highly sensitive smell receptors, pressure-sensing organs, plus some other sensory modality we are still researching, perhaps electrical in origin.

The snakes were infected with a parasite, possibly from the salamanders, that had adopted them as its host. We believe that either through biting or being fed upon, the snakes transferred the parasites into the hominids. Once inside the hominids, the parasites flourished, having a far more mobile and adaptable host, with access to a great many new food sources both inside and outside the caves.

Over time, the parasites re-engineered the DNA of these early *Homo sapiens*, as they had that of the water snakes. The chief effect of the parasites' action was to vastly increase the ability of the humans to access energy from their food sources. Oxygen and glycogen conversion increased ten-fold, so that every calorie of food consumed resulted in perfect 100% conversion into one kilojoule of energy made available, rather than the 10% common in normal human beings. In practical terms, this gave the human hosts dramatically increased physical strength. A second effect was to improve longevity, and through radio-carbon dating combined with bone density analysis, we have demonstrated conclusively that *Homo sapiens lamia* is capable of living for up to 375 years.

The parasite

Name: *lamia multigena* (vampire brood).

Type: Endoparasite

The parasites are blood-sucking arthropods, of a maximum length of 0.01 mm. They travel into the host bloodstream in an injected anticoagulant fluid. It is suspected that the parasites are themselves hosts to microscopic pathogenic organisms (probably viral in origin) that may be the root cause of the infection and subsequent DNA modification in the human host.

What does the parasite get in return?

From the host, the parasite gets what all parasites get: life and the opportunity to multiply.

How has the infection changed human behaviour?

In order to reproduce, the parasite needs a new host to infect. They have modified the human brain so its primary food drive is cannibalistic blood-drinking – hematophagy. In the act of feeding, the parasite travels into the new host's bloodstream in an anticoagulant injected through hollow fangs.

Extreme sensitivity to sunlight, most likely UV radiation, means *Homo sapiens lamia* are restricted to closed environments using artificial light during the day.

Possibly owing to the metabolic changes wrought by the parasite, the creatures need very little sleep – perhaps as little as two hours in every 24.

Libido is increased. The *lamia* are highly sexed and

prefer *Homo sapiens* partners. In sexual congress with their own kind, the increased blood flow and hormonal changes create extremes of aggression, which result in one or both participants feeding on, and therefore destroying, the other. See note below.

How has the infection changed human physiology and anatomy?

The parasite has altered human DNA to produce a range of anatomical and physiological changes.

Bucco-mandibular anatomy: behind the upper incisors, two long hollow fangs have evolved. These are erectable at will, as in members of the *Viperidae* family, such as bush vipers and puff adders. They are connected to individual sacs that produce a secretion containing an anticoagulant chemical.

The connective tissue and ligaments attaching the mandible to the styloid and mastoid processes have become hyper-flexible, allowing the lower jaw to partially dislocate without injury, facilitating a wide "gape" during feeding.

The tissues of the gingiva, soft palate, tongue and cheeks have developed into an extendible ring that forms a vacuum seal when feeding.

Digestion: *Homo sapiens lamia* feeds exclusively on human blood. The parasite DNA enables the host to extract 100% of the available energy from the calories contained in the blood.

Musculature: the extreme diet has produced dramatic increases in muscular strength. Muscular appearance is ultra-lean, and when hunting, physiological changes engorge muscles with blood giving the *lamia* a "ripped" appearance.

Keratin: fingernails and toenails are extendible – a variant on the mechanism used to erect the fangs.

Skin pigmentation: *Homo sapiens lamia* has extremely pale, though not pure albino, skin pigmentation.

Body's ability to repair itself: multiplied exponentially through unknown metabolic and cell regeneration mechanism.

Reproduction: The mutation has rendered the *lamia* sterile. They do not reproduce sexually, as explained below.

How has the infection changed human cognition and consciousness?

Lamia are hyper-predatory. They do not see *Homo sapiens* as creatures worthy of consideration in emotional terms and they do not experience empathy for human victims.

Their senses of smell, hearing and vision are all heightened, possibly as a result of the predatory impulse. Taste is blunted, touch is unchanged.

Death and injury

Homo sapiens lamia are affected by both salicylic acid, found in willow wood and bark, and wild garlic oil. The biochemical effects of both substances, especially in combination, cause catastrophic damage to blood cells, and the cells of the circulatory system itself. The effect has been likened by observers to an "explosion of blood". Even hard tissues such as teeth, bones and talons contain enough of the affected cells to be obliterated.

Attacking the heart is the most effective method of killing, for obvious reasons, though any major blood vessel is effective in a very short space of time.

Exposure to direct sunlight is also an effective way of killing *lamia*. The UV radiation destroys cell membranes throughout the body, resulting in a similar effect to that of the bioactive agents described above.

Owing to the fast, self-repairing nature of *lamia* body

tissues, assault by conventional means, whether armed or unarmed, results in slight and extremely temporary damage, if any.

Reproduction

In common with other closed societies that, for reasons of culture or biology, do not practise sexual reproduction, the *lamia* recruit new members of their "families". They do this through a less intense feeding strategy than that used purely for replenishing energy.

The victim is bitten and their blood is consumed, during which time the parasites migrate into their bloodstream in the manner previously described. But the *lamia* stops feeding before the victim dies from blood loss, allowing them to recover and the parasite to multiply inside the new host. The process takes anywhere from a few weeks to a few months, during which time the parasite inserts copies of its DNA into the host's cell nuclei and begins anew the process of reengineering the host's DNA to alter its structure and expression.

Cultural and mythological references in literature and art

There are widespread representations of *Homo sapiens lamia* in art and literature, from the Sumerian and early Semitic cultures onwards. In Latin America, a god, Ixctal, was usually depicted as a snake-headed human with a gaping mouth crowded with long pointed teeth. The Aztec and Mayan traditions of removing still-beating hearts from sacrificial victims is now thought to be a direct connection to the hematophagy of the *lamia*.

In African cultures, particularly those of sub-Saharan Africa, we find repeated references in stories and artworks to the *damu mnywaji* (Swahili for "blood drinker").

For more background on vampire folklore by region,

this Wikipedia entry is helpful. https://en.wikipedia.org/wiki/Vampire_folklore_by_reg ion

Of most relevance to current research is the long tradition in Eastern Europe of stories concerning vampires. Named *strigoi*, they led directly to the canon of western literature concerning blood-drinking undead monsters. Two western vampire stories have achieved global significance: *Dracula*, by Bram Stoker; and *Carmilla* by J Sheridan Le Fanu.

It hardly needs adding that the 21st Century has spawned a thriving vampire industry that has led to, among other things, a cult of "real vampires" – a loosely federated network of city-based clubs whose members believe themselves to be actual vampires.

ACKNOWLEDGMENTS

To Abraham "Bram" Stoker: your magnum opus, *Dracula*, was the inspiration for this humble homage.

To Christopher Lee, Bela Lugosi and Max Schreck: the vampires of my youth.

To Peter Cushing: you were always Van Helsing.

To Ingrid Pitt, Madeleine Smith and Valerie Leon: nobody bit or got bitten more beautifully.

To those who stay up late reading: you are the true "children of the night".

To my Sniper-Spotters: your eyes are as sharp as vampires' teeth.

To my first readers, Claire Quarm and Sandy Wallace: thank you for your insightful comments on the text.

Thank you all, from every chamber of my heart.

COPYRIGHT

© 2018 Sunfish Ltd

Published by Tyton Press, an imprint of Sunfish Ltd, PO Box 2107, Salisbury SP2 2BW T: 0844 502 2061

ABOUT THE AUTHOR

Andy Maslen was born in Nottingham, England, home of legendary bowman Robin Hood. Andy once won a medal for archery, although he has never been locked up by the sheriff.

He has worked in a record shop, as a barman, as a door-to-door DIY products salesman and a cook in an Italian restaurant. He eventually landed a job in marketing, writing mailshots to sell business management reports. He spent ten years in the corporate world before launching a business writing agency, Sunfish, where he writes for clients including The Economist, Christie's and World Vision.

As well as his novels, Andy has published five works of non-fiction, on copywriting and freelancing, with Marshall Cavendish and Kogan Page. They are all available online and in bookshops.

Andy lives in Wiltshire and can be seen during daylight hours, although he keeps to the shady side of the street.

ALSO BY ANDY MASLEN

The Gabriel Wolfe series

Trigger Point

Reversal of Fortune (short story)

Blind Impact

Condor

First Casualty

Fury

Rattlesnake

The DI Stella Cole series

Hit and Run

Hit Back Harder

Hit and Done

Non-fiction

Write to Sell

100 Great Copywriting Ideas

The Copywriting Sourcebook

Write Copy, Make Money

Persuasive Copywriting

WANT TO KNOW MORE?

To get two free books, and exclusive news and offers, join Andy Maslen's Readers Group at www.andymaslen.com.

Email Andy at andy@andymaslen.com.
Follow and tweet him at @Andy_Maslen
Like his page "Andy Maslen, Author" on Facebook.

Printed in Great Britain
by Amazon

46353288R00203